Rebellious Young Ladies

Finishing school was meant to turn them into perfect aristocratic ladies...but these four friends can never be contained by Society's expectations!

To conform to what Society deemed correct for females of their class, Amelia Lambourne, Irene Fairfax, Georgina Hayward and Emily Beaumont were sent by their families to Halliwell's Finishing School for Refined Young Ladies—which they soon dubbed "Hell's Final Sentence for Rebellious Young Ladies"!

Instead, the four found strength in their mutual support to become themselves and a lifelong friendship was formed...one they'll need to lean on when each young woman faces the one thing they swore never to succumb to—a good match!

Read Amelia's story now in
Lady Amelia's Scandalous Secret

And watch for Emily's, Georgina's and Irene's stories, coming soon from Harlequin Historical.

Author Note

Lady Amelia's Scandalous Secret is the first in my new series, Rebellious Young Ladies, featuring four young women who are sentenced to a finishing school for the crime of behaving in a manner unbefitting a young lady.

In Victorian England, young aristocratic ladies had one purpose: finding a husband—preferably one who would elevate the social status of the family. Young women were sometimes sent to finishing schools, not to receive an education but to learn the feminine arts of embroidery, watercolor painting and polite conversation—all with the purpose of making them ideal wives for aristocratic men.

That is the fate of the Rebellious Young Ladies—four round pegs in square holes who no amount of "finishing" will turn into demure young women.

In *Lady Amelia's Scandalous Secret*, Amelia's rebellious nature soon finds her in conflict with Mr. Leo Devenish, a self-made man who is equally determined to follow his own rules and not those dictated by society.

Irene Fairfax and the notorious Duke of Redcliff feature in the second book, while mischievous Georgina Hayward becomes entangled with the Duke of Mansfield in the third book, and the headstrong Lady Emily Beaumont finds Mr. Matthias Richardson to be equally indomitable in the fourth book of the series.

I hope you enjoy the first book in this series. I love hearing from my readers and can be reached at evashepherd.com and Facebook.com/evashepherdromancewriter.

EVA SHEPHERD

Lady Amelia's Scandalous Secret

Recycling programs for this product may not exist in your area.

ISBN-13: 978-1-335-72392-5

Lady Amelia's Scandalous Secret

Copyright © 2023 by Eva Shepherd

For questions and comments about the quality of this book, please contact us at CustomerService@Harlequin.com.

Harlequin Enterprises ULC
22 Adelaide St. West, 41st Floor
Toronto, Ontario M5H 4E3, Canada
www.Harlequin.com

Printed in U.S.A.

After graduating with degrees in history and political science, **Eva Shepherd** worked in journalism and as an advertising copywriter. She began writing historical romances because it combined her love of a happy ending with her passion for history. She lives in Christchurch, New Zealand, but spends her days immersed in the world of late Victorian England. Eva loves hearing from readers and can be reached via her website, evashepherd.com, and her Facebook page, Facebook.com/evashepherdromancewriter.

Books by Eva Shepherd

Harlequin Historical

A Victorian Family Christmas
"The Earl's Unexpected Gifts"

Rebellious Young Ladies

Lady Amelia's Scandalous Secret

Those Roguish Rosemonts

A Dance to Save the Debutante
Tempting the Sensible Lady Violet
Falling for the Forbidden Duke

Young Victorian Ladies

Wagering on the Wallflower
Stranded with the Reclusive Earl
The Duke's Rebellious Lady

Breaking the Marriage Rules

Beguiling the Duke
Awakening the Duchess
Aspirations of a Lady's Maid
How to Avoid the Marriage Mart

Visit the Author Profile page
at Harlequin.com.

To the Christchurch Eastside Writers
in thanks for their support, enthusiasm
and good advice.

Chapter One

London 1894

Amelia was determined to maintain her professional façade, but deep down she knew her quest was hopeless. How was she ever expected to succeed when the odds were all stacked against her?

'I'm sorry to disappoint you, my dear,' the bank manager said with a sanctimonious smile, as if he had not just taken a pin, thrust it deep into her dreams and left them deflated. 'But you must know it is most irregular to grant a loan to a woman.'

Amelia was tempted to point out that Queen Victoria was a woman. Did that mean the bank would not lend to her? But she suspected such cheek would not be appreciated and would get her no closer to achieving her goal.

'I'm sure if you asked your father, he would give you the money to pursue your little hobby.' The bank manager quickly looked her up and down. 'Or perhaps you could use some of the money that you spend on those pretty dresses,' he waved his hand in a circle in front of her face, 'and hats and other whatnots.'

If it was that simple, did he not think that she would have come up with such a solution herself? But, while her father was more than happy to pay for endless pretty gowns, hats and those so-called whatnots, just like the bank manager, her father would neither finance nor lend her the money for anything else, and especially not so his daughter could continue to publish a monthly magazine aimed at educated gentlewomen.

If she was foolish enough to tell him what she was doing, her father would be outraged. Such an enterprise would be deemed an absurd pursuit for a young lady, one who should be focusing all of her energy on finding a suitable husband before it was too late. But unlike the bank manager, her father would not dismiss it as a little hobby. Nor would he see anything amusing in such behaviour. He had made his feelings very clear, on more occasions than Amelia could remember, regarding what he thought of educated women. Even those two words caused his lips to turn down, his nose to rise in the air and his body to shudder as if a woman with an education was an abomination against nature.

That was one of the reasons she was so determined to make the magazine succeed. Even if her father never knew, she would prove him wrong. Prove that women could be successful. That they could be interested in more than just fripperies. That finding a husband did not have to be their only goal in life.

While her father had no faith in her—or any woman, for that matter—her lovely aunt had extended her the original loan to start her magazine, *The Ladies' Enquirer*. She had insisted that Amelia use the small nest egg she had managed to squirrel away over the years and put it towards achieving her cherished dream. Amelia had been reluctant to take the money, but Aunt Beryl had insisted, saying it would be what Amelia's mother would have wanted. Now she wished she had been firmer in her opposition. She should never have risked her aunt's savings.

The magazine had been going for less than a year, and already it was running into financial problems. It was not as if it required much money to stay afloat. Amelia worked for free. The office she used was poky, run-down, and it would be a compliment to say it was in a rather unfashionable part of town, and many of the contributors did not expect payment. They were women beavering away in academic pursuits or fighting hard to change social injustices. Seeing their work in print was reward enough, and that was something her magazine provided. She had promised those women that *The Ladies' Enquirer* would provide them a channel through which their voices could be heard, and she would not let them down.

But she could not do that without money for printing and distribution, and to pay for the services of her one employee who filled the roles of secretary, accountant, salesman, office manager and anything and everything else that needed doing. And, oh, it would be so lovely if they could actually expand. Something that looked impossible unless she could convince this man to actually have faith in a woman's ability.

She sat up straighter in the chair, determined not to let her father or this bank manager thwart her plans. Too much was riding on her succeeding. She was loath to have her aspirations destroyed so quickly, but more than that, what she most certainly could not do was let down Aunt Beryl.

'As you will see in the ledgers,' she said, pointing to the account book open on his desk, '*The Ladies' Enquirer* is a relatively new publication, but the subscription numbers have continued to grow every month since we were first launched, and with additional investment and a bit more time I am confident—'

'Yes, my dear, but growth from nothing to slightly more than nothing is hardly growth at all. And as for the advertising revenue…' His finger ran along the columns of figures. 'Well, that's all but non-existent.'

His condescending smile became paternalistic. 'Sales are not growing, are they? You need to be able to prove that *The Ladies' Enquirer* is a viable proposition before the bank will consider lending its money, and these sales figures do not show that. You have to get your numbers up. It's as simple as that.'

If increasing sales was simple, do you think I would not be doing that? Amelia wanted to say. Instead she smiled as the manager continued to lecture.

'I'm afraid you've entered into a very competitive market. Magazines, journals and newspapers are opening and closing every day.' He looked down at the copies of *The Ladies' Enquirer* she had brought with her, picked one up from his desk and adjusted his horn-rimmed glasses. '"*A magazine for women with enquir-*

ing minds",' he read off the masthead, frowned and looked at Amelia over the top of his spectacles. 'A rather small market, I would have thought.'

Amelia quashed her anger at his insulting attitude and continued smiling politely. It was the only publication of its sort on the market and that was exactly why she had begun publishing it. *The Ladies' Enquirer* was the magazine *she* wanted to read and she was certain there were many other women out there just like her, if only she could reach them. 'As I said, the numbers are growing and I'm positive—'

'But not fast enough.' He slammed shut the thick black account book and placed the folded copies of *The Ladies' Enquirer* on top.

'If you can't show me that sales are improving, then there is, of course, another option,' he said as he handed the pile back to Amelia.

'Oh, yes?' Amelia sat forward in her chair, hoping against hope that he was going to suggest something that was actually useful.

'You could ask your father to act as your guarantor. The bank would not hesitate to do business with the Earl of Kingsland.'

'Thank you. Yes, what a good idea,' she said, still with that false smile. 'But would you be so kind as to agree to the loan now, then I will discuss it with my father tonight?' Amelia hoped this didn't constitute fraud. Her father knew nothing of her enterprise, and she intended to keep it that way. Not so much for herself as for Aunt Beryl. Her aunt had already had to bear the brunt of Amelia's father's wrath for allowing her to acquire an education. If he discovered that she had provided the initial funding for the magazine, Amelia hated to think what he might do.

'Yes, do that, Lady Amelia. Speak to your father. My office is always open to the Earl. When the two of you return and when he agrees to act as guarantor, then I think you'll find the bank will offer you very favourable terms on your loan. Very favourable indeed.'

In other words, the bank would lend to her father, who did not need the money, but not to Amelia, who desperately did.

She took the account book and magazines from his outstretched hands.

'Good afternoon, my lady, and I look forward to doing business with you and your father, or extending you a loan if and when you can show me that this magazine of yours is worthy of the bank's investment.'

Amelia forced herself to continue smiling as she said goodbye and walked out of the office. She maintained her professional demeanour as she passed through the bank, where male bank tellers working behind grilles were serving their male customers, but the moment she was out of the office and back on the bustling London streets her shoulders slumped and she released a loud, despondent sigh.

Somehow, she was going to have to find the money to keep *The Ladies' Enquirer* going. If she was a man, Amelia knew there would be no problem. The bank would have extended her a loan. Her father would have little objection to backing her. She would have an allowance from the family fortune, and friends in the same position who could act as investors.

Instead, she had no money of her own. If it hadn't been for Aunt Beryl's small contribution, she would never have been able to start her magazine in the first place.

Perhaps the bank manager was right and she was foolish to have embarked on such a venture. But she *had* embarked on this venture. She *had* borrowed all the money Aunt Beryl had in the world. She had made promises to all those women who gave their time to write for the magazine. She had to make this work. Standing up straighter and marching down the street with a confidence she was determined to feel, she recited to herself that she would not, could not fail, and she would do everything within her power to ensure that *The Ladies' Enquirer* was a roaring success.

Her next engagement was to be a much more enjoyable one than the appointment with the bank manager, and hopefully would push all thoughts of failure out of her head. Several hansom cabs clattered past on the cobbled streets, the drivers looking hopefully in her direction, but she was still full of angry energy and needed to walk it off. By the time she arrived at the Mayfair townhouse of her friend Lady Emily Beaumont, she was starting to relax and was looking forward to spending a pleasant time with her three closest friends.

Miss Georgina Hayward and Miss Irene Fairfax had already arrived and were laughing and chatting together when the footman showed her into the drawing room. All three turned in her direction.

'How did it go?'

'What did he say?'

'Did you get the loan?'

The questions came at her so fast she was unsure who had asked what, but the answer was generally the same for all. 'It went badly. He said no. I didn't get the loan.'

'That's terrible.'

'So unfair.'

'Appalling. I wager you would have secured the loan if you were a man.'

Amelia could only agree with all three statements. She took a cup of tea from the footman, and helped herself to a slice of Battenberg cake, hoping the sweet pink-and-yellow confection would cheer her up.

'Never mind. I'll think of something,' she said with as much determination as she could muster. '*The Ladies' Enquirer* is not dead yet.' She smiled at her friends. She would not let her mood ruin theirs. 'So, what have I missed out on? What other gossip have you to share?'

All three rushed to tell of their latest adventures and they were all soon talking animatedly and laughing loudly, behaviour which they knew would be frowned on by many in society and considered gauche for young ladies. Something about which they cared not one jot.

Her friends had seen her through many despondent days. They had met at Halliwell's Finishing School for Refined Young Ladies, which Emily had dubbed Hell's Final Sentence for Rebellious Young Ladies. The four young women had all been sent there to finish them off. In other words, change their natures so they would conform to what society deemed correct for a female of their class.

In Amelia's case, she had been sentenced to Halliwell's for the crime of being far too educated. Her father, who took little to no interest in his daughter, had been horrified to return home unexpectedly one day to find Amelia sitting in the study with her brothers' tutor going over a list of Latin verbs. Once again, her brothers had abandoned their lessons and were out playing somewhere. And once again, the tutor, with nothing else to occupy his time, could see nothing wrong with teaching the Earl's daughter, especially as she was the only member of the household eager to learn.

Her father had not been angry with his sons—saying 'boys will be boys'—and he had agreed with them when they'd said, 'Who needs Latin verbs anyway?' But he was furious with his daughter. No man wanted an educated wife, he had bellowed. 'It's unnatural. You're a disgrace to me, to the name of Lambourne, to your ancestors.'

Poor Aunt Beryl, the woman who had raised Amelia since her mother died, had been blamed. Amelia had argued long and hard, trying to convince her father that her lovely aunt knew nothing about her secret studying. She had promised he would never again find her doing something so shameful, but that hadn't stopped him from sending her away to a finishing school where she would learn the feminine arts of embroidery, watercolour painting, deportment and how to converse with prospective beaus, which as far as Amelia could see consisted of smiling a lot, agreeing with men and laughing at their jokes.

If not for Emily, Georgina and Irene being sentenced to the same school for equally outrageous crimes, Amelia doubted she would have survived the tedium. They had remained friends after they were released from school, supporting each other through the good and bad times, and today was no different. Irene shared her good news, that she had been accepted by an art school. Lady Emily discussed her plans for a children's hospital she was hoping to establish in the East End of London, and Georgina regaled them with a funny tale in which she evaded the attentions of yet another amorous young man who had fallen hopelessly in love with her enormous dowry.

By the time afternoon tea was over, Amelia had almost forgotten about her terrible day. Almost.

But any good cheer she felt was destroyed when she arrived home and found her father waiting for her in the hallway of their Belgrave townhouse. And he did not look happy. She braced herself, hoping and praying the bank manager had not contacted him. Weren't they bound by some sort of privacy agreement, or did that only apply to their male clients?

'Where on earth have you been?' he asked before she had even handed her hat and coat to the maid.

She released a held breath. He didn't know. Thank goodness for small mercies. 'I've been having afternoon tea with—'

'Yes, yes, yes. All right. We're running late. We're expected at Leo Devenish's for dinner this evening.'

This was the first time she had heard of such an invitation, but Mr Devenish was known for sending out invitations on the day of his dinner parties. It was highly irregular, and everyone knew it was yet another way of him expressing his power. No one invited would turn down such a summons.

She had met Leo Devenish on several occasions and he was everything she despised. Arrogant, superior and far too handsome for his own good. He had an appalling reputation, not just as a ladies' man, but as a ruthless businessman as well. Amelia doubted he ever had to go cap in hand to a bank manager. They probably fell over themselves trying to throw money in his direction. And to make things worse, he had recently moved from acquiring railways and industries to purchasing newspapers, and had a portfolio that included many of the leading publications in the country.

The last thing she felt like doing was spending time in the company of a man who saw newspapers and magazines as a commodity to acquire in his pursuit for greater wealth and power. Especially on a day such as this.

'Come along, make haste,' her father said, actually pushing Amelia towards the stairs. 'Mr Devenish is not a man who appreciates tardiness.'

Mr Devenish was one of the few men her father was wary of, while at the same time despising him for his lowly origins. As an earl, her father was all but untouchable, but he supported many a politician, men who could further his own interests, and a bad word in one of Mr Devenish's many publications could destroy a politician's career. So when Mr Devenish commanded attendance at one of his dinner parties, her father accepted, no matter how inconvenient it may be to his schedule.

Amelia suspected Devenish enjoyed making these titled men come running when he commanded.

'Do I really have to go?' Amelia was unsure why she had asked, as she already knew the answer.

'Of course you do. Prebbleton and Bradley will be there.'

Her heart sank further. Lord Prebbleton and Lord Bradley had both expressed interest in courting Amelia, or at least in courting the daughter of the Earl of Kingsland, a woman likely to come with a substantial dowry. Having to spend an evening with Mr Devenish would be bad enough but having to endure the company of the two Vacuous Viscounts really was the limit.

Amelia had no illusions about herself when it came to men and marriage. Men were certainly not attracted by her beauty, or lack thereof, and her father was not the only man to have informed her that men did not like intelligent women. At an early age she had come to the realisation that if she wanted love, wanted a husband and children, she was going to have to bury part of herself and become the sort of woman men did find attractive. One who listened rather than spoke, agreed rather than argued, and always, always made the man feel as if he was in every way her superior.

That was something she would not do and had long ago come to accept she would not be marrying. But her father still had illusions that he would one day walk his daughter up the aisle and palm her off on a titled man of his choosing.

'And don't shame me tonight by trying to be intelligent. It's bad enough that I have an unmarried daughter of twenty-three—I don't want them to think I was lumbered with a bluestocking as well.'

Amelia knew better than to come back with a clever refrain. That would only make her father even more irritable. Instead, she went upstairs to dress for an evening of tedium and torment.

Chapter Two

Leo Devenish stared at his reflection in the full-length mirror. It had been a good day, and he could think of no better way of ending it than to invite members of the aristocracy to dinner to celebrate his latest acquisitions.

He smiled to himself, thinking of those dukes, earls, viscounts and barons receiving his late invitation and having to quickly rearrange their social calendar so they could dance to his tune.

'Thank you, James,' he said, as his valet finished brushing down his evening jacket and handed him his gloves. 'How is the new scullery maid feeling now? Is she over her illness?'

'Much better, sir. She appreciated the time off you gave her to visit her family. I believe that was all it was. The poor girl was homesick.'

'Good, and how are her lessons proceeding?'

'Excellent, sir.' The usually impassive James gave a small smile. 'She wrote her first letter home to her mother and was very proud of her accomplishment. Her mother can't read, but she said the local clergyman will read it to her.'

Leo nodded, turned back to the mirror and adjusted his cravat. Education had changed his life, and it was an opportunity he would not deny to his own servants. Although he would never inflict on anyone the horror of being the only child from an impoverished background at a school for England's wealthy elite. He had barely survived the ordeal himself. Although it was enduring such unending cruelty that had made him the man he was today. So perhaps, in a strange way, he owed a debt of gratitude to those merciless bullies.

But those days were long behind him. No one dared try to bully Leo Devenish now. Not if they knew what was good for them. And tonight he would celebrate another business success with the very class of men who had once seen him as their prey. The magazines were a small addition to his empire, but a significant one. And yet another step away from being that frightened little boy who had first arrived at the elite private boys' school, the charity child who might as well have had a target painted on his back for all the bullies to see.

The guests had already assembled in the drawing room when he entered, and with satisfaction he registered the drop in the level of conversation as everyone looked in his direction. He spotted several viscounts, an earl or two, a duke, several barons and the men who had previously been owners of the magazines that were now his. Lady Madeline, his latest mistress, was also in attendance. Her husband was absent, giving his tacit approval of his wife's indiscretion.

That was something that never failed to amaze him, how aristocratic young ladies had to remain chaste until they married, but once they had provided the heir and a spare or two, their husbands often couldn't care less how many lovers their wives took. It might be surprising, but it worked out well for Leo. He had no intention of marrying but had to admit he gained a certain satisfaction in providing the excitement that the bored wives were not getting from their aristocratic husbands.

The only problem was that it was never too long before he tired of each woman, and that was what was happening with Lady Madeline. Thankfully, there would always be another dissatisfied married woman ready and willing to take her place.

He circled the room, greeting his guests, and was pleased to see that each man responded with the requisite fawning smile. The dinner gong rang out just as he was tiring of this polite conversation, and he escorted Lady Madeline down the hallway to the dining room. She was not the highest-ranking woman present, but Leo knew no one would dare comment on this breach of protocol.

When they entered the dining room he was filled with satisfied pleasure, as he always was when he was presented with evidence of how far he had come. The table was set for the thirty guests and they were about to dine on food that was out of season but grown by his team of gardeners in the hothouses at his Cornwall estate. Orchids, also grown at his estate, made an exotic centrepiece. The fine China, crystal glasses and silverware were lined up with military precision, and a team of liveried footmen were poised ready to respond to his guests' every need.

Not bad for the son of a blacksmith and a servant.

He stood at the head of the table, with Lady Madeline at his side. Once they were all seated and the wine poured, Lord Addington rose to his feet.

'I believe we must congratulate you,' he said, raising his glass. 'Ladies and gentlemen, you are looking at the new owner of *The Ladies' Home and Hearth, The Gentlewoman's Home Journal* and *The Fireside Chat.*'

Leo had to concede it was gracious of Lord Addington to make such a toast, as yesterday he had been the owner of *The Fireside Chat.* Or was the man being shrewd, and knew it was wisest to keep in Leo's good graces, in case he went after other magazines the man owned? Leo nodded his thanks to Addington.

'Bit of a change for you, isn't it, Devenish?' Lord Bradley said. 'Women's magazines.'

Leo stifled his annoyance. Bradley was a buffoon who wouldn't know a profitable business deal if it sat up and begged. That was why, like so many members of the aristocracy, he was sitting back and idly watching his fortune diminish. For generations, men like Bradley had relied on owning countless acres of productive land. Now that that land was no longer providing a healthy income, they were sinking deeper and deeper into debt with no idea of how to rectify the situation, other than marrying a woman with a significant dowry.

'All three are successful women's magazines with wide readerships,' the young lady next to him said.

'Indeed, you are right, Lady…' What on earth was

her name? She was the daughter of the Earl of Kingsland. He must have been introduced to her, but for the life of him he couldn't remember her name. After all, one debutante looked much like the next.

'And, therefore, extremely profitable,' she continued, looking at Bradley, who merely shrugged, as if thinking about profit was beneath a man of his status. An attitude that had seen the downfall of many a long-established aristocratic family.

'Although they do tend to be full of mindless gossip and cater to women with very limited interests and education,' the young lady added.

What was her name?

Amelia Lambourne, that was it.

'Perhaps you are right, Lady Amelia, but they sell in large numbers, and that's all I'm interested in.'

She gave a huff of disapproval. It seemed she was yet another aristocrat who saw making a profit as beneath them.

'And what magazines do you read, Lady Amelia?' he asked.

'Well…' She looked over at her father, who frowned and gave a small shake of his head, then she turned back to Leo. '*The Ladies' Enquirer* is an excellent publication. It contains fascinating articles on politics, scientific discoveries and some interesting, serious debates on the changing position of women in today's society.'

Leo was momentarily taken aback. A debutante interested in politics, science and serious debate was a rare creature indeed. 'I admit that *The Ladies' Enquirer* is a worthy publication, but, like everything else, it needs to make a profit. The important question is, does the magazine actually sell?'

'Well, obviously it does. As I just said, I read it.'

'But I very much doubt that many people do. Worthy topics are all well and good, but unless it widens its appeal it will no doubt soon go to the wall, like so many other minor publications. Particularly now that it is up against the stable of women's magazines that I have bought, which of course will suit me, as it reduces competition.'

'Magazines like *The Ladies' Enquirer* are essential,' she said, her voice rising with indignation. 'They discuss important issues, such as votes for women.'

Her statement caused a howl of laughter from the men and a stern look from Lady Amelia's father, while the lady herself kept her head high and her lips tightly pinched. Lips, he had to admit, were a rather tempting shade of cherry red and, if they weren't pulled together in a moue of irritation, he suspected would be full and somewhat enticing.

'That's something women should be reading about,' she stated loudly above the men exchanging the predictable jokes about how you couldn't give the vote to someone who was scared of mice, or how if women had the vote they'd probably want the economy based on the price of a new bonnet.

'Women have the vote in New Zealand,' she stated, while the men continued to laugh as if this too was highly amusing.

'Isn't that the sort of insanity you'd expect from the colonies?' a man at the end of the table shouted out.

'They'll probably be giving the vote to their sheep next,' another responded to howls of laughter. 'And the sheep will probably make better choices than the ladies ever would.'

'I wager that New Zealand will come to regret such foolishness,' another man added, to calls of *hear, hear* from the group. 'Women simply cannot think logically. It's a proven fact. Education is wasted on them.'

A sudden shudder ripped through Leo and he was immediately cast back to being a ten-year-old child. Wasn't that a similar argument to the one that Lord Fitzherbert had made when he'd found the scruffy son of the local blacksmith in his library? Lord Fitzherbert had claimed that education was wasted on the lower classes, a view disputed by his friends. Those men had argued as virulently as these men were now arguing over a woman's right to education and the vote. It had led to Fitzherbert's sending Leo to a private school to receive the best education money could buy. All so he could win a bet and prove that an expensive education would be wasted on the son of a blacksmith. A bet he not only lost but also eventually came to regret.

The men continued to harangue poor Lady Amelia, and Leo's sympathies went out to her as their loud arguments raged around her.

If the right to vote was dependent on intelligence, many of these fools would be denied that right. Lady Amelia gave every appearance of being an astute woman but none of these men would accept that, just as Lord Fitzherbert could not accept that a blacksmith's son could have a modicum of intelligence, no matter how many opportunities he was given. He had proved the Earl wrong, and maybe one day Lady Amelia would prove these men wrong as well, but right now she was wasting her breath arguing with mindless imbeciles.

'Lady Amelia deserves to be listened to,' he said, cutting through the boisterous voices.

The men all quietened down and looked eagerly in his direction. Their predatory expressions were familiar to him. He had seen them many times when he'd been at school. They were expecting him to go on to ridicule her arguments and tease her mercilessly for their entertainment. They were about to be disappointed.

'If women were given the vote, who is to say whether the world would not be a better place? It's unlikely they'd do a worse job than some of the so-called educated men that presently sit in parliament.'

This was met with howls of laughter, causing Leo to shake his head in disbelief. They were evidently unaware that many of those buffoons to whom he was referring were seated around this very table.

He caught Lady Amelia's eye. She was staring back at him in assessment, as if unsure what to make of him.

'A magazine is a business like any other,' he said, returning to a subject close to his heart. 'Noble causes alone do not sell magazines. If this *Enquirer* magazine is not attracting readers, then it will fail, no matter how worthy it is. It's as simple as that. And when it does fail, a more astute businessman, such as myself, will be able to scoop it up for a song and turn it into one that actually makes a profit.'

This caused Lord Addington to squirm uncomfortably, likely knowing that was exactly what had happened with his own publication, and Lady Amelia to place her hands over her heart as if she had been personally affronted.

'Surely you would not do that? Buy out *The Ladies' Enquirer?*' Her voice was unaccountably choked.

'It is something I would certainly consider. After all, I am a businessman. Buying up failing magazines and turning them into something profitable is how you succeed in the competitive media industry.'

'By making it just like every other magazine on the market,' she said derisively, as if this was an affront to human decency.

'No, by adding content that a wider audience will read, such as a social page.'

'A gossip column?' She gasped. 'Is that all you think women want to read?'

He'd hoped to take the heat out of the argument she'd been having with his male guests by discussing the publishing industry, but it seemed Lady Amelia was as equally hot under the collar about that subject as she was about votes for women.

And when Lady Amelia was hot under the collar her attractiveness improved remarkably. Odd, as he was never usually interested in unmarried women. She was pretty enough, he would give her that, with her blue eyes sparking with anger and her creamy white cheeks flushed a pretty shade of pink. He was not usually taken with blondes either, but a curiosity as to how those thick honey locks looked when released from that ornate hairstyle was piquing his interest somewhat. Not that he would ever act on that interest. And she was certainly intelligent, with a lively mind. But none of that mattered. One thing no man could get away with, even him, was dabbling with debutantes.

'Everyone likes to read gossip,' he continued.

His statement caused a few huffs of disagreement from the braver men, all of whom spent much of their time at clubs where gossip and scandal were discussed avariciously. 'If *The Ladies' Enquirer* included a Society page, which in reality is a scandal sheet, it would greatly improve its readership, but I suspect its owners are too intellectually superior to demean themselves in such a manner, even if it means the survival of their business.'

Lady Madeline leaned over towards him, her breasts brushing his arm. 'As long as they're not gossiping about us,' she said in a mock whisper, while staring at Lady Amelia. 'If they knew what we got up to it would really shock those bluestockings and make them jealous over what they're missing out on.'

Lady Amelia's blushing cheeks flushed a deeper shade of red and she quickly turned to the man sitting next to her and began chatting animatedly.

Leo continued to watch her as Madeline prattled on about something. She certainly was intriguing. It was unusual to meet anyone, never mind a young lady, who was prepared to disagree with him and challenge his opinions. Few men present this evening would have dared to be so bold.

Despite that, he had no interest in pursuing Lady Amelia and, if he needed a reminder why he did not get involved with debutantes, those blushing cheeks would provide it. Debutantes were innocents. She might have piqued his interest, but Lady Amelia Lambourne was definitely not for him.

Chapter Three

Amelia had not wanted to come to this dinner party and that odious man had just reminded her why. She despised everything he stood for, and, despite having been introduced to him several times in the past and again when they had first arrived, she had seen how he had struggled to remember her name.

Probably because she wasn't like his mistress, simpering and hanging on his every word as if he was the most wonderful man in the world. And didn't he just love it? He was so arrogant it was staggering. He thought just because he was handsome, just because he was so tall, with that thick black hair and those full lips, that strong jawline and high, chiselled cheekbones, that women were going to fall at his feet. Well, she would not.

Yes, perhaps he was more open to the idea of votes for women than the other men at the table, but it didn't take much to be more enlightened than this group of philistines.

And that most certainly did not excuse the way he

had talked about her beloved *Enquirer*. How dare he talk about buying up newspapers and magazines as if it were a casual pursuit, and not the destruction of people's dreams and aspirations? Well, there was no way he would ever get his hands on *The Ladies' Enquirer*. Her eyes lowered, she took a quick look in his direction, at his long, slender fingers holding his glass of red wine, then raised her eyes to his face. Those dark brown eyes, which were almost black in the subdued light of the candelabra, were staring straight at her. Studying her.

She quickly looked away. The peculiar tingle that his gaze had sent rippling through her made her wonder if it had been wise to disagree with Mr Devenish. Certainly none of the men at the table seemed prepared to do so. But why should she allow him to cower her? She had said nothing that she didn't believe with all of her heart and had every right to express her opinion. She tilted up her chin, turned to face him, and held his gaze with all the defiance she could muster. She had spoken her mind and would regret nothing of what she had said.

He held her gaze a moment longer then turned to Lady Madeline. Amelia held his and then turned towards Lord Prebbleton, wanting to dismiss Devenish as casually as he had dismissed her.

It was all so easy for Leo Devenish, she continued to silently fume, while giving Lord Prebbleton the impression she was listening to him. He was a man, and even though he had no interest in newspapers and women's magazines other than as a means to make more money, he had been able to purchase three of the biggest publications just so he could add them to his media empire.

How many magazines, newspapers and journals did this man need to possess? And how dare he say that *The Ladies' Enquirer* was worthy, as if that was an insult. She had started the journal because there were no magazines that appealed to women like her, educated women who wanted an intelligent read. That was a worthy cause, and one she was proud to be associated with.

Unfortunately, the arrogant cad was right about one thing. *The Ladies' Enquirer* was not a success and if she didn't do something soon to increase readership numbers it would indeed go to the wall.

'Like reading, do you?' Lord Prebbleton asked. 'Can't much see the point of it myself,' he continued before she had a chance to answer. 'Had enough of that in school to last me a lifetime, what?' He laughed as if he had made the most hilarious joke.

Amelia took another furtive look at Mr Devenish. Those penetrating brown eyes were once again looking at her, causing the heat on her cheeks to intensify. Drat it all. She hated him for making her blush. She was no simpering coquette. Never had been and never would be. So what if it meant men were rarely interested in her, and when they were, it was her marriage settlement that attracted them, rather than her charms, looks or grace?

It was who she was and she would never change. She would never be like Lady Madeline, who was pouting and preening at Mr Devenish as if he was some godlike creature who had deigned to mix with mere mortals. She turned back to Lord Prebbleton and tried to focus on what he was saying, something about looking forward to the shooting season once the social season was over. 'Balls and that are fine for you ladies, but us gentlemen are never happiest than when we've got a gun in our hands.'

Amelia sighed. It was going to be a long evening. Fortunately, or unfortunately, depending on how you looked at it, Lord Prebbleton did not expect her to contribute to the conversation, other than smiling and nodding. She flicked another look at Mr Devenish. Once again, he had turned his attention back to Lady Madeline, who was leaning towards him, exposing a scandalous amount of cleavage, and whispering in his ear. She couldn't help but give a moue of censure at his obvious enjoyment of such adoration. Typical man. Well, she would waste no more of her time thinking about him. She would instead use this time to contemplate what was really important—her financial problems.

She wanted to keep *The Ladies' Enquirer* true to its original aims, but dash it all, Leo Devenish was right, she needed to do something to attract a wider audience, especially as it would bring in more advertising revenue. And, dash it even further, he *was* probably right about everyone loving gossip. She considered herself an intelligent, educated woman but there were few things she enjoyed more than getting together with her friends and having a good old gossip.

Maybe she *should* include a Society page. The only problem was, who would write such a column?

Few of her contributors moved in the type of social circles the public wanted to read about. And those who did come from the higher echelons of society would be insulted if Amelia asked them to write a gossip column.

They were serious women who dedicated themselves to serious academic pursuits.

She took another furtive glance in Mr Devenish's direction. Lady Madeline was still leaning towards him, brushing herself against his jacket and whispering in his ear in a none too subtle manner. She smiled to herself. Amelia moved in the correct social circles. It might kill two birds with one stone if she started attending Society events to gather gossip, as her father would be happy— he would assume she was finally making more of an effort to attract a husband—and no one would suspect what she was doing. It would be perfect.

Still smiling, she turned her attention properly to Lord Prebbleton and asked him for the news from the various clubs of which he was a member. He instantly started regaling her with a story of an aristocratic woman who had run off to the Americas with her footman. Then, laughing to himself, he informed her of another club member who had lost all of his money investing in a dubious railway company in South America.

Once started, there was no stopping him, and he recounted a seemingly endless stream of gossip, some of which concerned people he considered friends. Amelia mentally shook her head. Men always claimed that it was women who liked to gossip, but, if Lord Prebbleton's revelations were anything to go by, there was nothing men enjoyed more than indulging in tittle-tattle.

She lifted her glass and made a silent toast to herself. That was what she would call her column: *Social Tittle-tattle*.

When the next course was served, she turned to Lord

Bradley and did the same. He too instantly launched into a litany of gossip, rumour and tales of scandals about friends and enemies alike.

Amelia raised her glass once again and this time made a silent toast to Mr Devenish. That arrogant man had inadvertently answered her prayers and shown her a way to save her magazine.

Leo removed Madeline's hand, which was slowly moving up the inside of his inner thigh, as he watched Lady Amelia chat and flirt with those two ninnies, Prebbleton and Bradley. He would have expected her to have better taste, but then, as an earl's daughter, her primary role in life was to find a husband. Both men were unmarried, both had inherited titles, and that alone gave those two imbeciles appeal, even to a young woman as bright as Lady Amelia.

He turned back to his mistress, who was cooing about something. What it was he cared not. After all, conversation was never Madeline's best attribute. He stifled his boredom. Now that he had celebrated his latest triumph, he rather wished they'd all leave. Including Madeline.

He looked along the table. The aristocracy were so predictable. The conversations were always the same, and everything they did followed a never-ending, never-changing routine. And Madeline was no different. She had married a man old enough to be her father, who was a crashing bore, but he was an earl with several prosperous estates, so, in her eyes, the perfect husband. Love never came into it for either of them.

He winced as a familiar pain ripped through him,

one that he hadn't felt for some time. Lady Lydia's face appeared in his mind's eye. He closed his eyes briefly and drew in a deep breath.

Love? Why on earth was he thinking of that? Hadn't he put those foolish notions well and truly behind him? The aristocracy knew nothing of love. That was something they left to the lower orders. For them, marriage was only about one thing—advancing your position in society. No, perhaps two things: advancing your position and increasing your wealth. While he now had the second requirement, he would never have the first. Lydia had made it clear that his lack of a title or a family he could trace back countless generations meant she could never marry him, and, despite having money that he had made himself through his own hard work, he would never be considered good enough.

His love had not been enough. When he had proposed she had actually laughed at him and informed him that women like her married titled men. And that was exactly what she had done. Despite his wealth and his power, he knew that the aristocracy would always consider him beneath them.

Once again, he looked down the table at his guests. He was under no illusions. These people might come to his dinner parties and treat him like a friend because they knew he was too powerful to ignore, but they would always regard him as a man who was 'not one of us'.

And that suited him perfectly. He did not want to be 'one of them' and would rather they feared him than truly befriend him. And as for the women, they might not see him as a potential husband, but that did not mean they weren't eager to become his mistress, and that too suited him perfectly.

'Perhaps we'll get a chance to slip away once the meal is over,' Madeline whispered. 'My husband has demanded that I return to the estate tomorrow for some boring family occasion, so we might not get another chance for a while. You're going to have to give me something to sustain me while I'm away from you.' She giggled, and her hand returned to his inner thigh.

Finally, she had said something that interested him. Madeline's husband had called her home. He would be free of her for some time. And he realised he did want to be free of her. It was time he ended this.

If he wanted to make it very easy on himself he could let her return home with the expectation that they would resume their affair when she came back to London, but he could not do that. He did not lie to his mistresses, and hopefully she would appreciate his honesty.

After tonight, he would be in search of another woman to warm his bed. His gaze returned to Lady Amelia. It was a damn shame she was not already married. Leo could tell he had affected her. The way her cheeks blushed when she looked at him and the way her lips parted and she gasped as if she was catching her breath were undeniable signs of her attraction. But he did not seduce debutantes. In fact, despite his reputation, he did not seduce any woman. All of his mistresses had clearly shown that they were willing. Some, like Madeline, had even unashamedly propositioned him. He knew what attracted them—his reputation and the excitement of being made love to by a man who came from the rougher, lower orders.

'Let's make an excuse and slip away now,' Madeline continued. 'I've learnt a few new bedroom antics that I think might delight you.'

Leo suppressed a huff of irritation.

'Yes, we need to talk. I'll join you in the green drawing room as soon as the ladies retire,' he said.

'Is that what you want to call it?' She laughed. 'You are right. We do need to talk, and I believe you will be excited by what I have to say.'

Leo stifled an exasperated sigh, knowing that Madeline was going to be far from excited by his response.

The final course over, the ladies retired to the drawing room while the men remained to take port and cigars. Amelia followed the swishing line of women dressed in an array of silk, satin and taffeta as they paraded down the hallway. Lady Madeline lingered at the back of the line, then instead of entering the drawing room kept on walking.

Amelia paused at the door as she watched her disappear around the corner. She presumably had arranged an assignation with Mr Devenish. It was none of Amelia's business, and she couldn't care less who he was meeting with in secret and what they were up to. But then, she was supposed to be gathering information for a gossip column. Wasn't this exactly what she needed to save her magazine—some really juicy gossip? For that reason, and that reason only, she quietly followed Lady Madeline. It would serve Mr Devenish right if he became the topic of *The Ladies' Enquirer's* first gossip column.

When Lady Madeline entered another room and shut the door, Amelia was unsure what to do next and she hovered in the hallway. Male footsteps heading her way forced her to make a quick decision and she secreted herself in an alcove.

The footsteps stopped, the door opened and closed and there was silence. Amelia emerged from her hiding spot. She looked up and down the hallway. Was she going too far in the pursuit of gossip? If she was caught spying the mortification would be more than she could bear. She should return to the drawing room. Now.

As quietly as possible, she tiptoed down the corridor, but raised voices and the mention of her name halted her in her tracks.

'Don't be ridiculous,' Mr Devenish said, his voice containing barely controlled anger. 'This has nothing to do with Amelia Lambourne.'

Amelia gasped and her hand flew to her chest where her heart had seemingly skipped a beat, but despite her shock she leaned closer to the door.

'I saw you looking at her,' Lady Madeline snapped. 'I can hardly believe you would stoop so low. She's twenty-three and unmarried. My God, the woman is practically a spinster and not exactly a beauty. I'd expect you to have higher standards than her.'

Amelia stiffened at the insult.

'As I said, I have absolutely no interest in Lady Amelia.' Amelia tried not to be offended. After all, he was saying no more than she knew to be true, and she had no interest in him either.

'Or is it because she's a virgin?' Lady Madeline continued, her voice rising. 'Is that what appeals to you? That's so typical of a man.'

Amelia covered her mouth, too late to stop another gasp escaping. But no one would have heard. Their voices had become so loud, their tempers so obviously inflamed she doubted they would hear if she was banging a bass drum outside the room.

'I have already said I have no interest in Lady Amelia. No interest in virgins, and no interest in debutantes,' Mr Devenish replied, each word stated slowly and clearly. 'The fact is, it is over between us. You knew it would end one day. We have had fun. Now it is time you returned to your husband.'

'How dare you? You are nobody, while I am the daughter of a baron, the wife of an earl. Who do you think you are, ending it with me? I'm the one who will end things when I'm good and ready.'

'It seems, madam, that, despite your exalted position in society, in this you are wrong.' Amelia could hear suppressed anger in his voice, and something else. Was it pain? Had Lady Madeline's venom wounded him? She had no time to contemplate this, as she heard footsteps coming towards the door.

As quickly and as quietly as she could Amelia ran down the hallway. When she reached the drawing room, she took a few steadying breaths, forced what she hoped was a carefree smile onto her lips, and entered. The women were taking coffee and chatting in small groups.

The men had already joined them and many were nursing brandy balloons.

Amelia took a seat near her father and smiled at him, hoping that nothing of what she had just heard was reflected on her face.

Mr Devenish entered the room, looking in her direction, and dash it all, flames of embarrassment engulfed not just her cheeks but also her entire body. He had already made it clear what he thought of her, so why did he have to look at her in that unsettling manner? She hoped—prayed—it was not because he knew what she had been up to.

The door opened again and Lady Madeline entered, her cheeks blazing in much the same manner as Amelia's. Without looking around, she strode across the room to where Mr Devenish was pouring himself a glass of brandy from the crystal decanter on the sideboard.

'Lady Madeline, may I offer you a brandy?' he said, his voice level as if their fraught exchange had not just taken place.

'No. This one will do.' Lady Madeline picked up his brandy balloon and threw its contents in his face. 'That's no less than you deserve, you bastard. I did everything for you, and this is how you treat me?'

Like a physical presence, silence descended on the room. All heads turned towards the angry woman and the man whose face was dripping with amber liquid. Mr Devenish removed a silk handkerchief from his top pocket, shook it out and casually wiped his face.

'This won't be the end of this, you no-account upstart,' Lady Madeline screeched. 'No one treats a woman like me as if she were a…a…common…'

Amelia waited to discover how Lady Madeline would describe her treatment. As did Mr Devenish and the entire room.

'I will teach you your place if it's the last thing I do.' Seemingly oblivious to the scene she was causing, she continued to glare at Mr Devenish, who had dried his face and was placing his handkerchief back in his top pocket.

He signalled to his footman. 'Lady Madeline is leaving. Please make sure she gets home safely.'

Shrugging off the footman, she turned from Mr Devenish, sent a ferocious look in Amelia's direction and stalked out of the room.

'And some foolish people think women should get the vote,' Lord Bradley announced. 'That just shows that they're far too emotional and prone to hysterics. Not rational at all.'

The men in the room all laughed uproariously, except Mr Devenish, who was still looking at the door through which Lady Madeline had just departed. Then he turned to the assembled guests.

'My apologies for that unpleasantness. It's lucky there are no journalists here tonight. That is just the sort of scandal I would like to see written up in one of my publications. It would send readership soaring.'

His nonchalance caused everyone in the room to laugh more heartily. Everyone except Amelia, who was secretly revelling in the knowledge that Mr Devenish would come to regret everything he had said and done tonight.

Chapter Four

Aunt Beryl was waiting up for Amelia when she returned from dinner, anxious to hear the day's news. While Minnie, her lady's maid, helped her undress, Amelia recounted her meeting with the bank manager, with a few artful modifications. She hated lying to her aunt but wanted to save her from any unnecessary worry.

'He didn't actually give his final approval for a loan at this afternoon's meeting,' Amelia said as Minnie unlaced her corset, keeping her voice light, as if completely unconcerned by the banker's refusal. 'But nor did he say no. He's a bank manager after all, so they like to consider things carefully, but there is definitely good reason to be optimistic.'

Provided I turn around the magazine's fortunes immediately, or tell Father and get him to guarantee the loan, which I will never do, and to which he would never give his consent.

'That is excellent news.' Aunt Beryl clapped her hands together. 'I just wish I had more money to give you, so you didn't have to borrow from a bank.'

Amelia raised her arms and Minnie lowered a night-gown over her head. Thankfully, the folds of embroidered linen hid her expression from Aunt Beryl, which she knew would expose her guilt.

'Thank you, but you've done more than I could ever wish for,' she said as her head emerged. 'And I promise I will pay back your loan with interest as soon as I can. And as the first investor in *The Ladies' Enquirer* I intend to pay you a healthy dividend once the magazine becomes profitable.'

If it ever becomes profitable.

'You don't have to do that. I'm just pleased I was able to help. Your mother would be so proud of you. *I'm* so proud of you.'

Amelia crossed the room and kissed her aunt's cheek. She had to make *The Ladies' Enquirer* profitable, not only so she could reimburse her aunt, but also so she could go some way to paying her back for all that she had done for Amelia and for the faith she had shown in her ability.

Amelia's mother had died when she was but two years old, and she could hardly remember her. Aunt Beryl had moved in to care for her sister's children and was the only real parent Amelia had ever had. Her father had remained aloof, only paying cursory attention to the boys, particularly Edwin, who was the eldest and the heir.

'And how was this evening's dinner party? Did you meet anyone interesting?' Despite Amelia being three and twenty and all but officially on the shelf, Aunt Beryl still harboured hopes that she would eventually marry.

While she hated disappointing her aunt regarding the loan, her lack of interest in eligible young men was something about which she had no regrets. She had dutifully attended social events each Season, keeping her father happy, but was yet to meet any man for whom she would surrender her cherished single state.

'No, nobody interesting, as usual.'

'Are you sure? Those blushing cheeks seem to be telling another story.' Her aunt smiled, her eyebrows raised in question.

'What? No. Not at all.' Her hurried response caused her aunt to add a tilted head to the raised eyebrows.

'I was seated next to Lord Prebbleton and Lord Bradley. It would be stretching the truth to breaking point to say that either of those gentlemen were interesting. And I'm afraid I got into a bit of a ruckus over votes for women. Father was most upset.'

She gave a little laugh, trying to dismiss the long, haranguing lecture she'd endured on the journey home. From the moment they were in the carriage until they reached their front door, he had lectured her on all the reasons she would never find a husband unless she changed her behaviour and how men did not like women who argued, telling her they did not want a clever wife, and that, as she was now three and twenty, she should be making more of an effort to be agreeable. Her father also reminded her, several times, that Amelia was not the only young woman available this Season with a sizeable marriage settlement.

'And was there no one else there that caught your eye?' Aunt Beryl asked.

Amelia sat at her dressing table and busied herself with vigorously brushing out her hair. 'No, no one. Everyone else there was married or otherwise spoken for.' That was not entirely true, as the exchange between Leo Devenish and Lady Madeline made it clear to everyone that they were no longer involved.

'Hmm,' was all Aunt Beryl said, as if suspecting there was more to Amelia's blushes and her sudden, frantic activity than she was letting on. But her aunt was wrong. The only reason why Amelia was thinking of Mr Devenish at all was because of what he had said tonight about her magazine, and the exchange she'd witnessed between him and Lady Madeline. It had nothing to do with whether she found him *interesting* or not. And even if she did find him *interesting,* which she did not, he certainly did not feel that way about her.

'I have absolutely no interest in Lady Amelia,' he had said to Lady Madeline. Her cheeks flamed further at her memory of their references to her status as a virgin and a spinster.

'Well, there's still plenty of time left this Season,' Aunt Beryl said, rising from the chair and kissing Amelia on the cheek. 'I'll let you get your rest, then. And I am so pleased everything is working out for you with regards to the magazine.'

Once her aunt had departed, Amelia dismissed her lady's maid and threw her hairbrush onto the dressing table. She had no intention of retiring to bed. Not yet. She was far too restless and still had important work to do. To that end, she moved to her desk, took out a stack of papers, opened her inkwell and dipped in her pen to write *The Ladies' Enquirer's* exciting new addition, the *Social Tittle-Tattle*.

Whether the new column was a success, and whether Mr Devenish was right that it would increase subscription rates, was yet to be seen, but as Amelia's pen flew across the page she could not deny that using that arrogant man's words against him provided her with a great deal of pleasure.

Leo Devenish's day always started the same way. No matter what the previous evening had entailed, no matter with whom he shared his breakfast, he always used the time before going to the office to scan the morning's newspapers and recent editions of all the magazines and journals.

This morning was no different, although he was dining alone. Since Lady Madeline's recent departure, he had not taken the opportunity to replace her. He'd had an offer or two, but frankly, none had piqued his interest. He would merely be replacing one bored married aristocratic with another.

Once he had perused the publications he owned and made notes on essential changes he wanted made immediately, he turned to the pile of rival publications. His casual skimming halted. He replaced his coffee cup and resumed reading *The Ladies' Enquirer* with renewed interest.

The highlight of a dinner party at the home of a certain Media Lion was watching said Lion wiping the contents of his brandy balloon off his face,

*which had been thrown at him by one Maddened
Lady. It was so kind of the Lion and the Maddened
Lady to put on such a show for the entertainment
of his guests.*

This was interesting. Very interesting indeed. It
would not take a genius to work out that the Lion was
Leo and the Maddened Lady was Lady Madeline. He
cared not that he had been featured in a scandal sheet,
and it was unlikely to affect Lady Madeline. Everyone
already knew of their affair, including her husband,
who had all but condoned the relationship. Her husband
might not like it appearing in print, but Leo doubted he
read such magazines and, tucked away in the country,
it was unlikely he would hear about it.

No real harm had been done. There was only one
thing that irked Leo. One of the men at his dinner party
had either written this column or passed on the information to a journalist at *The Ladies' Enquirer*. The fact
that it was a man he had no doubt. Along with a report
on his public encounter with Madeline was information of conversations that had taken place in the back
corridors of the Houses of Parliament. To be privy to
such information, one would have to be a politician or
a member of a gentlemen's club.

The question was, which man would be brave enough
to risk having him as an enemy? Few of the men who
had dined at his home were involved in the newspaper
industry, but that did not mean they didn't have con-
tacts in the media. There were some he knew to be short
of funds, people who had never expected to work for

a living but needed money. Such men would have no reservations in resorting to such subterfuge as selling information to a newspaper.

There were, of course, the owners of the magazines he had recently bought, including Addington. They had good cause to try and take revenge on him, although it did seem a rather petty way of doing so.

Whoever it was, he would come to regret trying to get the better of Leo Devenish. But before he could exact his revenge, he first had to find the culprit. And he knew exactly how to do that.

He would host a ball.

It was not something he had done before, and that alone would be of interest to a Society column like this *Tittle-Tattle* nonsense. He generally avoided balls, seeing them as a tedious waste of his valuable time, but this ball would have a purpose. He would invite everyone who had attended his dinner party and before long he would know the name of the informer.

His thoughts moved to Lady Amelia Lambourne. Her father was perhaps the least likely of the men present to have provided such gossip to a journalist. He was not involved in the media, and certainly did not need the money. However, there was always the possibility that, like most members of the aristocracy, he saw Leo as an upstart and wanted to put him in his place. So he would extend an invitation to the Earl of Kingsland, and his rather delightful daughter.

It wasn't the first time his thoughts had turned to her over the last few weeks. They had in fact strayed in that direction more than he knew was prudent. He, of course, would not be replacing Lady Madeline with a debutante, to even think such a thing was ridiculous, but she was the most intriguing woman he had met in a long time. And maybe, one day, when she was no longer an innocent young lady, when she was married to one of those ninnies, Bradley or Prebbleton…

He coughed to clear his mind of such diversions. He would also have to invite those two ninnies. He doubted either of them had the wit or the courage to be foolish enough to make an enemy of Leo, but you never knew, and they did need the money that selling such a story would bring. So they would be on the guest list.

For the first time in his life, Leo was actually looking forward to attending a ball, though he would not be wasting time indulging in mindless chit chat with the idle rich. No, he would be on a quest to find and punish the person who had the gall to attempt to embarrass him.

And there was nothing he enjoyed more than exacting revenge on stuck-up aristocrats who thought their position in society gave them the right to ridicule people they considered their inferiors.

Chapter Five

Amelia flicked the thick white card between her fingers. Under most circumstances an invitation to a ball would be received with despondent resignation, but not today. It was perfect timing on behalf of her nemesis, Mr Leo Devenish, even if he didn't know it.

All in all, today had been a good day, and things finally seemed to be looking up for Amelia.

Sales figures for the latest edition of *The Ladies' Enquirer* had arrived on her desk that morning. They were up on previous editions. Substantially. As were subscriptions, and several new advertisers had signed contracts. All of whom had insisted their ads be placed on the *Social Tittle-Tattle* page.

She looked at the invitation bearing Mr Leo Devenish's signature and smiled. That despicable man had been right. A gossip column was exactly what *The Ladies' Enquirer* needed.

She flicked the card one more time then placed it back on the mantelpiece. There was only one downside to this success. Another column had to be produced next month, and until Amelia could find a social butterfly who also enjoyed writing—a combination she doubted existed—it would be up to Amelia to continue producing the monthly column.

During the Season, she avoided as many social events as possible. She would avoid them all if she could but had to attend enough to keep her father happy, and to stop him from criticising Aunt Beryl and blaming her for Amelia's lack of suitors. But Mr Devenish's ball was one she most certainly would be attending. It would be the ideal place to gather plenty of gossip to entertain her readers.

On the night of the ball, Amelia discovered she was actually excited. That too was a new experience. As was dressing for a social event with such care. She even encouraged Minnie to give her corsets that one extra pull to accentuate her waist as pleasingly as possible, and selected her mother's ornate pearl combs to adorn her hair.

This newfound vanity had nothing whatsoever to do with Mr Devenish, she told herself. Of course it did not. Nor was it because she cared what anyone thought of her, especially not arrogant men like him. It was just that she needed to give the appearance of a young debutante enjoying a ball, so no one would suspect what she was really up to. It was just a coincidence that the first social occasion that she would be attending in a professional capacity was that man's ball.

Amelia had carefully chosen her pale salmon silk gown with cream embroidery and once Minnie had buttoned up the long line of pearl buttons at the back of the gown Amelia turned to inspect herself in the mirror. Her hair had been elaborately styled in the latest French manner and was piled high on her head, with several tendrils curling artfully round her bare shoulders. The neckline was perhaps a little lower than she would normally wear, and the delicate cream lace seemed deliberately placed to draw the eye to her decolletage.

Her dressmaker had recommended this style, claiming that such a daring neckline was entirely suitable for a lady of Amelia's age. Amelia had known what she really meant; when you reached the advanced age of three and twenty and had still not married, you needed to be more obvious in your determination to attract a man's attention.

Amelia had put up no objection at the time, assuming that the gown would, like so many others, remain unworn. But tonight was not a night to be cautious, and her gown reflected that. Tonight she would be on a mission and she needed to look her best. She stifled a small giggle at the thought of her decolletage distracting men while she extorted an endless stream of gossip from them.

Thanking Minnie, she picked up her gloves and fan and walked down the hallway to Aunt Beryl's room, her embroidered silk train providing a swishing accompaniment to her steps.

She entered her aunt's room and was greeted by a beaming smile. Her aunt rushed towards her and took her hands. 'Oh, Amelia, you are the picture of beauty and elegance. No one is going to be able to resist you looking as you do tonight.' The smile became brighter. 'Especially a certain someone.'

'There is no certain someone,' Amelia responded more curtly than she intended. 'There is no one special,' she repeated in a gentler tone.

Aunt Beryl raised her eyebrows but thankfully made no further comment on that subject. Since returning from Mr Devenish's dinner party, Aunt Beryl had got it into her head that Amelia was smitten with some man. It was ridiculous. If her mood had altered since the night of Mr Devenish's dinner party, it was simply due to all that had subsequently happened with *The Ladies' Enquirer*.

Yes, she had expressed her excitement about attending tonight's ball, and confessed to a few nerves, but that was only because of the task ahead. If she *was* interested in seeing Mr Devenish again, it was merely because he mixed in interesting circles and could perhaps provide the information she needed for her column.

'Turn around,' Aunt Beryl said, her hands clasped to her chest. 'I want to see how your gown looks from every angle.'

Amelia did a slow pirouette. When she returned to face Aunt Beryl the older woman's smile had grown even larger, if that was possible. 'Just beautiful. You are going to be the belle of the ball tonight.'

Amelia smiled, strangely pleased by the compliment, but that was not what tonight would be about. All her gown was doing was providing suitable camouflage for her real purpose. If any man happened to be distracted by the way she looked then that was all for the good.

Not that she expected Mr Devenish to notice her, no matter how pretty her gown. She was unlikely to spend any time in his company, and if she did pay him any attention at all it would be merely in the hope of witnessing a repeat performance of the sort of drama that had occurred at his dinner party. Though it was unlikely Lady Madeline would be attending the ball. She was back in the countryside with her husband and Mr Devenish had no doubt moved on to some other woman by now.

She placed her hand on her stomach, which had suddenly tied itself up into tight knots.

'You've nothing to worry about,' Aunt Beryl said quietly. 'You look lovely and I'm sure he will appreciate the effort you've gone to.'

'No, I—'

'But we had better not keep your father waiting,' she continued, taking Amelia's arm and leading her out of the room and down the stairs to the drawing room. Her father gave Amelia a quick look, nodded his approval, then escorted them out to the waiting carriage.

The nerves gripping Amelia's stomach tightened as they drove through the jostling London streets to Mr Devenish's Mayfair home. That had never happened before. When forced to attend a ball, she was usually consumed with ennui, dreading the evening to come. It must be because tonight she would be working and so much depended on her finding something to amuse her readers and hopefully draw in more subscriptions and advertising revenue.

That had to be the reason for the strange fluttering

sensation that had possessed her. It could not be because she would soon be seeing Mr Devenish again. Even thinking such a thing was ludicrous.

Their carriage pulled up in front of his townhouse and joined the mayhem of carriages and horses, all jockeying for position so the elegant occupants could alight on the doorstep.

Finally they entered the brightly lit home where musicians were already playing a lively dance tune, handed their cloaks to the waiting servants, then passed through the bustling, noisy crowd and entered the ballroom. All of Society seemed to be in attendance, and the room was filled with women dressed in elegant gowns of every colour of the rainbow—their hair bedecked with ribbons, jewels and feathers and men in formal black evening suits, white shirts and white ties, the men's only concession to colour being their embroidered brocade waistcoats in various shades of cream, silver, gold and red.

Amelia knew that many members of Society looked down their raised noses at men like Leo Devenish, whom they regarded as new money, but that snobbery had not stopped them from accepting his invitation. Amelia suspected some were here out of curiosity, some were indebted to Mr Devenish, and some, like her father, knew it was in their best interests to keep on the right side of a man who wielded such power, even if they did not entirely approve of him.

The reasons why each was here would be something else Amelia would set about trying to discover, as it would make an excellent *Tittle-Tattle* article. She was sure people would love reading about the foolish snobbery of the upper classes, and she could even tie it in with some social commentary, thus making it more than just gossip.

She scanned the room for Mr Devenish. He was standing in the corner, deep in conversation with Lord Prebbleton. What on earth those two men had to discuss she had no idea but was certain it would not be her. Perhaps he was apologising for the scene at the dinner party, although she also doubted Mr Devenish ever apologised for anything. His nonchalance when Lady Madeline threw the brandy at him was staggering and his subsequent behaviour had been anything but apologetic.

Her scanning of the room moved on. As she had predicted, Lady Madeline was nowhere in sight. That was no surprise, but there were many other attractive women present.

Despite her exquisite gown and the time she had taken to style her hair, Amelia was suddenly feeling very dowdy compared to those sophisticated, elegant women, one of whom had surely taken Lady Madeline's place on Mr Devenish's arm, and even in his bed.

Not that it mattered to her which woman he chose, except as fodder for the *Tittle-Tattle,* of course.

'There's Lord Smythe,' her father said, releasing her arm. 'I must have a word with him. You two will be all right on your own for a while, won't you?' Before Amelia had time to answer, her father was off, moving through the throng and disappearing into the crowd.

'So, who is that man?' Aunt Beryl asked.

'Lord Smythe? He's an old friend of Father's. I thought you had been introduced to him.'

'No, not him. The man you keep staring at.'

'What? Who? I'm not staring at anyone.'

'That rather dashing man over in the corner talking to Lord Prebbleton.'

Amelia flicked a quick glance towards the corner. 'Oh, him—that's Mr Devenish. He's the host of to-night's ball.'

'Is he, now?' Aunt Beryl said, adopting a self-satisfied smile that Amelia had never seen before.

Amelia looked towards Mr Devenish, who was now walking across the ballroom floor, heading in their di-rection.

Amelia swallowed a yelp of consternation and re-sisted the inclination to hide behind her aunt. That would never do. She was a bold journalist in pursuit of a story and would act accordingly, so she forced herself to hold her ground.

'It looks like your Mr Devenish is coming our way,' Aunt Beryl said.

'He's not *my* Mr Devenish,' Amelia said through the side of her mouth just before he joined them.

'Lady Amelia,' he said with a bow. 'I am pleased you accepted my invitation.'

Amelia swallowed a lump that had strangely formed in her throat and forced herself to smile up at him. The fluttering in her stomach intensified, as if a flock of birds had just been released from their cage. Such a re-action just had to be because of her fear that he might know she was responsible for telling the world about his altercation with Lady Madeline.

It couldn't be anything else. It certainly was not because he looked devilishly handsome tonight, with his olive skin and black hair appearing even darker against his crisp white shirt, or because those brown eyes staring down at her appeared like deep dark caves, full of hidden mystery.

She coughed lightly to drive out that thought. *Deep, dark caves, hidden mystery.* Ridiculous.

'I was delighted to receive the invitation,' she said with a curtsey. 'And may I present my Aunt Beryl? Miss Simpson, Mr Devenish.'

Aunt Beryl curtseyed, still with that strange, smug smile on her lips. 'If you'll excuse me, I will join the other chaperones and leave you young people to enjoy the ball.' And with that she scuttled off, as if she couldn't get away from Amelia fast enough.

Amelia continued to watch as her departing aunt was swallowed up by the crowd, then slowly turned her attentions back to Mr Devenish.

Remember what you're here for. You need to gather some suitable gossip. And Mr Devenish would be the perfect place to start.

She forced herself to smile, horrified that her bottom lip trembled.

Be brave, Amelia, be brave. You're a fearless journalist, remember? The owner of a soon-to-be successful publication. You will not be intimidated by anyone, even a man like Mr Devenish.

Her smile became strained as she desperately tried to think of something to say that would cause him to share some titbits of gossip which would entertain her readers and encourage advertisers to spend lavishly. But her mind remained a blank.

'I have not seen your father tonight,' he said as she fought to get her mind, which she had previously considered quick and nimble, to actually start working. 'I was hoping to talk with him,' he added.

Amelia's stomach clenched tighter. It was not her that Mr Devenish wished to talk to but her father. Of course. Men like him did not speak to young women like her. They went in pursuit of women like Lady Madeline.

'He is here, but I'm afraid he seems to have disappeared. It looks like you're stuck with me.' She gave a little laugh, but he neither smiled nor laughed in response.

'That will be no hardship.' His dark eyes swept quickly over her and Amelia swallowed a gasp as heat rushed to her cheeks and radiated throughout her body. No man's look had ever elicited such a powerful response from her. Never before had she been more conscious of her appearance, more aware of her feminine shape, and more in need of a man's approval.

She blinked to brush away such silliness. She needed no man's approval, and Mr Devenish's less than most.

'You are looking particularly lovely this evening, Lady Amelia,' he said.

She gave a forced smile, as if it were merely a compliment made out of politeness that meant nothing, which it surely was.

He did not smile back. Did this man ever smile?

'Thank you.' She bit her lip, racking her brain for some meaningless conversation that would give her time to regain her composure. 'And you're looking… I mean, the ballroom is also looking particularly elegant this evening.' She gazed around the room, smiling inanely, then back at Mr Devenish.

He raised his eyebrows and Amelia blushed brighter. She really was burbling. She never burbled but tonight she was burbling. And she had never seen this ball-room before so didn't know whether it was looking particularly elegant or not. For all she knew, the large central chandelier with its myriad candles always sent light sparkling around the room, the parquet floor always shone to perfection, and the enormous bouquets of scented lilies, lavender and gardenia were a regular feature.

'Perhaps you'd do me the honour of the next dance. Then you can familiarise yourself with the room,' he said, offering her his arm. He was making fun of her, but as she could think of no witty comeback, or any comeback at all for that matter, she mutely placed her hand on his and let him lead her out to the centre of the dance floor.

Chapter Six

Calm down, Amelia admonished herself as they lined up with the other couples. *It's just one dance.*

But any attempts to calm herself were thwarted when he placed his hand on her waist for the waltz, causing a warm tingling to radiate out from his touch. Despite the fabric of her dress, her corset and chemise providing a barrier between them, it was as if his hand was stroking her naked skin, causing it to burn.

She had waltzed with many men over the last five seasons but had never noticed what an intimate dance it was. Was he standing closer than propriety demanded? Amelia wasn't sure. All she knew was the warmth of his body seemed to be burning into her, and that masculine scent of musk and bergamot was overwhelming her senses.

The music started and they glided across the floor. He was a sublime dancer. Of course he would be. She suspected he did everything sublimely, unlike Amelia, who had never been particularly graceful. She knew the steps but had always gone through them in a formal manner. But dancing with him was different. Never before had she been so conscious that she was a woman in the arms of a man, and that she was surrendering to his lead. It was not like mere dancing. It was more like she was participating in a ritual that was almost primal. That reaction was surely because she had never before danced with a man who exuded such raw masculinity, one whose body was so strong, whose face was so ruggedly handsome. Even his scent seemed more masculine than that of other men.

She closed her eyes briefly, and her body continued to follow where he took her, as if they were not just a man and a woman dancing but had joined and become one.

Her eyes flew open and she coughed lightly. Once again, she was becoming fanciful. It was just a dance, nothing more. They were doing the same as every other couple on the floor, and no one else was behaving as if they were partaking in an intimate act.

Focus, Amelia, focus.

But what should she focus on? Her hand moved along the strong muscles of his shoulder, feeling the contained power under her fingers. She had heard that he was the son of a blacksmith. Did that account for the physical strength that emanated from him? Once again, she closed her eyes, imagining him with his sleeves rolled up, exposing the knots of muscles in his forearms. She pictured him pushing back his black hair from his sweat-slicked brow then returning to his work, and rhythmically pounding red-hot metal into submission.

'Oh, my,' she whispered as she released a small sigh. She cast a quick look up at him to see if he had registered her odd behaviour. He was looking down at her, but his gaze did not suggest disapproval. Quite the contrary. His look held an intensity unlike any she had seen before. She wanted to look away, knew she should look away, but couldn't. It was madness, but like a mesmerist, his gaze was seemingly holding her enthralled.

Was this how he looked at his mistresses? As if he wanted to possess them? Was this why Lady Madeline had behaved in such a manner when he had finished with her—because she had fallen under his spell?

She shook her head slightly and forced herself to look away. She was being ridiculous. He was just a man. A man who was sublimely handsome, she had to admit, but still just a man. He was not capable of ensnaring a woman with one look, and no man, not even Mr Devenish, would ever possess her.

She had to get herself under control and stop acting in this uncharacteristically featherbrained manner. This ball was the perfect opportunity to gather material for her column, and she was wasting it with silly fantasies about blacksmiths and mesmerists.

What she had to do was get Mr Devenish to open up and reveal some information that would be perfect for her column. Once again, her mind went blank, which seemed to be its natural state this evening.

She looked up again and forced a smile. Even if she could think of an opening that would get Mr Devenish talking, she doubted he would be inclined to gossip anyway, but she had to try, otherwise it would be a waste of an evening.

'I see you were talking with Lord Prebbleton earlier,' she said with as much composure as she could summon.

Her comment merely elicited a slight nod of his head. She would have to push harder. 'May I be so bold as to enquire what you were discussing so avidly?'

She smiled up at him in what she hoped was innocent nonchalance. He held her gaze. Her smile became strained, as did her nerves, and she suspected she did not have what it took to become a real journalist.

'You have no need to concern yourself, Lady Amelia. We were not discussing you. Although I am sure that you still have Lord Prebbleton's affections.'

'Oh, no, no, that wasn't what I meant,' she blurted. 'I have no regard for Lord Prebbleton at all.'

That eyebrow was raised once more and she knew that she was burbling again.

'And yet you are curious to know what he and I were discussing?'

'Not that curious,' she mumbled, wishing she had tried another approach to get information out of him.

'Is it Lord Bradley, then, that you are more interested in?'

'Bradley? No, of course not. I'm not interested in either of the Vacuous Viscounts.'

As he continued gazing down at her, the strangest thing happened. A smile quirked the edges of his lips. It turned into a full smile, and then he actually laughed. Amelia smiled back as warmth coursed through her. It was as if he had just bestowed on her a precious gift and he really did have a rather wonderful smile. It lit

up his face, made those dark eyes sparkle and trans-
formed his appearance.

'"The Vacuous Viscounts" describes them perfectly.
I'd always thought of them simply as the ninnies, which
is not nearly as apt.'

Amelia bit her top lip, suddenly ashamed of herself.
'We really shouldn't be so cruel. It's not their fault if
they're, well, rather shallow.'

His face was once again serious. It was as if he had
never smiled, let alone laughed. 'I've known both of them
since we were at school, and I believe when it comes to
being cruel, you couldn't possibly begin to match them.'

There it was again, that pain underlying his brusque
manner. She looked up into his eyes, trying to read what
had caused that pain, but it was as if a shutter had come
down and he was determined not to reveal anything,
at least not to her.

'Unfortunately, my father rather likes both men,' she
said.

'Of course he does.' His words were crisp, dismissive. 'They have titles, estates. That alone makes them
perfect husbands.'

'But not for me.'

He looked down at her, his lips once again quirking
into a slight smile. 'And what sort of man would make
a perfect husband for you, Lady Amelia?'

*One who is so handsome he makes my insides quiver.
One who intrigues me with his contradictions. A man
who is so strong, so self-composed, but every so often
lets his mask slip and shows there is a vulnerable core
under that hard, steel-like exterior.*

'I have no interest in marrying anyone.'

'And yet you attend Society balls, such as this one. Don't all young ladies attend such events to find a suitable husband?'

'Not this young lady.'

He cocked his head slightly as if he didn't believe a word she was saying.

'And what of you, Mr Devenish? Are you hosting this ball to find yourself a wife?'

She could see she had shocked him with her boldness. Good. Maybe she'd shock him into revealing some gossip. 'If you are able to ask such a question of me, then surely you can have no objection if I do the same,' she added.

He nodded in acquiescence. 'Indeed, and I will answer in the same vein. I too have no interest in marrying anyone.'

No, but you do have an interest in married women, she would have liked to say, but that demanded a level of courage she did not possess.

'Is Lady Madeline present tonight?' she asked instead with feigned innocence, surprised she was able to summon even that level of boldness when dealing with such a man.

'I believe Lady Madeline has retired to the country with her husband,' he replied, his voice dismissive as if it was of no importance to him.

And been retired as your mistress.

'What have you been occupying your time with lately?' he asked, taking her by surprise. Was he actually making small talk, or was he just trying to distract her from asking any more questions about Lady Madeline?

'Oh, nothing that would interest you.'

Apart from running a magazine and increasing the subscriptions rate at your expense.

'But I'm sure you've been having an exciting time with your newspapers.' She smiled up at him, all coquettish simpering. Miss Halliwell would be pleased with her. She was making small talk, complimenting a man, and smiling mindlessly. In other words, doing everything she was taught at Halliwell's Finishing School.

He gazed down at her, his dark eyebrows drawn together. 'I'm sure you don't wish to discuss business.'

I most certainly do, as it is my business as well.

'Perhaps we should just enjoy the dance.' He pulled her in slightly closer towards his chest and Amelia almost gasped.

No, talking would be much better. Then she would have something to distract her from the effect being near to him was having on her frazzled nervous system. They were almost touching. If she just leaned forward, ever so slightly, she would actually be up against his chest. What would that be like? Would the muscles of his chest be as firm as the ones of his shoulder? Would it be all hard planes and tough brawn, like those of the bare-knuckle boxers she had seen in newspaper sketches?

As if she no longer had a will of her own, her body moved closer to his. Her head was almost resting on his shoulder, her breasts were all but skimming his evening jacket. This was not how she was taught to waltz at Halliwell's Finishing School. Miss Halliwell always insisted that it was essential to be able to see plenty of light between a couple. If Amelia moved any closer, she was in danger of completely extinguishing all light.

The music came to an end, freeing Amelia from her inappropriate thoughts and behaviour. But then he placed his hand on the small of her back to escort her off the dance floor. The touch was feather-light but once again it seemed to scorch through her dress, through the layers of her undergarments to her naked skin.

And, once again, she knew she was being ridiculous and acting out of character. But that was the effect Mr Devenish had on her, and possibly had on all women. She just had to remember how Lady Madeline had behaved. Something about him was capable of causing women to embarrass themselves in public. She would be wise to remember that, if she wasn't to find herself also behaving like a foolish, impulsive woman.

He returned her to Aunt Beryl, who had left the other chaperones and was standing on the edge of the dance floor with Amelia's father, watching the approaching couple.

Aunt Beryl was beaming a smile, unlike her father, who bore a look of decided distaste. Mr Devenish bowed politely, thanked her for the dance, and departed, no doubt off in search of some other woman to enchant.

'Oh, my,' Aunt Beryl said, fanning herself. 'You two make a lovely couple.'

'We're not a couple,' Amelia blurted.

'Don't be ridiculous, Beryl,' her father added. 'Mr Devenish is hardly suitable for Amelia.'

'He certainly looks suitable, very suitable indeed. And he appears to be rather wealthy.' Aunt Beryl looked around at the large ballroom, one that would be the envy of many a duke, earl or baron.

Her father sent Aunt Beryl a disapproving glare, then leaned in closer to whisper, 'He purchased this house.' It was a simple statement that said so much. Her father was informing Aunt Beryl that Mr Devenish had committed the unforgivable transgression of being newly rich, rather than having inherited all of his property. Unlike the Lambournes, and most of the other people present, he did not come from a family that had been wealthy for countless generations.

Aunt Beryl looked at Amelia. 'He is rather handsome. Don't you think, Amelia?'

'I hadn't really noticed,' Amelia replied, hoping her blushing cheeks would be attributed to the heat of the ballroom.

'Handsome or not, I hope he doesn't ask you to dance again,' her father said, still scowling. 'Won't do. The man has a reputation, you know.'

'Yes, Father. I was at the dinner party, remember?'

'Yes. Quite. Anyway, Lord Bradley has asked for the next dance. I, of course, accepted on your behalf. A much more suitable young man. A viscount. I'd prefer an earl or a duke, but needs must, and his family does go back generations.'

Amelia could see Lord Bradley approaching from the other side of the room. 'That's most unfortunate, Father. You're going to have to make my excuses, as I really must go to the ladies' retiring room. Now.'

Before her father could make an objection and before Lord Bradley could reach her, she skirted round the edges of the ballroom, and escaped to the adjoining withdrawing room, where many of the guests had congregated to converse, away from the sound of the orchestra. Including Mr Devenish.

Amelia pinned herself to the wall, hoping Mr Devenish would not think she was following him. But she had nothing to fear. He was deep in conversation with Lord Addington and seemed oblivious to everyone around him, including her.

At least he's not in pursuit of another mistress.

Amelia mentally chastised herself for that thought. That was precisely the sort of gossip she was after, and exactly what she would expect from Mr Devenish. Surely that was the reason for this ball, so he could peruse the available women and take his pick.

So why wasn't he flirting? Why was he engrossed in conversation with Lord Addington? Were the two discussing business? Both were newspaper men, so if they were, then it was Amelia's business as well, and she needed to hear what they were saying.

To that end, she quietly and discreetly edged herself through the milling crowd and placed herself behind a chatting and laughing circle of guests. Despite the burble of conversation flowing around her, she could catch snippets of Mr Devenish and Lord Addington's conversation.

'...the Lords have approved the bill but I believe that might be due more to Lord Somerfield's son being kept out of court than to any real support for law reform,' she heard Mr Devenish say.

'Appalling, just appalling,' Lord Addington replied, before Mr Devenish moved off through the crowd.

Lord Addington turned, strode off in the opposite direction, joined his wife and led her back into the ballroom.

That was strange. Why on earth would Mr Devenish tell Lord Addington something so scandalous and potentially libellous as to suggest that Lord Somerfield was corrupt?

Mr Devenish had moved to the other side of the room, speaking just as intently to Lord Montgomery. As unobtrusively as possible, Amelia slipped through the crowd, smiling at each person she passed, so if Mr Devenish did spot her, she could pretend she was part of a group and oblivious to his presence.

When she was within earshot, she stopped, and lingered on the edge of a rather large, exuberant group, and concentrated hard to block out their raucous laughter so she could hear what Mr Devenish was saying.

'His debts are said to be momentous, and it won't be long before he's carried off to the debtors' prison.'

'That's terrible, poor man,' Lord Montgomery replied, shaking his head ruefully.

Mr Devenish was doing it again, spreading gossip and possibly setting himself up to be sued for libel. What on earth was the man up to? Whatever it was, she was determined to find out.

To that end, she continued to follow him, moving slowly and quietly through the crowd, but always ensuring that there were enough people between them to conceal her presence.

When he took Lord Sanderson by the arm and led him to a corner, Amelia once again did her best to position herself within hearing distance, but not so close that she would be seen by either man.

'I must apologise for that scene Lady Madeline made at my dinner party,' Mr Devenish said with a level of bonhomie that she had never heard before.

'Not at all, old chap. Women can be so emotional,' Lord Sanderson said, causing Amelia to grimace her disagreement.

'That's so understanding of you, but Lady Madeline's scene was nothing compared to what happened to Lord Addington.'

'Really? Do tell.'

Amelia quietly huffed her annoyance.

And men accuse women of being gossips.

'He's been sharing the same mistress with the Prince of Wales. When the Prince found out apparently there was quite a scene, with the Prince threatening Addington with a fire poker.'

'My goodness, poor old Addington,' Sanderson said with a chuckle. 'Serves him right.'

Mr Devenish turned, and Amelia quickly darted behind a rather portly gentleman, who smiled at Amelia, as if such antics from a young woman were perfectly normal behaviour.

As Mr Devenish passed by, she slowly moved around her rotund cover, keeping him between herself and her quarry. Once Mr Devenish was out of sight, she smiled at the confused gentleman in thanks, then continued her pursuit.

She quickly surveyed the crowd to see where he had got to, then just as quickly gasped. Her father had entered the room and was standing in the doorway looking around, presumably in search of his errant daughter. Amelia slowly squatted down and peeked between the shoulders of two women wearing conveniently concealing ostrich-feather boas around their necks. As much as she wanted to pursue Mr Devenish, she was just as determined not to be dragged back to the ballroom and handed over to Lord Bradley.

Mr Devenish approached her father, and she would have so loved to hear what they were saying but the risk was too great. Instead, she moved to a conveniently placed marble pillar, and like a spy watched the two men in conversation.

Mr Devenish was leaning close to her father, all but whispering in his ear. Her father's eyes grew wide, then a schoolboy smile crept across his lips, indicating that he too was the recipient of some rather salacious gossip.

What Mr Devenish was up to was now so obvious, Amelia was surprised she had not spotted it immediately. Mr Devenish was no gossip, and if he was, it was most unlikely he would gossip with Amelia's father. He was planting false information with every man who was at his dinner party in order to expose the person who had tattled to *The Ladies' Enquirer*. Amelia was unsure whether to be amused, insulted or to feel smug that she had duped Mr Leo Devenish, a man who struck fear into politicians and rival business leaders throughout the land.

She decided smug was the best option, with a dash of pique that he did not see her as capable of such subterfuge. It served him right. He had arrogantly assumed it had to be a man who had the audacity to print gossip about him. He presumably also thought a man was behind *The Ladies' Enquirer*, and it was a man who had been listening when he had inadvertently given advice on how to improve the magazine's finances.

Now that she knew what he was up to, she would leave him to his pointless endeavour, and return to her own pursuit, finding some genuine gossip with which she could fill her *Tittle-Tattle* column.

That, at least, was what she should do. Instead, she continued to watch him as he accosted Lord Hainsworth and engaged him in conversation. Amelia did not have to hear what was said to know that it was something rather titillating. Lord Hainsworth's expression was almost identical to her father's. His eyebrows rose, a gleeful smile spread across his lips and then he rubbed his hands together in pleasure at whatever lies he had just heard.

Amelia slowly shook her head, but the men's reaction further proved Mr Devenish correct. He had said everyone loved gossip, both men and women. If the men's reactions were anything to go by, they would happily part with their coins to buy a magazine that provided it, even one aimed at educated ladies.

Mr Devenish parted from Lord Hainsworth and left the room. Amelia should just leave him to his fruitless pursuit, and resume her own, more important work. But she was enjoying this intrigue far too much to give up now. She edged through the crowd and slipped out of the door, just in time to see Mr Devenish turn the corner at the end of the hallway.

As quietly as possible she walked down the hallway, saying a silent thanks to her satin ballroom slippers that seemed designed for such clandestine behaviour. Still smiling to herself, she slipped round the corner then froze as a mortifying sight greeted her.

Chapter Seven

'Are you going to tell me why you have been following me?'

Amelia stared at the man standing in the middle of the empty hallway. All she could think of was how those dark brown eyes were glaring at her.

'Oh, I… I was… I was just…' She looked over her shoulder and pointed as if somehow the hallway could provide a reason for why she had found herself so far from the ballroom.

He stepped towards her. She fought the temptation to take a step backwards.

'You were what, Lady Amelia?'

Amelia now knew what a startled rabbit felt like when confronted with a fox. She should do something. Turn tail and run, fight back, something, anything. Not just stand in the middle of the hallway racked with indecision.

'Does your father know that you are stalking men as if they are your quarry? Is that how you usually behave at balls?'

Stalking? Quarry? Was the fox accusing the rabbit of being up to no good?

'No, I mean, no, I wasn't stalking you, I was…'

Stalking you.

He took another step closer. 'I'm sure you are aware that it is most improper behaviour for a young lady.' His gaze moved from her startled eyes and slowly, inch by agonising inch, raked down her body. 'You could give a man the wrong impression as to what it was you wanted from him.'

She should be outraged. He accused her behaviour of being improper. Well, the way he was looking at her was decidedly improper. But what was even more improper was the unexpected reaction of her body.

Her heart, whose beating had seemingly come to a halt on first encountering him, now pounded back into life, thumping hard and fast against the wall of her chest. Breathing had become much more difficult, as if the room was suddenly short of air. But worse than that, the pulsating was not confined to her heart, but a deep, throbbing sensation had taken over her entire body. This was unlike anything Amelia had experienced before, and it was all because Mr Devenish was looking at her, in *that* way.

His gaze slowly moved back to her face, pausing at her lips before once again fixing on her eyes. 'Or are you following me to give me the right impression?'

She placed her hand lightly on her stomach to try and still the fluttering and pulled in a long, calming breath. The arrogant man was playing with her for sport, and thoroughly enjoying the effect he was having on her.

She slowly exhaled and tilted her chin. He was about to discover that she was no rabbit frightened of the fox, but a strong woman who would stand her ground and give as good as she got.

'I have no idea what impression you have, Mr Devenish, right or wrong. But I can assure you I most certainly was not following you.' Good. Despite the heat in her cheeks, despite the tension in her stomach and the unfamiliar reactions in parts of her body best not thought about, her words came out strong and defiant.

He raised his eyebrows as if to say he did not believe a word of what she was saying.

How presumptuous of you, Amelia wanted to say.

He assumed that she was following him because she found him attractive. Well, yes, she did find him attractive, but she was certainly not following him because she wanted to sacrifice her virtue to him. After one dance he thought she had fallen so hard that she had lost all sense of reason and was about to throw herself at him. The man's arrogance seemingly knew no bounds.

'So why are you in this hallway, so far from the ballroom and the other guests?'

Damn. There was that question again. The one she still couldn't answer. The truth would not do. She could hardly say she was the owner of *The Ladies' Enquirer* in search of more gossip. That she was the person he was attempting to flush out by planting false gossip with all the men who had attended his dinner party. No, that was something he must never know. But she needed to say something. He stared down at her, waiting for her answer.

Think, Amelia, think.

But thinking was something she was finding all but impossible to do. Instead she stared back at him like the innocent woman she was, a woman completely out of her depth, a woman she desperately did not want to be.

'I'm sure the Vacuous Viscounts would be most upset if they discovered that you got free of your chaperone and were all alone, with me.'

Damn him. She would not let him treat her like a little girl who was misbehaving. She was the owner of a magazine, a woman of some importance, and more than a match for this man.

Ignoring her inconveniently inflamed cheeks, she attempted a nonchalant laugh. 'Are you worried that you might feature in another gossip column?'

His jaw hardened. His eyes became cold. Amelia shivered, suddenly doubting the wisdom of raising the subject of the *Tittle-Tattle*.

'I take it you read *The Ladies' Enquirer* and realised who they were talking about in their scandal column.'

She nodded. 'It must have been simply awful for you,' she said, aiming for outraged shock.

He shrugged. 'I care nothing for that.'

So why have you been trying to find the source of the gossip all night?

'All that concerns me is that one of the men who attended my dinner party passed on the information. I intend to find the guilty party and deal with him accordingly,' he said, answering her unspoken question.

Amelia forced her eyes to grow wide in innocent curiosity. 'Oh, and do you have any leads?'

'No, but I've planted a few seeds. Now I just have to watch to see which one germinates.'

She furrowed her brow and nodded as if considering this piece of information. 'That's very clever of you.'

He gave her a long, considered look and she swallowed. Had she gone too far, playing the innocent young lady impressed by the much more intelligent man?

'But what I said was correct. You should return to the ballroom and not be alone with any man. Especially me.'

'Do you think they might write that I am your latest mistress?'

He laughed as if such a thing was absurd. Amelia recoiled. Was the idea so ridiculous that it was a source of mirth for him? Apparently so. Not that it mattered to her. She too considered the idea of her becoming Mr Devenish's latest mistress an absurdity, and yet the gripping pain in her stomach suggested something entirely different.

Amelia forced herself to smile, as if sharing this ludicrous joke. 'Well, perhaps I could help you in your search for the person who wrote that article. After all, no one is going to suspect a young lady of doing such a thing.'

Including you.

Her smile became genuine. He might consider her a joke, an innocent woman he could not take seriously, but she was the one having a joke on him. Amelia took comfort in that and it went some way to assuaging her embarrassment over his laughing at the idea of her becoming his next mistress.

'I need no one's help,' he stated.

'We all need someone's help some time.'

'You are wrong. I need the help of no one.'

Amelia wanted to be offended by his statement, wanted to take umbrage at his rejection. To see it as yet another personal affront to her and to women in general, as if they were not capable of offering assistance. But she couldn't. Once again, he had exposed more than he intended. His words were strong, but this arrogant, powerful man had given her another glimpse of the man underneath, a man capable of feeling pain.

'I will find the person responsible.' His jaw lifted as he looked over her head. 'And I will make him regret his actions.'

A twinge of guilt rippled through her. He was seeking the person who had tricked him, and that person was standing right in front of him, and she was still tricking him.

She pushed down that thought, reminding herself that she should have no pity for Mr Devenish. He would happily take over her magazine given half a chance and destroy her dreams, just as he had done with so many other publications. If he did so it would inevitably expose Aunt Beryl's involvement, and bring ruin to that kind, trusting woman. No, she could not feel pity for him. He did not feel pity for the owner of *The Ladies' Enquirer*, or the owners of any of the other publications or businesses he had acquired.

He looked back at her and that predatory smile returned. 'But you still haven't answered my question. Why are you stalking me? What is it you want from me?'

I want you to promise to leave my magazine alone.

'What does a woman usually want from a man?' The

words came out before she had time to think of what she was saying.

His eyes grew large, just as the eyes of the men who he had been gossiping with had done, then he composed himself. It may have been a risky thing to say, but it was rather nice to have disconcerted this man.

'Have I shocked you with my boldness?' she continued, starting to enjoy herself.

He stepped even closer, took hold of her chin, tilted it up and stared down into her eyes. 'You need to be careful. Young women who play with fire are liable to get burnt.'

Amelia's temperature certainly was soaring, as if she was standing far too close to a roaring fire.

'Is that what you want? To burn?' he asked, his voice menacingly quiet.

Yes, no, yes.

Amelia didn't know what she wanted. All she knew was she didn't want to leave. Didn't want to return to those boring men in the ballroom, didn't even want to go back to her ordinary life, the one without him in it. He might be frightening, but there was something so intoxicating about Mr Devenish that she wanted to stay right here, no matter what the consequences.

'Maybe,' she whispered, so quietly she could barely hear her own response.

'Are you sure?' Still holding her chin, he leaned closer, his face merely inches from hers. 'Once the fire begins there is often no means of controlling it. Is that what you want? To lose control?'

Amelia couldn't answer, couldn't think. Even if she

could speak, her heart was pounding so fast and loud she was sure it would drown out anything she might say. Instead, she swallowed, trying to relieve her dry throat, and ran her tongue lightly along her bottom lip, to soothe her equally dry lips.

'I believe you have completely forgotten what is proper for a young lady.'

That was something Amelia did not need to be told. She knew young ladies were not supposed to behave like this and was equally certain they were not supposed to feel like this. Their lips were not supposed to yearn to be kissed. Their skin was not supposed to ache for the touch of a man's caressing hands. They were not supposed to be pulsating deep within their core, with a demanding need that was almost painful.

He was now so close, his breath was a gentle stroke, warm on her cheek.

Hang what is proper, she wanted to say. *If being with you will cause me to burn, then let the inferno rage.*

He continued to stare into her eyes, his face so close all she had to do was lean forward and they would be touching. As if pulled by an invisible thread, her parted lips inched towards him.

She held her breath and closed her eyes. Her mind was almost blank, with only one thought possessing her, the one that was calling to him, willing him to do something—anything—to relieve her of this desperate craving building inside her.

His lips lightly touched hers and she gasped, causing them to part further. She tilted back her head and waited. His masculine scent and the heat of his body enveloped her. The material of his jacket lightly skimmed her breasts, increasing their aching sensitivity. She moved in slightly closer, wanting to feel the hardness of his body against the softness of her own. Unable to resist, she pressed her lips more firmly onto his. Her tongue escaped from her mouth and lightly ran along his bottom lip. He tasted wonderful, like brandy and something intangibly male.

Then his lips were gone. Her eyes flew open. Had she imagined that brief, light kiss, conjured up their touch out of some fevered part of her brain?

He had stepped back and smiled down at her.

'Run along, Lady Amelia. Back to your chaperone, back to your young gentlemen. Girls like you should not be left unchaperoned. You never know what trouble they might get into.'

Was he laughing at her? Had that kiss been a joke, a prank played on a silly debutante or, even worse, an old maid? At the very least he was treating her like a child. She was not a child. She was a grown woman, and a businesswoman.

How dare he?

She took a step backwards, disgusted with him, but even more appalled by her own behaviour. She had exposed herself to him. She had let him know that if he wanted her, he could have her. That her virtue was his for the taking. And he had made it equally clear that he did not want her.

He really was despicable. Not only was he out to ruin the owner of *The Ladies' Enquirer* by planting libellous gossip, but he had also just used her for sport, for his own entertainment, and had the audacity to now laugh at her.

She turned and strode back to the ballroom without another word. He may have humiliated and made fun of her, but she would be the one to have the last laugh.

Chapter Eight

Leo stared down the corridor, trying to make sense of what had just happened. How had he come perilously close to entangling himself with Lady Amelia? How had he forgotten, for one dangerous moment, that she was an innocent young lady—in other words, untouchable?

He shook his head slowly, as if to shake some order into his confused thoughts. He did not seduce debutantes. In fact, he rarely even spoke to that protected breed of females. There was no reason for him to do so. He did not want a wife. Nor was he like some men who were tempted by forbidden fruit, and he most certainly was not the sort of man Madeline had accused him of being, one who was drawn to virgins.

For all those reasons he should not have been tempted by Lady Amelia, but by God, he had been. Despite knowing it was wrong, he had been unable to resist tasting those cherry-red lips. Thank goodness he had been able to stop at one chaste kiss. If he had not stopped when he had, heaven knew what might have happened. If he had given in to his baser nature he would have been lost completely. He doubted he would have been able to fight the desire to take her, here, up against the wall of this empty hallway and satisfy a primal need unlike any he had ever experienced before.

He exhaled a long, slow breath. This was not like him at all. He liked women, of that there was no doubt, but never before had a woman made him feel as if he was losing control. And she wasn't even his type. She was not conventionally beautiful, and despite her clumsy attempt at sophistication she was inexperienced. He might not know what it was about her, but she was a temptation. Was he ever going to forget the sight of those inviting lips parting, or those full, luscious breasts falling and rising as she drew in rapid gasps? He certainly hoped so.

He should at least give himself some credit for resisting the irresistible. She had been so ripe for the picking. All he would have had to do was take what she was so naively offering, lead her away, up to his bed chamber, and have her. But he knew where that would end up. Marriage.

That was something he did not want. Although he had to admit, in some ways he envied the man who would one day marry Lady Amelia. If it was one of the Vacuous Viscounts it would be a tragedy. She needed a man who knew how to strip away all the remaining barriers that prevented young women from giving vent to their sensual natures. A man who would guide her, helping her explore her passions to the full. And tonight, Lady Amelia Lambourne had shown him clearly that she most definitely had passions worth exploring.

But unfortunately he would not be the one to do so.

He gritted his teeth as the image of those parting lips once again invaded his mind. This would not do. He needed a distraction to rid himself of that memory.

What he needed was another mistress. That would stop him from thinking about plucking forbidden fruit. That would stop him from fantasising about releasing those lovely breasts from their trusses of whalebone and tightly stitched cloth.

He ran his tongue along his bottom lip, savouring the memory of the soft touch of her lips, her scent as delicate as gentle rain on spring flowers, and her sweet, feminine taste. Surely that behaviour only proved her innocence. She could not have known what effect she had on him, how she was driving him mad with desire, and causing him to lose sight of the rules by which he lived.

He coughed, determined to be done with such thoughts. He needed to get his mind under control. One thing he prided himself on was his discipline, of never breaking his own rules. That was what had got him to such heights in the world of commerce. He had never before had to exercise that discipline when it came to women, had never needed to, but he was going to have to do so now.

It was time to forget all about Lady Amelia, and he knew exactly how he should do that. He needed another woman. Right now.

That had not been his goal for tonight. All he'd planned to do was entrap the man who had betrayed him to *The Ladies' Enquirer.* Then he'd intended to return to his study and work, only emerging when it was time to say goodbye to his guests.

But Lady Amelia had ruined all that. He needed to replace Madeline. To that end, he entered the ballroom and scanned the array of beautiful women. His gaze took in Lady Amelia, who was dancing with Lord Bradley. Good. That was where she belonged, with her own kind.

Several women caught his eye, their smiles speaking volumes, including Lady Sarah, the Duchess of Penderville, who was watching him from the other side of the ballroom. She was everything he was after—beautiful, elegant, married and known to have taken several lovers already. All she would want from him was a bit of meaningless fun, and that was all he would ever offer a woman. She smiled at him and ran her fan lightly over her lips, signalling her availability.

He flicked a quick look at Lady Amelia before walking across the room with determination and bowing in front of the Duchess. 'Lady Sarah, would you do me the honour of granting me your next available dance?'

'I'm available now,' she gushed, not looking at her dance card.

He smiled politely and led her onto the floor, where couples were lining up for the polka.

'It's a shame it's not a waltz,' Lady Sarah said in a breathy whisper. 'Lady Madeline tells me that your technique is unsurpassed, and you can show a woman how such a dance really should be performed.'

This was going to be so easy. Too easy.

'My husband is not much of a dancer,' she continued, with much fluttering of eyelashes. 'He never has been, even when we first married. Now he'd rather play cards. That's where he is now, and I know he doesn't care one bit with whom I dance.'

She gave a quick wink in case he had missed her none too subtle innuendo.

He looked over Lady Sarah's head and saw Lady Amelia lining up with Lord Prebbleton. The dance commenced and a laughing Prebbleton spun her around as if she were a child's spinning top. The buffoon.

But he should be paying no heed to Lady Amelia. It would not be long before she married a man like Bradley or Prebbleton. That was what women of her class did. He knew from bitter experience that titled ladies only ever married titled men, even if the men were complete dolts. He looked down at Lady Sarah, who was chattering on about something. She too had married the man chosen for her and in doing so had elevated her own and her family's position in society. The fact that the two held no attraction for each other was neither here nor there. Now Lady Sarah was looking for some fun, and that was why he was suddenly of interest to her. Something that suited him perfectly.

He cast another quick glance at Lady Amelia. He was more than happy to provide beautiful young women with some excitement, as long as none of them expected any more from him than that.

The dance over, he escorted Lady Sarah off the floor, then departed as quickly as possible. She was beautiful, she was available, and had sent every sign that she was willing, but she was not the distraction he craved.

Lord help him. It had been more than a month since Madeline and he had still not replaced her. Was he tiring of women altogether? He cast another glance towards Lady Amelia. She was talking to her chaperone, and it seemed the two were preparing to leave.

Good. With women, he knew that out of sight meant out of mind, and Lady Amelia would be no different. Refusing to watch her any longer, and determined not to think any more of her, he looked around, certain that there had to be a woman present who would serve his needs.

'Are you sure you wish to leave so early?' Aunt Beryl asked yet again as they took their cloaks from the servants. 'I thought, perhaps, that Mr Devenish might ask you for another dance.'

Amelia flicked a look at the maid who had just placed the cloak around her shoulders. Hopefully, Mr Devenish's servants weren't the type to gossip. It would be just too embarrassing if it got back to Mr Devenish that she was hoping for another dance with him.

'We have already had one dance. You can hardly expect me to endure another,' she said, just in case the servants were indeed the gossiping type. 'And it would be most improper to dance more than once with the same man.'

And even more improper to kiss him and all but thrust yourself upon him.

Aunt Beryl frowned slightly, either in censure of Amelia's tone, or in confusion over her sudden bad mood. Whatever it was, Amelia could not worry about that now. She needed to be away from this ball, away from Mr Devenish, and away from her humiliation.

It was bad enough being rejected by him, worse that he had laughed at her, but even more humiliating that he had then immediately commenced flirting with other women. She might be fleeing like the frightened rabbit she had been determined not to be, but that was better than remaining in the ballroom to be further demeaned by the sight of him in obvious pursuit of a new mistress.

'He seems a very presentable young man,' Aunt Beryl continued as they waited outside in the cool evening air for their carriage, the light, music and laughter spilling out from the townhouse into the otherwise quiet Mayfair street. 'Very presentable indeed.'

Amelia looked at her aunt, who was wearing a small, coquettish smile. Was she too falling under his spell? Was no woman immune to his charms? She had seen the way Lady Sarah had looked at him, as if greedy for his attention. The Duchess was a beautiful woman, unlike Amelia. She was experienced, unlike Amelia, and tonight she would probably discover what it was like to be really kissed by Mr Devenish, unlike Amelia.

What on earth had she been thinking when she had all but thrown herself at him? She wasn't thinking, that was the problem. It was so unlike her to be bedazzled by a man just because he was handsome, charming and so damn manly. Finding herself alone with him had addled her brain and caused her to forget just what sort of man he was. He had endless women in his life, and when he tired of them he disposed of them the way she would cast off last season's bonnets. She had seen that in the way he had broken up with Lady Madeline. He was also a hard-headed businessman who cared nothing for who got hurt in his endless pursuit of power. And had she forgotten he was the man who could destroy all of her dreams, put an end to *The Ladies' Enquirer* and financially ruin her beloved aunt?

She had no right to criticise Aunt Beryl for falling under his spell. Hadn't she done the same? Despite having so much to lose?

'Or would you prefer Lord Bradley or Lord Prebbleton?' her aunt said with a knowing smile.

Amelia rolled her eyes, which caused Aunt Beryl to laugh.

'I have no interest in any man,' she said emphatically, and it was Aunt Beryl's turn to roll her eyes.

'Well, Mr Devenish appeared to have an interest in you. He was looking at you rather a lot when he was dancing with the Duchess. We chaperones notice such things,' Aunt Beryl said as the carriage arrived and the footman lowered the steps and helped them inside.

Amelia had also noticed Mr Devenish looking at her. She also knew it meant absolutely nothing. The man thought she was a joke. Not only did he find her clumsy attempt to kiss him a cause for great amusement, but he also didn't even have the slightest bit of respect for her intelligence.

She huffed out a sigh of annoyance. He had made the assumption that it had to be a man behind the *Tittle-Tattle* column. He wouldn't imagine for a minute that it was a woman who owned *The Ladies' Enquirer*.

She looked out of the window as the carriage drove

them home through the London streets still bustling with hansom cabs, carriages and people doing heaven knew what at this late hour. Amelia watched the passing traffic as she tried to calm her thoughts and her agitated body.

Her father had said he would find his own way home and not to wait up for him. That suited Amelia just fine. She could not endure the inevitable questions about whether Bradley or Prebbleton had made their intentions known, and, if not, what Amelia intended to do to ensure that she had a proposal before the end of the Season. She had far too much on her mind to pay heed to such trivia.

When they arrived home, she said goodnight to Aunt Beryl, claiming she wished to retire immediately. But once Minnie had helped her undress, she sat at her writing desk, pulled out some paper and dipped her fountain pen into the inkwell.

This was what she was supposed to be doing. Saving her magazine. Not attempting and failing to flirt. Not trying to be someone she most certainly was not. Not being distracted by a man. She was a serious woman with a serious job to do.

That was something Mr Devenish would never appreciate about her. He saw her as a silly young woman of no substance. He really was the most infuriating man she had ever met, and there was a lot of competition for that honour. Tonight he had insulted her intelligence, laughed at her and rejected her. Those were three crimes for which he was going to pay dearly.

Mr Devenish might not know it, but he had made an

enemy tonight. He thought she was a source of amusement. Well, he was soon going to find out the true extent of her sense of humour.

She would have her revenge on that arrogant, insulting man. As her pen scraped across the page, she smiled to herself, savouring the pleasure of the sweet, satisfying feeling.

Chapter Nine

The familiar pile of newspapers and magazines, stacked neatly beside his breakfast setting, greeted Leo in the morning a month later. As they did at the start of every day. He poured himself a cup of thick black coffee from the silver coffee pot and picked up the first newspaper. The latest edition of *The Ladies' Enquirer* would be in the pile, but he resisted the temptation to read it first. Discovering the identity of the rat who had the temerity to try and best him was a pleasure he wanted to save till last. It would provide him with a warm feeling of satisfaction that he could savour as he travelled to his office.

Then he would take his time to consider how to exact his revenge. It would have to be a punishment suited to the guilty individual. That too was something to which he was looking forward, and something that was not to be rushed into. After all, wasn't revenge reputedly a dish best served cold?

He sipped his coffee and moved on to the next newspaper. Once again, he was taking his breakfast alone, as he had every morning since Madeline's return to her country estate. It was something upon which he was trying not to dwell, but this behaviour was certainly out of character. It was more than two months now. That was the longest he had been without a woman in his bed for as far back as he could remember. And it was not as if it were something which could not easily be rectified.

Lady Sarah had made her availability clear by sending him suggestive notes and she hadn't been the only married woman to inform him that her husband was out of town, or even out of the country, and she was in need of some diverting company.

Was he tiring of aristocratic women? Or worse, tiring of women altogether? he asked himself again. It was a ludicrous thought, but one that niggled at him on occasion.

He continued to peruse the papers, trying to give his unfamiliar state of celibacy no further thought. Eventually, he reached the bottom of the pile and picked up *The Ladies' Enquirer*. Before the identity of the traitor could be revealed, he poured himself another cup of coffee. Then, as if performing a pleasant ritual, he sat back and opened the magazine. He skimmed through several articles—on fossil hunting, the health benefits of cycling for women and the need to improve the working conditions of Lancaster miners—until he got to *Tittle-Tattle*.

As he read the column his smile died. He sat forward, gripping the magazine, and read the column again with greater concentration.

His fists tightened, ripping the edges of the page. This was an outrage. He slammed down the magazine,

causing the coffee cup to rattle in its saucer and the mar-
malade pot to jump. Someone was going to pay. And
pay dearly. Grabbing hold of the tattered magazine, he
raced out of the breakfast room to his waiting carriage
and informed his driver that he would not be going to
the office this morning.

His ruse had failed, and Leo hated to fail. No one had
taken the bait of all the false gossip he had planted, and
someone at the ball had committed an even greater act
of betrayal, one that he would never forgive. But first, he
had to put his own lust for revenge aside. He had to make
this right. An innocent woman's reputation was at stake,
and he had to do everything in his power to save it.

To that end, his carriage pulled up outside the address
of *The Ladies' Enquirer.* He bounded up the narrow,
dark staircase, which smelled unaccountably of boiled
cabbage, passing countless closed doors, to the top floor,
and burst into the magazine's small, cluttered offices.

'I demand to see the owner of this rag,' he shouted
from the doorway, waving the ripped magazine above
his head. 'And I demand to see him now.'

Amelia reacted before she could think and somehow found herself hiding under her large desk in her
office, which was just off the main room in which Mr
Devenish now stood.

She knew he'd be annoyed that his plan had failed,
and somewhat chagrined that he had once again been
the subject of *Tittle-Tattle*, but such anger was surely
unwarranted. After all, it was just a harmless gossip
column that no one was likely to take too seriously.

She now had two choices. Emerge from the office and deal with his wrath, or continue hiding.

'I said, I demand to see the owner, and I demand to see him now,' his voice boomed through the door. Amelia made her choice. She would remain hidden. Not because she feared Mr Devenish, and not because she knew she was going to look a fool climbing out from under the desk, but because it was obvious he still had no idea that she was the owner of *The Ladies' Enquirer* and still thought it was a man behind the *Tittle-Tattle* column.

'Lady Amelia?' Charles, her secretary, accountant, sales executive and virtually everything else in the office, moved around the back of her desk and looked down. 'Lady Amelia? What are you doing?' He looked up. 'And who is this man?'

'You're going to have to pretend that you're the editor of *The Ladies' Enquirer*,' she whispered, hoping above hope that Charles would do as she said and be a convincing actor. 'I'll explain everything once he's gone.'

Amelia knew she was taking the coward's way out, but at least it would preserve her anonymity, and she could take some comfort in knowing she was once again triumphing over Mr Devenish and using his prejudices against him.

He had thought himself so clever, planting all that false gossip in the ears of the men at the party. If he didn't have such a low opinion of women's intelligence, he would not have immediately assumed a man had to be behind *The Ladies' Enquirer*. Well, now his low opinion of women, and of her in particular, had come back to bite him.

All he thought a woman was good for was to serve as his mistress. And in Amelia's case, he didn't even think that.

'Good morning, sir. How may I be of service?' Charles said, moving to stand in the doorway of Amelia's office.

'I demand to see the owner of *The Ladies' Enquirer*.' Mr Devenish's boots pounded across the floor of the outer room and his voice grew closer.

Charles looked over towards the desk, and Amelia stared up at him in appeal, circling her hand to indicate that he should play along with her scheme.

'I'm afraid the owner is not here, but I am the editor.' Charles reached out his hand. 'Charles Harrison. And how may I assist you?' His hand dropped to his side, unshaken.

'You can start by printing a retraction and admit that there is no truth in the lies you've printed in this edition of your scurrilous rag.' His fist hit the table, causing Amelia to start with surprise.

'A retraction?' Charles said slowly. 'Lies?'

'Yes, lies, man,' Mr Devenish seethed. 'You will either print a retraction admitting that your article was all lies or I will be suing you.'

'Was there something in the magazine that was inaccurate?' Charles asked, without prompting from Amelia. He picked up a copy of the magazine and began flicking through it, obviously wondering which article could contain inaccuracies, and why it should so anger this man.

The magazine disappeared from Charles's hand, pulled away by an irate Mr Devenish. Paper rustled above her head and once again the desk shuddered as Leo's fist hit it hard. 'This is what I am talking about. This has ruined a young woman's reputation and I demand that you retract it.'

Amelia frowned and tried to gather her thoughts. This was unexpected. Why on earth should he care that the article made reference to her? He hadn't reacted so violently when she had written about him and Lady Madeline. He had not demanded a retraction then or claimed that the column was all lies. Surely this was no different. And it wasn't a lie. She had, perhaps, exaggerated ever so slightly, just for effect, but she hadn't actually told any outright lies.

'It doesn't mention the young lady's name,' Charles continued. 'It merely says, *"At a recent Society ball, the Lion was alone with the Lamb. Their passionate embraces suggest he has now developed a taste for feasting on the innocent flesh of—"'*

'I know what it says, man!' Mr Devenish shouted. 'And anyone who moves in the same social circles as the lady in question will know to whom it is referring.'

'And is it not true that the so-called Lion was alone with this Lamb person and seen in an embrace?' Charles asked.

Mr Devenish hesitated for a brief second. 'I'm not going to argue with you over that. You will print a retraction or you will rue the day that you attempted to challenge me. I don't know who your source is, but they too will be paying a heavy price for what they have done.'

Charles frowned. 'It is most irregular for a magazine to print a retraction unless something is shown to be incorrect.'

Mr Devenish leaned over the desk, his face inches from Charles's, the anger seemingly radiating off him. Amelia shuffled backwards further under the desk so he would not see her cowering in the corner.

'Either you do as I say or I'll tie this magazine up in legal knots that will ruin it,' he seethed through clenched teeth. 'By the look of this office I have much deeper pockets than this small enterprise ever could. Even if I lose, by the time that has happened it will be bankrupt. That will inevitably mean job losses. I suspect you do not want to be one of those unfortunate people who are out looking for a new job in an industry where I wield such power.'

Charles swallowed so loudly that Amelia was able to hear him from under the desk. This was not going at all well.

'So you expect a retraction?' Charles looked down at Amelia, who nodded. 'Then a retraction is exactly what you will get, sir,' he said with a tremulous smile. 'Will there be anything else?'

'It will be on the front page.'

Charles looked back down at Amelia, who gave a resigned nod.

'Of course.'

'Banner headlines'

Amelia nodded again.

'Yes, sir,' Charles replied.

'Good,' Mr Devenish said. 'Now, thanks to you and this excuse for a magazine, I have a young lady and her father to apologise to. This,' his fist hit the desk again, 'has put me in an unenviable position. If I am unable to make this right with the young lady in question and her father, then, retraction or not, *The Ladies' Enquirer's* days are numbered.'

With that he left, slamming the door of Amelia's office behind him.

Charles reached out his hand. With as much dignity as possible, Amelia climbed out from under the desk, which for some reason was more difficult than her quick and efficient dive underneath it.

'I'm so sorry about that,' Amelia said, standing up and brushing down her dress.

'Who was that man? Why was he so angry?' Charles looked from Amelia towards the door through which Mr Devenish had departed.

'I'll explain as soon as I can, but first I have to get home as quickly as possible.' Amelia picked up her hat and coat and raced to the door. 'And thank you, Charles!' she shouted over her shoulder. 'You made an excellent editor.'

Charles sent her a confused smile, then slumped down into her chair behind the desk and rubbed his hands against his furrowed brow.

If she could she would take the time to console Charles, but she had other problems that needed her immediate attention. She had to stop Mr Devenish before he confronted her father and made a bad situation even worse.

Leo was stunned that such a wimpish man was the editor of *The Ladies' Enquirer*. The weakling could hardly even make eye contact. Instead, he had repeatedly looked down at his desk in that cowardly manner. Plus, he hardly seemed to know his own mind. But fortunately for him he had agreed to do as Leo demanded. But in many ways, getting a retraction was the least of Leo's problems.

He knocked on the door of Lord Lambourne's Belgrave townhouse while attempting to compose himself. This conversation was going to demand diplomacy, not anger.

While he'd known exactly what he wanted to say when he entered the offices of *The Ladies' Enquirer*, he was unsure what he was to say to Lady Amelia and her father. All he knew was he would have to agree to whatever they requested to make this right.

The door was opened by the Earl's butler, who accepted Leo's calling card. 'I am afraid neither Lord Lambourne nor Lady Amelia are home,' he said in that superior tone often adopted by senior servants.

'Please tell him I need to see him on a matter of some urgency.'

'Very good, Mr Devenish.' Had *Mr* been said with a note of disapproval, from a servant more used to addressing visitors as 'my lord' or 'your grace'?

The snobbery of senior servants always irritated him. When he was a child the butler and housekeeper had made his mother's life a misery, all because she was considered at the bottom of the heap, working as a day servant, doing the lowliest of jobs when the family needed the extra money.

In his own establishments, such behaviour was never

tolerated. Every member of his staff was treated with respect, no matter what their position.

But now was not the time to care about the snobbery of Lambourne's servants. Instead, he returned to his waiting carriage and sat staring out at the quiet street, without actually seeing anything.

For the first time in his adult life, he was unsure what to do next. He did not feel inclined to return to work while this matter remained unsettled. Lord Lambourne was possibly at one of his clubs, but Leo did not want to be seen pursuing the man around London. Nor was it wise to confront him in public. This was a matter that needed to be dealt with discreetly and in private.

So he sat, and he waited, drumming his fingers on his thigh and still fuming over the fact that one stupid article in an inconsequential magazine had put him in this onerous position.

A hansom cab drew up in front of the house, and a flustered Lady Amelia alighted and rushed up the path towards the front door.

Leo jumped out of his carriage, all but ran up the path and caught up with her on the doorstep.

'Lady Amelia, it is vital that I speak with you,' he said, reining in his anger at the magazine. He needed to maintain his composure and handle this with delicacy. He had to reassure this innocent young woman that she had nothing to fear, that he would do everything and anything in his power to preserve her reputation.

'Why, Mr Devenish, this is a surprise.'

Why it should be a surprise Leo could not imagine. She claimed to always read *The Ladies' Enquirer*.

She knew that in last month's *Tittle-Tattle*, the person referred to as the Lion was him. Could she be so dim-witted as not to know the Lamb was her? She had never struck him as dim-witted. Quite the contrary.

If she hadn't made the connection, perhaps he had no need to have this difficult conversation. Shame gripped him. Was he such a coward that he was prepared to shirk his responsibility? He *had* kissed her. That alone demanded some redress. Now it was public knowledge, even if she was unaware of that fact, she deserved an apology and reassurance that he would do whatever was required to satisfy her and her father's honour.

'I need to talk to you and your father.'

'My father?' She looked up and down the street as if expecting the man to suddenly appear. 'What on earth do you need to talk to him for?'

'Please, Lady Amelia, this is something we need to discuss inside and not on the doorstep. May I come inside?'

'Yes, yes. I suppose so.'

The butler opened the door. Lady Amelia swept in and handed her coat and hat to the waiting footman.

'Please serve tea in the drawing room,' she said to the butler.

'Miss Simpson is not at home. Shall I ask your lady's maid to join you?' the butler asked.

'No, that will not be necessary. Mr Devenish will not be staying long.'

She looked at him and he nodded his agreement. Leo did not know how long this conversation would take, and he did wish to wait until her father returned, but it would be better if they talked in private, without witnesses. And really, what harm could being alone together do now?

'But will you arrange for tea to be served, please?'

The butler bowed and departed. Lady Amelia showed him into what was obviously the ladies' drawing room, with its soft pink walls, comfortable chairs placed to make conversation easy, an array of potted plants and an abundance of the knick-knacks that ladies seemed to favour.

'To what do I owe this visit?' She indicated a chair.

He sat down opposite her, attempting to compose himself and consider what he was to say, and how he would say it. 'Have you read *The Ladies' Enquirer* yet?'

'Yes, it was a very interesting read, as usual. I particularly enjoyed the article on cycling. I think perhaps I might take up that sport. It sounds like such fun.'

'Did you read the *Tittle-Tattle* column?'

'Yes, I ran my eye over it, but I care nothing for gossip.'

He drew in a breath to prepare himself for what was to come. If there were tears or hysterics, he would have to take it like a man. Although he was unsure how men were supposed to deal with such things. 'Lady Amelia. I am very sorry to have to tell you, but the article mentioned you, and our…exchange at my ball.'

Her eyes grew wide in innocent curiosity.

'I don't remember reading anything about us.'

'It didn't refer to either of us by name, but we are the Lion and the Lamb.'

'Oh, are we?' She was obviously still not taking in the full ramifications of what the column said.

'That's rather clever, isn't it? The lion for Leo, and the lamb for me, my family name being Lambourne.'

How could she possibly be so calm? An aristocratic lady's reputation was her most valuable possession. Without it, her chances of making a good marriage were ruined. Could she not see that her reputation had been besmirched in a highly public manner? 'Whether it is clever or not hardly matters.'

Surely that does not need to be pointed out.

'And there was nothing clever about anything else it said. I'm afraid it will have done terrible damage to your reputation, and your father will be furious.'

The butler entered with tea and conversation halted. 'Leave it, will you, please, Samuel? I'll pour the tea.'

They both watched as the servant departed.

'There's little chance my father will have read it,' she said, picking up the teapot. 'He avoids reading anything if he can, and certainly won't be reading a magazine aimed at women with enquiring minds.'

She gave a little laugh as she handed him a cup, which he placed on the side table, in no mood for refreshments. 'Be that as it may, others might read it and are likely to tell him.'

'Well, if that does happen, I can say it was someone else that you were seen kissing at the ball. You do have rather a reputation.'

'There was no one else.'

'Really? But you were seen dancing with Lady Sarah and—'

'There was no one else,' he repeated, fighting to keep his temper in check. Whether he had kissed anyone else or not was hardly the point and not something he wished to discuss with her. He had to make her see that she needed to take this matter seriously.

'When people work out who the Lion and the Lamb are, which they inevitably will, this will ruin your reputation.'

How many times did he have to say that before he made her understand?

'For that I am deeply sorry, but you and your father can rest assured that I have taken actions to put this to rights. There will be a full retraction in the next edition of *The Ladies' Enquirer* telling readers that the entire thing was a fabrication. If that doesn't happen, believe me, the owners of that magazine will come to regret what they have done. I will happily destroy the publication, and everyone who works there, particularly the guttersnipe who wrote the article.'

'No, don't do that,' Lady Amelia blurted, slamming down the teapot on the side table so fiercely Leo feared the fine porcelain might break.

'I mean, it's not really that important,' she said more slowly with a smile. 'No one is ever likely to know it's about me. My father will never know. And, as you have said before, you already have a reputation, so…you know. No real harm has been done, has it?' she asked, her voice trailing off.

'Of course harm has been done.' He leaned towards her, frustration growing at her lack of understanding. 'You're right that I care nothing for my reputation, but I do care about yours. I will not let that scurrilous magazine harm you or any other innocent young woman.'

'I don't mind, really.'

'That just shows how innocent and sweet you are.' And indeed she was. With her head tilted in supplication, her blue eyes wide and her cheeks flushed, she really was the picture of innocence, lovely, sweet innocence. He was a cad to have kissed such a virtuous young lady. And even more of a cad in that he wanted to do so again.

He coughed to drive away all thoughts of taking her in his arms and once again tasting those red lips. Such behaviour was what had got him here in the first place. Now was the time to make things better, not worse.

'As no harm has really been done, perhaps making that retraction will only draw further attention,' she said. 'I think we should just forget all about it and forgive those people at *The Ladies' Enquirer*. After all the…the man who wrote the column was just doing his job. And I'm sure there are lots of other people who work there who need their jobs as well. Not to mention investors who might have risked everything to make the magazine a success. It would be a shame for them to suffer, just for my sake.'

'Oh, Lady Amelia.' He stood up and moved towards the mantelpiece, too full of pent-up energy to remain seated. 'You don't understand just how serious this is. Those people have mistreated you and they deserve to pay for their actions. When they wrote that article they cared nothing for the effect it would have on you. They deserve to suffer for what they have done.'

She too stood, stepped towards him and to his surprise took hold of his hands. 'Please, for my sake, please don't do anything rash or cause anyone to suffer. I beseech you.'

'You really are a lovely, charitable young woman, always thinking of others and never of yourself.'

She cringed, as if he had insulted rather than complimented her on her kindness towards people who did not deserve it.

'I just don't want anyone hurt on my behalf, and I'm sure no one will know that the article was about me. I'm sure the lamb could be any one of a number of women who were at your ball.'

'You are wrong. I was not alone with any other woman during the ball.' He looked over her head and drew in a breath. 'Nor did I kiss any other woman.'

I didn't want to kiss any other, only you, much to my shame.

'Even if people don't realise the Lion and the Lamb refer to us, they will be able to work out which young lady was absent at the same time as I was. And there was only one such woman. You.'

'None of that matters. So please, don't take it out on the people at *The Ladies' Enquirer*.'

He looked down at the beautiful young woman gripping his hands with such urgency. 'You are far too kind for your own good. Those people at *The Ladies' Enquirer* have shown that they care nothing about you. Why should you care about them?'

'Well, because…because…'

'Exactly. There are no reasons.'

'Maybe I don't care who knows that we kissed.'

He stared at her. Had she really said that? 'But your reputation, your marriage prospects...'

She shook her head. 'I believe I've already told you I have no interest in marriage, and if this gossip column puts off the Vacuous Viscounts it will be all for the good.' She gave a small laugh. 'So, please, no more talk about making the people at the magazine suffer.'

He stared down at her in disbelief. This was not what he had expected. Where were the tears, the panic and hysteria? It was she who was seemingly trying to calm *him* down. But he had vowed he would do whatever she wanted, and if doing nothing was what she desired, then, against his better judgement, he would acquiesce.

'Please,' she repeated, clasping his hands tighter.

'If that is what you wish,' he said, still unsure if this was the right course of action.

'It is.'

'You are truly a remarkable young woman, Lady Amelia.'

She shrugged one slim shoulder. 'It's just a shame that the worst gossip that can be said about me is that I exchanged a rather chaste kiss with you.'

Unable to resist doing so, he moved his gaze to her lips. It *had* been a chaste kiss, but that did not mean Leo had not enjoyed the touch of her lips against his and would not give just about anything to feel them again.

'That was not how the magazine described it. The writer seemed to think our embrace was one of unbridled passion. That the Lion had feasted on the Lamb,' he continued, looking at her lips, the desire to feast on them firmly on his mind.

'You'd think that if my reputation *was* going to be ruined, I could have at least experienced a proper kiss, one that really was full of unbridled passion.' She laughed, suggesting the statement was made in jest, but the look she was giving him said something different. Those blue eyes darkened as she stared up at him, those tempting lips parted, and her quick, short breaths caused her chest to rise and fall rapidly.

'Surely you don't want to start a real scandal?' Leo tried to make it sound as if he was teasing, but his voice came out strangely choked, and despite himself he moved in closer.

'Well, we wouldn't be doing anything that the magazine says we haven't already done.' She smiled tentatively. 'And don't worry,' she added mischievously, 'there are no nosy journalists, editors or magazine owners anywhere in sight. It will just be between you and me.'

He reached down and brushed a stray hair from her forehead, tucking it behind her small, delicate ear. 'We shouldn't,' he whispered as his finger moved gently along her soft cheek. Even touching her in this manner was wrong, but by God it felt good.

She tilted her head, her eyes closing as he stroked her cheek.

'Lady Amelia, I…' His voice trailed off, unsure what he wanted to say, only knowing what he wanted to do, so desperately he could almost taste her lips, could almost feel the touch of her body.

Her hand moved to his chest, not to push him away, but in exploration. It rested on his heart, which pounded vigorously under her fingers, revealing how much he wanted to do what his mind knew he must not.

She opened her eyes and looked up at him, and her red lips parted, causing a groan of desire to surge up inside him.

He shouldn't do this, but he knew he was going to ignore his better judgement. How could he resist? He leaned down slowly, giving her ample time to protest, if that was what she wished to do. She said nothing, merely tilted her head back and once again closed her eyes. God, he was lost. He wanted to kiss her with a desperation that was frightening.

Before he could further question what he was doing, he wrapped his arm around her slim waist, pulled her towards him and his lips were on hers. Any lingering arguments were ripped away when those soft lips parted under his touch and her fingers wrapped themselves around his head, burrowing into his hair. She was holding him tightly, as if to ensure that he did not stop kissing her. But he did not want to stop. His arms encased her more tightly as he feasted himself on her lips, like a starving man finally offered life-giving sustenance.

As if under a will of their own, his hands moved down her back, to where her small waist flared out to the swell of her buttocks. A moan of desire escaped as he pulled her in firmly against his body and ran his tongue slowly along her bottom lip. Her lips parted further, as he had hoped they would, and, forcing himself to slow down, he gently entered her mouth, savouring her glorious, intoxicatingly feminine taste. She responded in the way he had hoped, by moulding her body in closer to his. Those luscious breasts, that he was desperate to touch, were hard up against his chest, her thighs were pressed against his, and she kissed him back with a hunger that matched his own. She might be inexperienced, but there was nothing innocent about her kiss. She was a woman in a state of arousal. A woman who wanted him, wanted him to do more than kiss her. His hands moved further down her body, cupping the roundness of her buttocks and pushing her in hard against him, to try and relieve his surging need for her.

She continued to kiss him back with a mounting intensity as her buttocks moved sensually under his touch. Whether she meant to or not, she was making it clear that she wanted him, and he wanted her so much it was physically painful. But he could not have her. This kiss was all they could share, and they should not even be doing that.

Before he lost his last vestige of control, he forced his lips from hers and fought to regain a semblance of composure, to take charge of himself and this situation.

He looked down at the woman in his arms. Her eyes were still closed, her lips parted in invitation, her breath coming in quick, panting gasps. She was so beautiful, the most beautiful woman he had ever seen, but she was not for him. This had to stop, now, before he went too far.

Chapter Ten

Amelia opened her eyes and gazed up at Mr Devenish, light-headedness making her vision misty. Why had he stopped? Had she done something wrong? Whatever it was, she could change. He could teach her what she needed to do to make him keep on kissing her. She wanted his kisses, needed them and needed so much more. Needed what only he could give her. She leaned in towards him, desperate to have him hold her close again, to relieve the surging desire building up inside her.

He continued to gaze down at her as if transfixed. She did not know much about men, but she could see in his glazed eyes that he wanted her as much as she wanted him. So why was he not doing what they both wanted and needed?

If he wasn't going to give her his kisses, then she would have to take them. To that end, she raised herself up on tiptoe and pressed her lips against his. His groan of desire encouraging her on, she parted her lips and kissed him again, losing herself in the sensation of those lovely lips on hers.

Letting him know how much she wanted him, she pushed her body up against his, stroking her breasts against his chest, loving the feel of his hard muscles, and wishing it were his hands that were caressing her.

Once again he cupped her buttocks, his hands moving in deeper towards the parting at the top of her legs. The pulsating that had captured her pounded harder through her body. She cried out, leaning back her head as his kisses ran down her neck, nuzzling the sensitive skin.

A crashing sound resonated behind her as his kisses returned to her lips. She rubbed herself against him as her tongue entered his mouth, desperate to taste him, wishing she could savour more than just his lips, and explore every part of his glorious body.

'Carruthers at the club said the strangest thing to me today,' her father's voice exploded in her ears. 'He claimed this magazine is referring to you and—'

Amelia jumped back and gripped the mantelpiece to steady herself. Her heart still beating fiercely, her breath frozen in her throat, she turned to face her father. Had he seen what she was doing?

His expression gave her an immediate answer. His eyes appeared to be bulging out of his head as he looked from Mr Devenish to Amelia and back again.

'Amelia, no,' he gasped, moving to the nearest chair and slowly lowering himself down as if the strength had gone out of his legs. 'Oh, my God, it's true.' He placed his head in his hands, rocking backwards and forwards, then slowly looked up at the two people standing in front of the mantel, as still as statues. 'Why, Amelia? And why him, of all men?'

Why him?

With her lips still tingling from his kisses, her body still aching for his touches, she could tell her father that it was because he was the most exciting, attractive man she had ever met and because he made her feel things that she had not known possible even in her wildest imaginings.

Her father waited for her answer, frowning and rubbing his hand along his forehead as if suffering from a splitting headache.

She looked up at Mr Devenish, her befuddled mind starting to clear, and asked herself the same question. Why him? He was arrogant, opinionated, and obviously didn't think a woman could run a magazine. He'd had countless mistresses and had an appalling reputation. Yes, his kisses could make her forget herself, who she was, what she wanted, what she believed in. But wasn't that to be expected from a man as experienced as him? When it came to *Why Mr Devenish?* that was a question to which Amelia couldn't give a clear answer.

I despise so much about him, but I also want him more than I can say.

That was hardly an answer worthy of a rational woman.

He stepped forward. 'Lord Lambourne, I—'

She placed her hand on his arm to stop him, worried he might make this worse, if that was at all possible. 'Father, this is not what it looks like,' she said, stalling for time.

'It looks to me as if you were kissing that man.'

In that case, I guess it is exactly what it looks like.

'What I mean is, it doesn't mean…it was just a kiss.'

'Just a kiss?' her father spluttered, his eyes once again bulging. 'Damn it all, Carruthers was right. That article was about you.' He placed his head back in his hands. 'Oh, Amelia, how could you?'

Mr Devenish took another step forward. She grabbed his arm, pulling him back towards her, and shook her head vigorously. She had got them into this situation and it was a problem best solved by her.

'You could have made a decent marriage,' her father continued. 'To Lord Prebbleton or Lord Bradley, but you've thrown it all away for him. Oh, Amelia, why?'

Amelia gave a little shudder at the thought of kissing either of those men and Mr Devenish shrugged off her restraining hand and approached her father.

'I take it you consider me beneath your daughter, and beneath you.' His voice was confrontational. Not what she'd expect from a man who had just been caught in a compromising position. 'I suppose if it were a titled man who had been kissing your daughter you would demand that he marry her, but not me—is that what you are saying?'

'What?' Her father looked up at him as if confused by all these arguments. 'No…yes. I don't know. Yes, I suppose you will have to marry her after what I've just witnessed.'

'What? No!' Amelia cried out, mirroring her father's confusion. 'It was just one kiss. No one has to know anything about it. It doesn't mean we have to actually get married.'

Surely both men could see how ridiculous this was. It *was* just one kiss. Well, just a few kisses. And she supposed no one could say it was *just* a kiss. It was sublime, earth-shattering, and more than Amelia would have thought a kiss could be, but it still did not mean they had to get married. After all, they hardly knew each other.

'Father, let's be reasonable,' she said, adopting a tone that she hoped sounded composed. 'It *was* just a kiss. No one outside this room knows anything about it. We could just forget all about it and pretend it never happened.'

She looked to Mr Devenish for his agreement, but he was still staring at her father as if he was the one who had somehow been deeply offended and wronged.

Men. What on earth was wrong with them?

'I might have agreed with you, Amelia, and I just might have been able to pretend this hadn't happened, if it wasn't for this gossip column.' He slapped the crumpled magazine against his leg. 'I thought the Lamb might be someone else, but it isn't, it's you. I was the only one stupid enough to think my daughter was too sensible to be caught up in a scandal.'

'No, Father, I'm sure you're wrong.' She took a step towards him. 'I'm sure lots of other people will be equally stupid… I mean, I'm sure no one else other than this Carruthers person will think I'm the Lamb.'

Her father looked at her as if she was the stupid one. 'My dear, someone saw you two together at the ball and reported it in this rag.' Amelia shuddered, not so much at the ludicrousness of the accusation, but at calling her magazine a rag. 'Even if you deny that it was you, this person could come forward and expose you.'

'I'm sure they wouldn't,' Amelia said, her shoulders slumping in defeat. Would now be the time to confess that it was she who had written the article, she who had besmirched her own reputation, and she who was to blame for all this mess? She kept quiet, hoping there was some other way out of this other than a full confession.

'And I am sure that they would,' her father responded. 'You must understand, your reputation is now completely ruined. No one else is ever going to want to marry a woman who is the subject of such public gossip.'

'Well, I can remain single.' That would solve everyone's problems. Her ruined reputation would save her from marriage to Lord Prebbleton or Lord Bradley. She could concentrate on her magazine. Mr Devenish would not be forced into a marriage he didn't want. Everyone would be happy. She smiled at both her father and Mr Devenish. Neither smiled back.

'You will not remain single,' her father stated emphatically. 'I will not have another spinster under my roof. You will marry him.'

'His name is Mr Devenish and I think he should have a say in this, don't you?'

She turned towards him, and nodded rapidly, wanting him to say he had no intention of marrying her, or anyone else. That was what he had told her at the ball. Now he just had to repeat it to her father. After all, there was nothing her father could do about it. He couldn't force Mr Devenish to marry her, and she had made her opinion clear that she had no desire to marry anyone, and certainly not to save a reputation that she cared not one fig about.

'I must apologise for compromising your daughter and I will of course marry her.'

'What?' Amelia cried out. 'No. We can print that retraction you wanted, say that it was all lies. That there was no Lion, no Lamb, no kissing.'

'Don't be ridiculous,' her father replied. 'Everyone would know that Mr Devenish had demanded it. The man wields such power in the publishing industry that no one will believe such a retraction. It will look even worse for you, as if he'd had his way with you and then didn't want you any more. Your reputation would be even more damaged than it already is.'

'I don't mind,' Amelia said, looking from one stern man to the other. 'Really, I don't.'

'Well, I do,' her father said, standing up and crossing the room and staring hard at Mr Devenish. 'I'll announce the engagement immediately and tell everyone that you have been courting for some time, and weren't going to announce it till we finalised the terms of the marriage settlement, but that foolish magazine forced our hand.'

Mr Devenish nodded once, as if that was a sensible agreement, while Amelia stood between her father and the man she was expected to marry, looking backwards and forwards between the two, knowing that this was her own fault.

She staggered to the nearest chair and collapsed into

it as the two men continued discussing the marriage as if it had nothing to do with her. But it had everything to do with her. It affected her more than it affected either of them. Her father would continue to live his life as if none of this had happened, pleased to have his wilful single daughter finally off his hands. Mr Devenish could also continue to live exactly as he had before. He'd be married, but, knowing what she did about so many married men, she assumed that would change his behaviour not one little bit.

She didn't know how exactly being his wife would change her life, but, judging from what she'd already learned about him, she suspected it would not be for the better. Under most circumstances she was able to trick her father, but she knew she would never be able to fool Mr Devenish, at least not for long. He would soon find out that she was the owner of *The Ladies' Enquirer*. Once he had got over his anger at her, he would just absorb her magazine into his empire and she would be left with nothing.

Plus, there was the danger that he would think she had deliberately tricked him into this marriage. She already knew how Mr Devenish reacted when someone tried to put one over him. She hated to think how he would react when he discovered his wife had done exactly that.

No, this could not happen and she would make sure it did not. Somehow, she was going to have to stop this marriage from ever taking place.

Mr Devenish turned towards her, his discussion with her father seemingly concluded, and made a formal bow, as if they had not, only moments earlier, been locked in a passionate embrace. It seemed he too did not know how to behave now that their circumstances had changed so dramatically.

The moment he left the room, she stood up and adopted her most defiant pose. Too much rested on her winning this argument with her father, so win it she most certainly would.

'Father,' she started, pleased that her voice sounded composed and full of authority, 'I will not be marrying Mr Devenish. We do not live in medieval times, so you cannot force me. I have to give my consent and I most emphatically do not.'

'We'll discuss this later,' her father said, moving towards the door.

She darted forward, pushed herself in front of him and stopped his progress. 'No, we won't. We will discuss this now. In fact, there is nothing to discuss. I have told you that I will not be marrying Mr Devenish. That is the end of the matter.'

Her father sighed loudly as if this was more an irritation than an argument that he was destined to lose. 'Amelia, you have made a spectacle of yourself and of me. It is beholden of you to make this right. I chose not to believe what was written in that magazine, thinking that it must be some other foolish young woman who had compromised herself with that man. Now I have seen with my own eyes that it was indeed my daughter. There is no option but for you to marry him so that we can end all this humiliating scandal.'

'As I have already said, I care nothing if people talk

about me—they will soon get tired of discussing this, and then something else will occupy their minds.'

'That is hardly the point. *I* care about what people say about *me*. If you don't marry him I will be a laughing stock. Everyone will see me as a man who can't control his immodest daughter. I am as disappointed as you that you have to marry Mr Devenish, but there is no option.'

'Father, you can't make me marry.'

'I can and I will. If you don't marry, I will cut off your allowance.'

'Then do it.' She stared him straight in the eye so he would know how serious she was. And it was no sacrifice. What did Amelia care for her allowance, which had to be spent on gowns and hats so she could attend Society events?

He narrowed his eyes. Amelia did the same.

'And I will cut off financial support for your aunt as well.'

They continued to glare at each other, but Amelia knew he had won, and that too was her fault. If Aunt Beryl hadn't lent her the money to start the magazine, then she would have had some money on which to survive, but without it she was completely dependent on her brother-in-law's good graces.

'But Aunt Beryl raised me,' she said, appealing to her father's better nature. 'You owe her so much,' Amelia added quietly, swallowing her fear and fighting to stay strong.

'If she had raised you correctly then you would be a young lady who was obedient to her father and would marry the man he told her to, without question.'

She stared at her father, who was smiling, knowing he had won.

'And I can't see why you are objecting. I caught you kissing him. You must have some feelings for him, or do you make a habit of kissing men?'

Amelia bit her lip, unsure how to answer.

'Well? Do you make a habit of kissing any man you happen to be alone with? Has your aunt raised a young lady of such low morals? If she has, then she does not deserve my support, even if you do marry.'

'No, neither. I have never kissed any man other than Mr Devenish.'

'There we are, then. You obviously have feelings for Leo Devenish, although why I cannot fathom, so you surely can have no objections to marrying him.'

Amelia knew this line of attack would not bring her victory. Her father would obviously not budge. Somehow, she would have to convince Leo Devenish not to do the honourable thing, to go against her father, and refuse to marry her. She just had to think of a way to achieve that.

Chapter Eleven

When faced with a catastrophe of such monumental proportions, there was only one thing that Amelia could do. She summoned her friends from Halliwell's Finishing School to the Savoy tearooms and told them the entire story, leaving out nothing, even the more embarrassing moments.

Her friends listened in rapt silence, the three-tiered serving plate of scones and cakes sitting untouched in the middle of the table, their cups of tea going cold.

'Any ideas?' She looked expectantly at her three friends, who all stared back at her with blank expressions.

'It is difficult,' Emily began, stating the obvious, but causing the other two to nod their agreement.

'Yes,' Amelia said, feeling increasingly deflated. 'And it's also important that Aunt Beryl should never discover that I am being forced to marry Mr Devenish against my will and am doing so to save her. You know what she is like. If she gets a whiff of this, she is likely to sacrifice herself so I don't suffer, and that too will never do. She has already sacrificed so much for me.'

Her three friends nodded again, their brows furrowed.

'What does Aunt Beryl think of this engagement?' Emily asked.

'She's actually rather happy about it,' Amelia said, her mood deflating even further at the memory of her aunt's excitement when she'd told her the news. 'For some unknown reason she likes Mr Devenish. She is a bit confused about why I allowed the magazine to print that article about us but has decided it doesn't matter as we are to wed. I haven't told her about my involvement in writing the *Tittle-Tattle* column, or the way Father has blackmailed me into this unwanted marriage.'

'Could you appeal to Mr Devenish's better nature?' Irene said.

Amelia scoffed at this. 'I don't believe the man has a better nature. He's a hard-hearted businessman. That's what got me into this predicament in the first place. If he hadn't been so determined to destroy *The Ladies' Enquirer* I would never have even noticed him.'

That was not entirely the truth. Amelia had most certainly noticed him at the dinner party, and if she was being completely honest she had noticed him at the other social occasions they had both attended. It was he who had never noticed her, and he still wouldn't have noticed her if she hadn't tried to get her revenge on him.

'Well, I suppose he has done the honourable thing in agreeing to marry you,' Irene said. 'The man's got so much power he could have just laughed in your father's face. And I'm sorry to say this, but if he had, there would have been little your father could have done about it. So, given that he is inclined to doing what is right, perhaps if you told him you didn't wish to marry him then he might be able to see things from your point of view.'

Her friends looked at her with eager expectation, but Amelia was unconvinced.

'So, you're suggesting I ask him to do the honourable thing by not doing the honourable thing and marrying me?' Amelia said.

'Yes,' her friends all answered.

'I suppose you realise that's a ridiculous, unworkable idea? He demanded a retraction from *The Ladies' Enquirer* and threatened to bankrupt the magazine and destroy everyone involved in it to save my reputation. He agreed to marry me, even though he didn't want to, to save my reputation. He knows I don't wish to marry, but, well, after that kiss he probably thinks I've got feelings for him.'

All three friends nodded.

'Not that I have, of course.'

She waited for the nods of agreement. None came.

'Have you thought about telling him the truth?' Emily said. 'The whole truth, about the magazine, Aunt Beryl, *Tittle-Tattle*, and why you behaved the way you did at the dinner and ball?'

That was an even more ridiculous idea than appealing to his better nature. 'Did I not mention that he wants to drive *The Ladies' Enquirer* out of business? He's hell-bent on acquiring more and more magazines and newspapers. I don't want him to take control of *The Ladies' Enquirer* as well.'

'It's either that, or you're going to have to marry him,'

Irene said. 'And once you marry him, everything you own will become his anyway, including *The Ladies' Enquirer*.'

Amelia crumpled in her seat. It was hopeless. No matter which way she looked at it, Mr Devenish won.

'It is quite the quandary,' Emily said, and the other two nodded.

'A dilemma, indeed,' Irene added. 'Marry him and you'll be trapped with a man you can't abide, don't marry him and you risk your aunt's future.'

'Well, it's not that I can't abide the man. He does have some good qualities. I just don't want to marry him.'

'It's still a dilemma, though,' Irene continued. 'If you marry him you will be miserable, if you don't, your aunt will be.'

Amelia touched her lips as the memory of that kiss returned. Would she be entirely miserable being married to such a man? Her hand shot back to her lap. Of course she would be.

Georgina raised a questioning eyebrow. 'Did you say you kissed him twice?'

'Yes,' she responded in her most matter-of-fact manner. 'But that is hardly relevant.'

The three friends exchanged a look, the meaning of which she could not tell.

'What was it like?' Georgina asked.

'It was…' Amelia paused. As she remembered the touch of Mr Devenish's lips a strange tremor ran through her. 'It was…'

'It was?' Georgina prompted.

'It was rather wonderful,' Amelia admitted and

lightly bit her bottom lip to stop herself from smiling at the recollection of just how wonderful it was.

The three friends raised their eyebrows in question.

'But that's not important. I do not wish to marry him,' she said, trying to get her friends to focus on her problem. She was not here to discuss Mr Devenish's kissing technique, sensational though it might be.

'But it will be some compensation if all else fails,' Irene said. 'Not every woman gets to marry a man who can cause her to simper and blush when discussing his kisses.'

The other two nodded.

'I am not simpering,' Amelia stated, unable to deny that talking of Mr Devenish's kisses had made more than her cheeks burn. 'But it matters not if his kisses did send me into…made me feel…caused me to want to…'

'Feel what?'

'Want to do what?'

'Sent you where?'

'I don't know. All I'm saying is; yes, Mr Devenish knows how to kiss, but he would, wouldn't he? He's had countless women in his life, and he's done a damn sight more than just kiss them.'

This statement should have got her friends back to discussing what was important, but instead they once again exchanged a look, as if they were unconvinced by Amelia's attempt to dismiss any feelings she might have about his kisses.

'The man's a rake,' she said, louder than she meant to. She looked around the dining room, but the mainly female customers were all engaged in their own intense conversations and none seemed to hear her. 'The man's a rake,' she repeated in a more controlled tone. 'He will make a terrible husband, especially as he doesn't want to marry me, or any woman.'

'And yet he has consented to marry you. At least he's an honourable rake, then,' Georgina said. 'I suppose that's something.'

'Is there such a thing? Isn't that a contradiction in terms?' Irene added.

'Well, surely people are capable of changing, even rakes,' Georgina countered.

'None of that matters,' Amelia interrupted before they got further off topic and into a philosophical discussion about the nature of man. 'The fact that he has agreed to marry me doesn't matter. Whether he's an honourable or dishonourable rake doesn't matter. How well he kisses does not matter. I do not want to marry him and I need to find a way out of this engagement. And I need your help.'

The three friends nodded in unison and muttered their apologies, finally getting back to the point of this emergency afternoon tea.

'So the best outcome will be to halt the marriage,' Emily said.

'Yes,' Amelia replied.

'And in doing so, you have to make sure that Aunt Beryl does not suffer.'

'Exactly. Any ideas?'

She looked expectantly at her three friends, who all looked at each other for an answer.

'I think what we need now is a fresh pot of tea,'

Emily said, signalling for the waiter, while Irene smothered a scone with jam and cream and passed it to Amelia in consolation.

Ideas continued to be thrown around, none of which
solved her problem. How she was to free herself and
Mr Devenish was eluding not only herself, but also her
otherwise intelligent, resourceful friends.

'I'm sorry. We haven't been much help, have we?'
Emily said, when they had discussed and discounted
each and every idea.

'You listened and you tried to help and for that I am
grateful,' Amelia said. 'But it seems unless something
miraculous happens I'm going to soon become a bride.'

She released a loud, despondent sigh, then tried to
smile. 'But in the meantime, let's just enjoy our tea and
talk of something else.'

Slowly, conversation moved on to other topics, but
while they chatted of this and that, Amelia continued
to lament her forthcoming marriage, and hoped and
prayed for a miracle, one that would present itself before her fate was sealed.

As she left the Savoy Amelia refused to be defeated.
The discussion with her friends had provided no clue
on what to do, but she had to do something. To that
end, she went straight from the tearooms to Mr Devenish's office.

She did not agree with her friends that she should
appeal to his honourable side, as she doubted he possessed one. She only had to remind herself how he had
discarded Lady Madeline, or how he had gone straight

from kissing her to dancing with Lady Sarah, to know that when it came to women he thought only of himself. No, he was not honourable, but he did have a keen sense of self-preservation. It was to that which she would appeal.

He had even less interest in marriage than she did and had absolutely no reason to want to tie himself to her for the rest of his life. There were many things about Mr Devenish of which she disapproved, but he was an intelligent man. Even if she couldn't come up with a way to end this farce of an engagement, she was sure that he could.

With renewed determination, she strode through the streets, certain that a solution would be found and she was worrying over nothing. Together, they would find a way to ensure that they did not marry. It was as simple as that. Once they had discussed it like rational, intelligent adults all talk of marriage would be over. She would triumph over her father, Aunt Beryl would be safe and they could both go on with their lives.

And she would never again know what it was like to be kissed by Mr Devenish. A frisson of regret rippled through her, causing her walking pace to slow.

She was letting her feelings rule, and now was not the time to get emotional. Now, more than ever, it was time to be sensible and rational. Too much was at stake.

With that in mind, she straightened her spine, lifted her head, walked through the opulent entrance of Devenish Enterprises and marched up the marble stairs to his office.

'Good morning,' the secretary said, rising from his chair. 'How may I be of assistance?'

'I'm here to see Mr Devenish.'

The man frowned and looked down at the diary open in front of him. 'Do you have an appointment, Miss…?'

'Lady Amelia. And no, I don't have an appointment, but Mr Devenish will see me. Now.'

She crossed the room towards the door which she assumed led to his office.

'Lady Amelia, I'm afraid Mr Devenish is busy and cannot see you,' the secretary called, rushing to place himself between Amelia and the door. 'If you would like to make an appointment, I will see when he is available.'

She stopped, her hand on the doorknob, as an image crashed into her mind of Mr Devenish in an embrace with Lady Sarah. Was that the reason for the secretary's panic, because he was with another woman? Ignoring the pain gripping her chest, she turned the doorknob with more defiance than she felt and threw open the door.

'Lady Amelia, what a pleasant surprise,' Leo said from behind his desk.

Her heart still pounding hard, relief flooded through her. He was alone. Not that it mattered really. They meant nothing to each other. She could hardly demand fidelity from a man who had been forced to marry her against his will, but she couldn't help but smile with relief.

He walked around the desk and guided her to the leather button couch. 'To what do I owe this visit?' he asked, seating himself beside her. A bit too close for

Amelia's comfort. If she was to continue to remain rational, it would have been better if he had stayed where he was, separated from her by the large expanse of a desktop.

'We need to discuss this marriage,' she said, pleased that her voice came out clear and precise, like a businesswoman discussing a deal.

'Of course. I see your father has already announced the engagement in all the leading newspapers. He has been true to his word, not wasting any time in nipping this scandal in the bud.'

This was news to Amelia and she so wished she had spoken to her father and discouraged him from taking such hasty action.

'What is it you wish to discuss?' He turned towards her, and his eyes held hers in such a disconcerting manner that she was in danger of forgetting what she intended to say.

'Well, everything. This has all happened so fast. We hardly know each other. It's all so ridiculous.'

He picked up her hand. She was wearing gloves, but he wasn't, and she could almost feel his skin through the light fabric.

'Then our courtship will be a chance for us to get to know each other better.'

'Courtship?'

He smiled. It was such a rare sight and one that always caused Amelia's breath to catch in her throat.

'Yes, courtship. And now that we are officially courting, I believe you should call me Leo. Don't you agree, Amelia?'

Her name had never sounded so seductive, like an offer, a promise of enticing things to come.

She nodded, knowing that this conversation was not going the way she had intended, but unsure how to get it back on track. She was supposed to be discussing how to get out of this marriage, not talking about courtship, not swooning simply because he was holding her hand.

'So, Amelia.' He smiled again. 'Perhaps we should begin our courtship in the traditional manner. Would you like to accompany me tomorrow for a ride in Hyde Park?'

'Hyde Park? What? Yes. No.' What was wrong with her? Why was she allowing herself to become so distracted?

'Look here.' She sat up straighter to indicate that she was now getting serious. 'This marriage has been forced on us. What we should be doing is finding a way of getting out of it, not discussing courtship, or rides in parks.'

He raised his eyebrow slightly. 'And how do you propose we get out of our engagement?' There was a spark of amusement in his voice, as if he was not taking this seriously. Did he no longer care that he had been trapped into a marriage he didn't want? But then, it was different for men. He would not really be trapped, would he? He could continue to behave exactly as he always had.

'You could tell my father you don't want to marry me.' She stared at him carefully to gauge his reaction. There was none.

'Your father is correct, Amelia. We have no choice but to marry. Your reputation will be in tatters if we do not wed, and I am not going to be the man responsible for ruining a young woman's reputation. It is hardly as if we will be the first couple to be forced into a marriage against their will.'

'But I don't mind.' Amelia was suddenly unsure whether she didn't mind being married to Mr Devenish or didn't mind that her reputation would be in tatters.

'Good,' he said, apparently assuming she meant the former. 'Then tomorrow we ride in Hyde Park and show the world what a happy couple we are.'

Amelia shook her head to clear the fog that always descended on her otherwise clear mind whenever she was in his company. She looked straight ahead, taking in his office, his masculine retreat of dark wood panelling, leather chairs and sofas, all dominated by his large oak desk in front of the floor-to-ceiling windows. 'No, we do not need to court. We do not need to try and convince the world we are a happy couple. We need to get out of a marriage that neither of us wants.'

'But I don't want to get out of this marriage.'

She turned to face him, so quickly it all but knocked the breath out of her. 'What? No. Yes, you do. You said you don't want to marry anyone. And you most certainly would not want to marry me if my father hadn't forced you.'

He shrugged. 'What you say is true, but this is the situation in which we find ourselves, so I believe the sensible thing to do would be to accept it. I have come to terms with it and I believe that is something which it would also be sensible for you to do.'

Amelia fought not to be offended by his honesty. He was saying nothing she did not already know. His reluctance to marry was as strong as her own. He was doing it under duress but had resigned himself to accepting it as inevitable. So why was she so offended that he had stated those facts so boldly?

'Look,' she said as firmly as she could, 'we don't wish to wed and we should not have to do something we don't want to. And I believe you have the ability to get out of it.'

He was about to counter her, but she held up her hand to still his words.

'I have already told you that I care nothing for my reputation as I do not wish to marry anyone, ever. But my father is determined that he will not be mocked by the men at his club, so you and I have to go through with a sham of a marriage just to save him from some embarrassment.'

He gave a grim smile and shook his head slowly. 'So it is your father's reputation he cares about more than yours.'

'Exactly.' Amelia leaned towards him, pleased that she was finally making him understand. Then sat back, remembering that getting closer to Mr Devenish was not a sensible idea. 'I'm sure you don't want to marry to save my father's reputation.'

'Of course I do not.'

'Good. So we are in agreement.'

'But what of my reputation?'

'What? Your reputation? But your reputation is…'

He gave a small laugh at her floundering. 'If we do not marry I will get the reputation as a man who seduces innocent debutantes, becomes engaged to them, then abandons them. Is that the type of man you think I am?'

'Well, um, you do have rather a reputation for your treatment of women… Lady Madeline and all that.'

His jaw tightened. 'You are nothing like Lady Madeline.'

Amelia recoiled at his hurtful words. No, she was not beautiful, experienced or flirtatious. She was not the sort of woman he would take as his mistress, and if she hadn't written that foolish column she would not be the sort of woman he would ever consider taking as his bride.

'I know.' She looked down at her hands, twisting in her lap. 'I'm sorry.'

He placed his hand under her chin and lifted it up so she was looking into his eyes. 'Amelia, believe me, you have nothing to be sorry for. But you are mistaken. You say you care nothing for your reputation but I know how harsh people can be. You will be ostracised, ridiculed and the subject of endless gossip. I will not see you become the victim of such cruelty.'

'But…' Amelia was unsure what she wanted to say— all she could think was how dark and velvet-soft his eyes were as he looked at her with compassion, and what could almost be described as affection.

'We are not the first couple, nor will we be the last, to be forced to wed,' he continued, still staring deep into her eyes. 'It is something that we should both accept and make the most of.'

'But wouldn't you rather marry a woman you loved?' she said quietly.

He released her chin and laughed as if she had made a joke. 'Love? I'm surprised a sensible woman of your class would talk of such things, especially in connection with marriage.'

Amelia had surprised herself as well, not in the sentiment that she had expressed, but in saying such a thing to Mr Devenish. But now that she had talked of love, she realised that was what she really wanted. She did not want to marry a man who did not love her. She did not want to marry a man who had been forced to marry her to save her reputation. And she did not want to marry a man because her father had blackmailed her into it. She wanted to marry a man she loved, who loved her in return, and that was not Leo Devenish.

'Now, if there is nothing more you wish to discuss?' he said.

'No, there's nothing else,' she said, her voice despondent.

'In that case, my secretary will see you out.' He stood up and escorted her to the door. 'I shall be at your home tomorrow afternoon for our ride in Hyde Park.'

Amelia nodded her agreement and left the office. When she was out on the street her fuddled mind started to clear. What had just happened? She was no closer to extraditing them both from this unwanted marriage, but it seemed she was now about to go through the charade of being courted by Mr Leo Devenish.

Chapter Twelve

A drive in Hyde Park. It was the traditional way in which a young couple displayed themselves in public so all of Society could see that they were courting. It was not what Amelia had expected from this Season, or from any Season, and as she dressed for the occasion she kept asking herself, *How has it come to this?*

All she had wanted to do was save her magazine and have the pleasure of embarrassing Mr Devenish in the process. She had expected him to get peevish when he read the column, then shrug it off and eventually forget about it.

At worst, she thought he'd renew his efforts to find the 'man' responsible, and she could sit back and quietly laugh at the way his prejudices had blinded him.

Now here she was, standing in front of a full-length mirror, dressed in her prettiest day dress of striped blue and white cotton with a high-necked lace collar, a feathered hat placed on her head at what Minnie insisted was the fashionable jaunty angle and her cream parasol clutched in her white, lacy gloved hands.

Minnie had taken an inordinate amount of care with Amelia's hair, as if it was the lady's maid herself who was betrothed, and had even given Amelia's cheeks a tight squeeze to bring colour to the surface.

'You look so pretty, my lady,' Minnie said, admiring her work. 'Like a young lady in love,' she added, placing her hands over her heart, and causing Amelia to frown at the lady's maid's silliness.

This was not a courtship. She was not in love. Her betrothed did not love her. All of this was a pretence. She was tempted to take off this pretty, fluffy outfit and change into something more appropriate. Mourning dress, perhaps.

She released a loud sigh, and it was Minnie's turn to frown. 'Does something not meet with your approval, my lady?'

'No, as always, your work is perfect, Minnie. It's just nerves, I suppose.' This courtship might be a lie, but both those statements were the truth. Amelia had to admit that she did look the picture of a young lady being courted, and her jittery stomach certainly suggested nerves at seeing her intended again.

'You have nothing to be nervous about,' Minnie said, her smile returning. 'You are glowing, just as a lady in love should.'

She forced herself not to sigh again or counter her lady's maid's claims. Until she found a way to untangle herself from this mess, Amelia would have to pretend that she was indeed a woman happy to be courted. That was the only way she could see to convince her father that she was being compliant.

She entered the drawing room and found Mr Devenish chatting with Aunt Beryl. He stood and stared at her, his brown eyes admiring, his lips smiling.

Oh, he was good. Anyone watching would think that he really was gazing on a woman who beguiled him. Although there was only Aunt Beryl and the footman present, so why he should make such an effort she did not know. Perhaps he was determined to play the role at all times, no matter who was watching.

She gave him a terse smile, determined not to return the besotted look, although in all honesty, it was hard not to. Dressed in a cream jacket, waistcoat and trousers, he looked magnificent. But then, didn't he always look magnificent? That was part of the problem. If he wasn't so damn handsome he wouldn't have had a string of mistresses. That scene at the dinner party with Lady Madeline would never have happened. She would never have written about him in *The Ladies' Enquirer.* Yes, this was his fault for being far too good-looking. And it was his fault that she had kissed him. Twice.

A little shiver rippled through her. Now that they were officially courting, there was no reason why he could not kiss her again, and maybe do more than kiss her. He did not know that she had no intention of actually going through with the marriage.

The thought sparked off another delicious thrill and did nothing to ease the butterflies that weren't just in her stomach but also fluttering throughout her body.

As her friends had said, his kisses were some compensation for this forced engagement, and she really did deserve some recompense for all the stress she was going through. A kiss or two, or three, or more was surely her due.

'Shall we?' he said offering an arm to both Amelia and Aunt Beryl, who smiled at him as if he was some sort of Greek god who had deigned to mix with mere mortals.

Amelia couldn't help but frown at her aunt, who had so easily fallen under his spell, just like so many other women before her. Just like Amelia.

Aunt Beryl returned her frown, which Amelia knew was a silent criticism of her bad manners. She forced herself to smile and take Mr Devenish's arm. Like him, she was supposed to be pretending this were a real courtship and needed to convince her aunt more than anyone.

He walked them out to the waiting landaus. The warm day was perfect for a drive in an open carriage, easily allowing them to perform their public display of courtship. Although couples would bear quite inclement weather if it meant being seen by the rest of Society.

They entered the park and joined the line of carriages rolling slowly through the tree-lined boulevards, while fashionably dressed people promenaded along the paths, and men exercised their horses. Like herself and Mr Devenish, they were all there to be seen and to watch others. A complete waste of time, if anyone had asked Amelia.

The sedate pace meant people could indeed see them, and once again, if anyone asked Amelia's opinion, far too many young women were casting a glance in Mr Devenish's direction.

Well, she would show them that they had no right

to do so. She slid along the carriage seat until they were almost touching. Just for appearances' sake, of course. Those young ladies, along with everyone else in the park, needed to think that this courtship was genuine, particularly any members of her father's clubs who might be watching.

Aunt Beryl sent her an approving smile. 'You young people should go for a walk,' she said with a quick wink. 'I'm happy to remain in the carriage reading my book while you two take a nice, long stroll.'

The implication could not be missed. Aunt Beryl had no intention of chaperoning them. Once again, that silly little shiver rippled through Amelia at the thought of being alone with Mr Devenish.

He signalled to his driver to halt, then helped Amelia down, taking her arm, and they joined the parade of people walking in the sunshine.

'I suppose we should make polite conversation,' she said. 'Isn't that what courting couples do?'

'I believe you are correct. What would you like to politely talk about?'

She stared ahead, her mind a blank. 'Well, we are supposed to be pretending to be courting. If we can't think of anything to say to each other, perhaps we should just look at each other with adoration.' She stopped walking and looked up at him, with wide eyes and a head cocked coquettishly, in a parody of a woman smitten.

He laughed, then returned the look, but she found it impossible to join in with his laughter. Not when those dark eyes were staring deep into hers. She blinked to break the invisible, imprisoning chains that seemed to be wrapping themselves around her and drawing her towards him. She attempted a dismissive laugh, but it came out as a rather odd, embarrassing squeak.

'Is that adoring enough for you?' he asked with a smile.

'Yes, I suppose that will do,' she said, ignoring the way the temperature had suddenly soared, despite the sun disappearing behind a cloud.

'Now, I believe it is customary to indulge in a bit of flirtation. I should compliment you on your beauty.'

He scanned her slowly, causing that heat to travel up and down her body along with his gaze. 'You are a picture today, Amelia. I have never seen a young lady look more beautiful.'

Amelia forced herself to smile, determined to join in with the jest. 'Oh, and you, my darling Mr Devenish, I mean Leo, have never looked more handsome,' she said in a teasing manner, although the words were completely true. 'Your hair, as dark as a raven's wing, is simply shining in the sunlight, and your eyes…my, your eyes are…why, they are simply perfect for seeing with.'

This caused him to smile, drawing her gaze to his lips.

'And your lips,' she continued. 'What can I say about your lips? They are perfect for…' Oh, God, how had she got herself into this? She knew exactly what his lips were perfect for, and his cheeky smile made it evident that he did too.

'I think that will do for flirting,' she said, staring straight ahead and resuming their stroll.

'I think you might be right. I'd be a bit worried about

what you might come up with if you continued discussing my body parts and describing what they are perfect for.'

The heat of the park shot up a few more degrees.

'But at least our flirting and a-adoring looks will have convinced everyone that we are a genuine courting couple,' she said, stumbling over her words in a failed attempt to sound nonchalant.

'More importantly, we have hopefully shown everyone, including those rats at *The Ladies' Enquirer*, that the gossip about us was false and our kiss was merely an exchange between a couple who have been betrothed for some time.'

She forced herself to continue smiling, even though her cheeks were now starting to ache from holding the false smile in place. 'I am so sorry for those gossip columns. It's so unfair that you have been forced into this engagement.'

He shrugged. 'It is hardly something for which you need to apologise.'

Oh, if only you knew how much I do have to apologise for.

'The fault lies entirely with me,' he continued. 'I knew the consequences but I kissed you anyway, which is why I am more than happy to take responsibility for my actions.'

By paying the price of marrying me, Amelia could add. *But none of it was your fault. It was all mine.*

'But it's still so unfair,' she said instead.

'Every man knows the penalty for kissing a debutante.'

'You make it all sound so romantic. Fault, penalty...' She laughed lightly as if this too was a joke.

'You're right; for that, too, I apologise. Any man would be honoured to be married to a woman such as yourself.'

'Any other man.'

He halted and turned to face her. 'I kissed you because you are a very desirable woman, and I have no regrets.'

Amelia's breath caught in her throat.

'Although I have been forced to marry, I can think of few women that I would prefer to have as my bride.'

It was almost a compliment, so why did it sound like such an insult?

'Well, I, too, did not wish to marry.' She stopped, unsure whether she could also say that if she had to, there was no man she would rather marry than Mr Devenish. Wanting to kiss him again was one thing, but marriage? The man was a rake, a ruthless businessman, one whose opinion of women was so low that he would never even consider that a woman could be behind *The Ladies' Enquirer*. Was that the type of man she would want to marry unless she was forced to?

He raised his eyebrows. 'No? Then tell me, what else does a young woman such as yourself want to do with her life besides get married, have children, attend social events, take tea with her friends, and then maybe…?'

His words also came to an abrupt halt, and she was sure he was going to add, *then find herself a lover?*

'I think, given the opportunity, women could do a lot more with their lives.'

'Such as?'

'Well, women are now involved in the sciences. They're becoming active in politics, advocating for better conditions for women and working people. All sorts of things.'

Including me. I own The Ladies' Enquirer! she wanted to shout out, letting him know that she was not the frivolous woman he thought her to be.

'Yes, some women, but not the women of my acquaintance. Can you name one woman who attended my ball who is doing anything other than indulging herself in social events, searching for a husband, or looking for another frivolous way to fill her time?'

Yes, me.

'Well, the men who attended your ball aren't much better,' she said, her voice sounding decidedly peevish.

He gave a small, mirthless laugh of agreement.

'So what makes you think it was one of those men who wrote that piece in *The Ladies' Enquirer* and not one of the ladies?' She was moving onto dangerous ground, but she couldn't help herself from challenging his disparaging view of women.

He laughed as if she had made a joke. 'For a start, most of the ladies who attended the dinner party and the ball have never written anything more complex than an invitation card. And why would they write such a thing? They're all the wives or daughters of wealthy men with sufficient incomes to buy all the gowns, hats and ribbons they require. They hardly need the money that selling such a story would give them, and, while many of the men have reason to despise me, believe me, none of the women do.'

'What about Lady Sarah?' she said, an emotion rising inside her, one that might be indignation but felt suspiciously like jealousy.

'Lady Sarah?' He laughed. 'She has many talents, but writing is not one of them.'

Amelia seethed. She would like to think it was on behalf of Lady Sarah, or because he was dismissing women in general, but knew it was the *other talents* comment which had her decidedly impassioned. When he had kissed her he must have known he was kissing an innocent, a woman who had never even been kissed before. Lady Sarah was an experienced woman, and that was no doubt how he liked his lovers. He liked them to have *other talents*.

Not that it really mattered what he felt about Lady Sarah. It mattered even less what opinion he had of Amelia or her kisses. This engagement was a charade that somehow had to be ended before they actually married. But, given her agitated state, it would be best to move the conversation away from discussing any of his lovers.

'Have you ever thought that the women you dismiss as incapable of writing for a magazine are that way because they are denied a good education, and are only ever taught how to make themselves agreeable to men?'

To have these other talents you seem to admire so much?

He stopped smiling. 'You are right.'

His agreement left her flummoxed. She wanted him to argue with her, so she could vent her wrath about his admiration of women like Lady Madeline and Lady

Sarah, without actually exposing the real reason for her anger.

'I more than most should know how an education can change a person's life,' he continued, his face serious. 'And I believe it is an education that has made you such an interesting woman.'

Interesting woman? Was that a compliment? Even if it was, she doubted it was anywhere near as desirable as *other talents*. Regardless, they were straying onto dangerous ground and it would be a disaster if he suspected she was the one behind the *Tittle-Tattle* column. She needed to move this conversation on.

'So,' she said, forcing a smile, 'which man do you think wrote the article?'

'Obviously not your father,' he said, warming to a subject to which he had apparently given much thought. 'The last thing he wanted was to have to marry his daughter off to a man like me. It is also extremely unlikely to be Lord Bradley or Lord Prebbleton. They were both vying for your hand. Yes, they are in need of the money that selling gossip to a magazine would bring, but would get more by marrying you.' He turned to face her, his look contrite. 'I'm sorry. I should not have said that.'

She waved her hand in dismissal. 'It's the truth. I know they had no interest in me other than my dowry.'

'Which merely shows what fools they both are.'

She shrugged off his compliment. 'So, it's not my father and it's not the Vacuous Viscounts. Then who else could it be?'

'I had assumed that it was someone who wishes to

do me harm, but with the second article it could equally be someone who wanted to harm your father.'

'My father? Why on earth would you think that?'

'Because it has forced a marriage between his only daughter and the last man he would want as a son-in-law. He wanted a titled man, and he's got stuck with a new-money upstart.'

'Then it serves him right for being such a snob.'

'Does that mean you agree that it is someone who wishes to punish your father?'

She shrugged.

'The other possibility is simple greed. *The Ladies' Enquirer*, like so many other magazines, is no doubt paying people for gossip, and the man responsible may have thought this was a profitable bit of gossip about me and didn't care what damage it would do to your reputation.'

'Is that why you demanded a retraction?'

He looked at her, his brow furrowed, and she quickly thought back. Had he mentioned that he had demanded a retraction? Yes, he had—thank goodness for that. She needed to think carefully before she spoke in future.

'Yes, and if I hadn't kissed you again, if your father hadn't caught us, that would have been the end of the matter.'

'That too was not your fault.'

It was mine and mine alone, and it will be my responsibility to free you from this position so you can go back to your married lovers.

'Of course it was my fault. As I said, I know the repercussions of kissing an unwed young woman of your class and I did it anyway.'

'There you go again, talking about fault and repercussions,' she said, trying to laugh it off.

'And there you go again, not focusing on the fact that I kissed you anyway. Doesn't that tell you how much I wanted to do so?'

He took both her hands in his and held them close to his chest. 'Amelia, we are now engaged. We will soon be married and spending our lives together. What brought us to this state no longer matters. What matters now is our future together. Agreed?'

She hesitated. He raised his eyebrows as he waited for her answer.

'Agreed,' she responded, knowing that in reality she was agreeing to nothing.

'So no more talk of what led up to our being engaged. Let's just accept what has happened and focus on enjoying our courtship.'

Amelia nodded then smiled. While she would never accept the inevitability of their marriage, focusing on enjoying the courtship was going to present no hardship. Especially as there was the tantalising possibility of getting some compensation in the form of more of his kisses.

Her smile growing wider in anticipation, they resumed their stroll.

Chapter Thirteen

Leo had not expected doing the right thing would give him such pleasure and found himself increasingly looking forward to the time he spent with Amelia. Evenings at the theatre and opera, along with dining together, followed on from their walk in Hyde Park. Outings were selected to ensure they were seen by members of Society. While the primary aim was to show the world that they were a courting couple, these social events became much more than a means to an end for Leo. The better acquainted he became with Amelia, the more he discovered his first impression of her to have been correct. She was an intelligent, lively young woman, one that any man would be proud to have as his wife.

There was a certain irony to the situation in which he found himself. He had been in love with a titled lady and had wanted to marry her, but had been rejected because of his lowly origins. Now he was attempting to show all of Society that he was willingly marrying the daughter of an earl and that this was a love match.

To prove that, all their interactions had been deliberately in the public eye, which meant no repeat of the kiss that had got them into this predicament. But there would certainly be time enough for that when they married, and surely anticipation would only make the final satisfaction even more rewarding.

Their wedding night was something he hoped Amelia was anticipating as eagerly as he was. He'd been given a tantalising glimpse of her delicious body when she wore that plunging neckline at his ball, and had explored her slim waist, rounded hips and delightful buttocks when he'd held her in his arms. Unwrapping her and gazing on her naked body alone would almost be worth giving up his bachelor status for. But on their wedding night, he would be doing much more than just indulging himself in an admiration of her naked beauty.

She may have said she had no wish to marry, but if he knew anything about women—and, having bedded a countless number of them, he believed he did—she certainly wanted him. Their kiss had shown him just how passionate she was. She had so quickly lost herself, given herself to him, and he was certain she would be eager to do the same on their wedding night.

He had every intention of making her happy, and not just in the bedroom. He did not want her to be like so many other women of her class, married and miserable. Especially if that unhappiness drove her into the arms of another man, as had been the case for his mistresses.

Until he had met Amelia, the fate of many aristocratic women was not something about which he had given much consideration. To his shame, all he had thought of was how those marriages had benefitted him, when those unhappy women fled to his bed. But it was wrong. And especially wrong for Amelia. Like so many other women of her class, she was being forced into this marriage by her father and by Society. That was something they both had to accept, but he wanted her to be happy and to see him as a good choice as a husband. And that was not just because the thought of sharing her with another caused his stomach to tense and his ire to rise against this non-existent man.

To convince her that this marriage could work, they needed to spend time alone together, without the scrutiny of Society. And there was no better way for that to happen than for her to visit with him at his country estate in Cornwall.

An invitation was extended to Amelia, Aunt Beryl and her father. Thankfully, her father declined, claiming that Aunt Beryl would be sufficient as a chaperone. Lord Lambourne had accepted him as a future son-in-law, but only begrudgingly. Leo was sure he would never fully reconcile himself to the disgrace of having a blacksmith's son in the family, but the snobbery of the aristocracy was something Leo had been dealing with his entire life and was no more than he expected. He would waste no more time thinking about it, not when he had a future wife to woo.

To ensure everything was perfect for his bride-to-be's visit, he arrived at his Cornwall estate the day before his guests. This also gave him time to inform his parents of his upcoming nuptials. They took it in much the same way as they took every announcement he had made since he had been taken from his family home and thrust into the world of the aristocracy, with humble acceptance, as if it no longer had anything to do with them.

Leo had long since learnt not to be hurt by this emotional estrangement.

When he'd become the subject of Lord Fitzherbert's wager he'd not only been forced into a world to which he was unprepared but had also lost the world into which he had been born. As the years had worn on and he had become wealthier and more powerful, connections with his family further unravelled until they hardly seemed related at all. There was now such an impenetrable barrier between himself and his parents that they treated him more like a respected guest than a son.

That was another reason why this marriage was turning out to be a good arrangement. He would have a new family now, one consisting of Amelia and the children he hoped they would one day have together.

On the day of their arrival, he waited at the entranceway as his carriage travelled up the long, tree-lined drive that led to his home. He'd given last-minute instructions to the butler and housekeeper to ensure that everything was to be perfect for his guests, had once more gone over the menus with Cook, and inspected the best bed chambers in the house to see for himself that they had been fully aired and prepared for Amelia and her aunt.

'Everything is as it should be,' his valet had assured him yet again as Leo dressed that morning. 'The servants know how important this visit is to you and they are just as anxious to make a good impression as you are.'

Anxious? Leo had dismissed his valet's statement as

ludicrous. Women did not make him anxious. He was not some innocent boy, but a man who had had more women than he could remember. But as he waited for her arrival, the churning in his stomach did suggest he was indeed nervous. Amelia was the first young lady he had invited to his country home, and the first since Lydia who had caused this rather unsettling state.

He frowned at that bizarre thought. This was nothing like his foolish attempt to court Lydia. He had been in love with her and had thought that she was in love with him. He had also naively thought that love was enough. That it could overcome his origins and his relative lack of wealth. With Amelia it was different. His origins had not changed, but the extent of his wealth and power certainly had. He was now in a position to offer his bride the best of everything, and the enormous stately home towering behind him was tangible proof of that.

Nor was he now the wide-eyed young man who had fallen hopelessly in love with a beautiful young lady, only to have all of his hopes and dreams crushed.

This courtship would be completely different and one which should not be causing him any undue agitation.

The carriage circled round the fountain in front of the house and with the crunching of gravel under the wheels came to a halt. He rushed forward to open the door before the liveried footman could climb down from the front of the carriage, and held out his hand to Amelia.

She smiled at him in greeting and stepped down, her smile growing larger as she looked up at his country home.

'It's magnificent,' she said, and the weight pressing down on his shoulders lifted and took flight.

He followed her gaze and it was as if he was seeing his home through her eyes, taking in the expansive ochre stone frontage, with its countless windows sparkling in the sunlight, the turrets standing proudly on each corner and the crenellated roof-line, a relic from a bygone age when the house had also been a fortification.

The estate had been in the Fitzherbert family for centuries, until they had fallen into a pit of debt that even their good name and connections couldn't dig them out of. Leo had taken great pleasure in buying the estate where he had grown up, where his parents still lived, and where his humiliation at the hands of the aristocracy had begun.

He rarely visited his country estate now and had only bought it as an act of revenge. It had once given him immense satisfaction to roam the many hallways and enter the countless elegant drawing rooms, dining rooms, breakfast rooms and ballroom, and declare to himself, 'This is all mine.' Then the satisfaction had started to wane. The house and estate felt far too big and empty for one lone man. So dust-covers had been placed over the antique furniture and vast art collection and he had returned to London.

Now it had been brought back to life and he was proud that he could use it to entertain the woman he was to wed and show her that marriage to him was in no way a step down for a woman from her class.

'And you said you grew up here?' Amelia asked as

he helped the equally impressed Aunt Beryl down from the carriage.

'Yes. As a child I loved playing in the woods, even though the servants' and tenants' children were not encouraged to do so. When I was a young boy, I imagined that the house was occupied by medieval knights. It was quite a surprise when I met Lord Fitzherbert and found him to be an overweight old man who constantly wheezed and had a walrus moustache stained yellow from smoking a pipe.'

She smiled slightly at his reminiscence, which had been intended to amuse, even though the memory of that man contained more pain than pleasure for him.

'It's a perfect place for a child to grow up,' she said quietly.

He looked out at the estate and imagined their children living here, running free and playing beside the river and in the wooded areas, places that were no longer off limits to the children of the tenants and servants.

Their children.

This engagement had been so sudden and so unexpected he had not considered that they would one day have children, that he would be a father, would have a son or daughter. If he had a son, or even a daughter, who could inherit his empire. If it were a boy, when he attended school, he would not be a charity case, being picked on by every oafish aristocratic son who thought himself superior because his father had a title. He would be a wealthy young man related to the aristocracy through his mother. He would be a young man to be reckoned with right from the start of his life and would not have to fight for everything he achieved, the way Leo had.

He might not approve of the aristocracy, might hold them in contempt for everything they had made him suffer at school and beyond, but if having connections to the aristocracy would give his son an advantage, then he was pleased to be able to give this unborn young man the best possible start in life that he could.

'Leo?' she said quietly, interrupting his thoughts.

He smiled at her. 'You are right. This is a perfect place for a child to grow up.' And this intelligent, lively woman would make the perfect mother for his children.

She blushed prettily, at the thought of their children or the manner in which they might be conceived, he did not know, but he too was looking forward to both.

After a polite exchange about their journey from London, he escorted Amelia and her aunt Beryl up the stone stairs, through the large doors and into the grand entranceway. Gone were the paintings of the ancestors that had once adorned the cream and gold walls. He had been unable to bear their smug faces looking down on those who were beneath them, both literally and figuratively.

When he'd purchased the estate, he had granted the paintings to Lord Fitzherbert's family. He had thought they would be pleased to have a memento of their forebears, but he later discovered the paintings had been sold to pay off the family's ongoing debts and so they could continue to live without the inconvenience of finding employment.

The servants were all lined up in the hallway to be

presented to his guests. Their deference was something he doubted he would ever get used to and he was pleased to see that Amelia did not treat them in a high-handed manner. She spoke kindly to each person, even chatting to the lowly scullery maid, and he could see that they warmed to her immediately.

She was going to make a perfect mistress of his estate. A perfect mistress for him. When he had first met her, he had dismissed her looks as pretty enough but lacking true classical beauty. It made no sense, but each time he saw her she appeared to grow more captivating, until now, in his eyes, she could rival any woman's beauty.

'The maid will show you to your rooms,' he said once the introductions were over. 'And I will see you at lunch.'

She reached for his arm. 'Oh, after sitting all morning on the train and then in the carriage, I'd really like to take a walk around the gardens.'

'Then it would be my honour to accompany you,' Leo said, feeling absurdly pleased. 'Both of you,' he added to Aunt Beryl.

'No, you two go ahead,' Aunt Beryl said, waving her hand in dismissal. 'I'd like to have a rest.'

Leo's absurd pleasure increased as he nodded politely and took Amelia's arm.

Amelia's excitement wound itself up another notch. It had started to escalate from the moment she had left London. No, that was incorrect. It had started when she selected her finest gowns for her lady's maid to pack. Or had it started when she received Leo's invitation to spend the weekend at his country estate? Yes, that was it. When she held that stiff white card in her hand, her pulse had started racing and she'd been infused with excitement, and that feeling hadn't stopped.

Now here she was, at his country estate, away from the prying eyes of Society and the disapproval of her father, with only Aunt Beryl as a chaperone. Now, hopefully, she would finally get that expected compensation for the inconvenience of this unwanted engagement.

The time she had spent in Leo's company had been enjoyable. The walks in the park, the nights at the opera and the theatre, the dinners at London's most fashionable restaurants…they had all been pleasant. They had conversed, laughed on occasion, but it had all felt like a show, a display to prove that they were indeed a courting couple.

Occasionally he had looked at her with something that bore a resemblance to desire, but she was yet to see the look in his eye that she had seen just before he kissed her. The look that made her feel that he wanted her and no one else. It was a look that set ripples of desire cascading within her, a sensation that overtook all ability to think. It was a look that was both frightening and intensely exciting, and one she hoped to see again during this visit.

Their engagement was just for appearances' sake. But they were still engaged, to all intents and purposes. Surely, he should feel free to kiss her again. And maybe, just maybe, do more than kiss her. Maybe she'd get to experience what Lady Madeline and so many other women had. That shimmer of excitement intensified even further as he led her back out through the entrance-way and down the stairs.

The wide vista opened up before them, with its grass-lands, wooded areas, and formal gardens. And there wasn't another person in sight. This was what she wanted. To be alone with him, away from prying eyes.

'What a glorious day,' she said, not just in reference to the sunshine.

'I'm pleased the sun has decided to come out so you can see the estate at its best.'

She laughed lightly.

'Where would you like to walk?'

'Anywhere.'

Anywhere that I'm alone with you.

She looked up at him, her heart pounding quickly within her chest, her body gripped in anticipation.

His gaze moved to her lips and *that* look passed over his face. The one she had seen before he had kissed her.

Her excitement rose up to an almost unbearable pitch. He *was* going to do it again. She just knew it. She parted her lips, hoping it sent him an unspoken invitation, one she would say out loud if she were a more courageous woman. After all, there was no one to stop them now, no ball guests, no Father, no anyone who might intrude. He could kiss her now and no one would know. Or even do more than kiss her, if that was his desire. Her heart pounding furiously, her skin came alive at the thought of his hands running over her. He could caress every inch of her and only the two of them would know, and she most certainly would put up no objection.

He had spoken of children. Was he too thinking of their wedding night?

But there would be no wedding night. Amelia knew that. Yet, oh, how she wanted this man to show her what it would be like.

'Perhaps we could walk to the woodland,' she said on a gasp, running her tongue over her bottom lip in what she hoped was a suggestive manner.

He coughed lightly and looked over her head. Anticipation rapidly changed to embarrassment as heat flooded her cheeks. Had she done that wrong? Had she just made a fool of herself and exposed her lack of experience with men?

'I don't think that would be appropriate,' he said, his voice terse.

What? Why not? she wanted to ask.

If it was appropriate to kiss her when they weren't even courting, why would it not be appropriate now? He could do what he wanted now and no one would object, certainly not her.

'The river is lovely at this time of year,' he said, still not looking at her as he led her down along the side of the house. 'That will make a pleasant walk and give you a chance to stretch your legs after your journey.'

He was suddenly so formal, and disappointment flooded through her. At least she had the pleasure of having him beside her. That, she supposed, was some consolation, but not the compensation she craved.

As they walked along the gravel path, over the stone bridge and along the gently flowing river, she moved slightly closer to him, relishing the strength of the arm holding hers and that masculine scent she remembered from when he'd held her.

She sighed lightly. Surely, some time over the next two days he would kiss her again. He just had to. Their marriage would never go ahead, of that she was certain. She could not do it to him. She would not force him into a marriage he didn't want, but it did not mean she could not taste the delights that other women had experienced in his arms.

After all, it was the first time, and it might be the last time she was with a man who held such a fierce attraction for her.

If he did kiss her again, thinking it was acceptable because they were engaged, it would add to her growing list of deceptions, but surely a little bit of extra guilt would be worth it. And if he kissed her again—and maybe, hopefully, did more—no one would be hurt. Least of all Leo Devenish. Somehow, at some time, during this weekend, she would have to make him aware of that fact.

'You're right, the sun really is showing off the estate quite gloriously,' she finally said, breaking the uncomfortable silence that had descended on them. 'It must have been lovely growing up here. I'm sure that river provided you with a wonderful place for many a childhood adventure.'

'When I was a child I didn't have free rein of the property.'

She could hear the hint of bitterness in his voice which always appeared on the rare times he mentioned his childhood.

'After all, I was merely the son of a blacksmith and a lowly servant. We lived in one of the tenant cottages and the children of the servants and tenants were expected to be neither seen nor heard by the lord of the manor.'

'So, how did you go from being the son of a tenant to the owner of this estate and so much more?'

He lightly patted her arm. 'You don't need to hear any of that. It's a rather boring story.'

'I doubt if any story which involves a man overcoming enormous obstacles to become the owner of a splendid estate like this could possibly be boring.'

He paused as if weighing up how much he should share with her. 'As my fortunes grew the Earl's declined, mainly due to his expecting the world to stay the same as it had for his forebears, for an income to continue to roll in without his having to do anything. He owned a lot of land, as you can see, but the traditional produce the land produced could no longer compete in price with ones coming in from the colonies.'

He was staring straight ahead, as if reciting a tale that had nothing to do with him, or at least one he wished to emotionally detach himself from.

'Rather than do anything about it, the family slowly fell deeper and deeper into debt, the way so many aristocrats are doing. He couldn't find a convenient heiress to bail him out, so I offered him a sizeable amount for the estate.'

'I don't imagine Lord Fitzherbert was happy about that, selling it to the son of someone who had worked for him.'

'He was happy about the money, but no, I think he

might have had to concede that I was not the man he wanted to see in ownership of his family estate.'

'And I assume you have now made it profitable.'

'Yes. That is what I do, turn unprofitable businesses into ones that make money.'

Amelia fought not to think of her unprofitable magazine that he wished to either acquire or drive out of the market.

'And what of your parents? Where are they now? Do they live in your house with you?'

'No. They did for a while, but they said they felt uncomfortable. They wanted to continue living with their friends and neighbours in the village and said they did not like putting on airs and graces by living in the big house. And they never got used to having servants, saying they felt awkward having people bowing and scraping to them. I built them a house in the village but they weren't too happy about that either. They felt it made them look as if they thought they were better than their friends. In the end I refurbished all the tenants' cottages so that it elevated the entire town. That way my parents were happy.'

'That was kind of you.'

'Nonsense. The estate was by then running at a profit, thanks in part to the hard work of the tenants. Providing them with good living conditions was nothing less than they deserved and taking care of your employees always reaps rewards. Happy workers are more productive.'

It had been a compliment, but it seemed Leo Devenish did not like to think that he was capable of being kind.

'So how do your parents feel about your being...?' She waved her hand to indicate the enormous estate.

'Filthy rich?'

'Well, yes.'

He exhaled slowly. 'They've accepted it with a certain level of fatalism.' He paused and drew in a slow breath.

Without realising what she was doing, she gripped his hand, wanting to soothe away the unspoken pain his words contained.

'Do you see much of your parents now?' she asked quietly.

He shrugged. 'On occasion.'

'Well, we must spend time with your parents while we are here.'

His eyes widened and he stared down at her as if she had made a startling proposition. 'Of course. I shall invite them to dinner.'

'But I thought you said they felt uncomfortable in the big house, that they didn't like putting on airs and graces or being waited on by servants.'

'That is true, but I am sure they will make an exception in your case.'

'I would not expect them to do so. We could visit them in their house, where they feel comfortable.'

'I'm not sure if that's a good idea,' he said, his voice becoming decidedly pompous.

'Why? Are you worried that I'll shame you with my fancy ways?' It was a joke, but he did not smile.

'Of course not.'

'Or are you ashamed of your parents, and as much a snob as my father?'

'Absolutely not,' he said, his voice rising.

'Good. Let's go there. Now.'

'What? No.' He looked around as if searching for excuses. 'Would you not rather wait? After all, you have had a long journey. I'm sure you wish to rest.'

'No, I don't. Now, in which direction do they live?' She did a small turn as if expecting his parents' cottage to appear before them.

'They live in the village, in a cottage next to my father's smithy. It's too far to walk. We'll have to take the carriage.'

Amelia suspected he was delaying but she would not allow such a thing. She wanted to meet his parents, wanted to know everything there was to know about this man who fascinated her so. It might not be a real engagement, but if it was, then of course she would meet his parents. So she had every right to expect an introduction.

'Then let's return to the house and take the carriage to your parents' home.'

She turned and walked back to the house, giving Leo no choice but to follow.

Chapter Fourteen

Amelia had not long been at his estate and already things were not going according to plan. Leo had intended to spend this time gently courting her in the manner a debutante expected. And yet, when she suggested the walk in the woodland, he had been overtaken with a surging desire to rush her into the secluded area, strip her naked and satisfy his raging lust. That was most certainly not how one treated an innocent debutante, and it was a reaction he was going to have to control if this visit was to be a success.

And now he was chasing behind her, back to his estate, trying to think of ways he could delay and hopefully postpone a visit to his parents' home.

He was not a snob, as she had suggested. At least, he didn't think he was. But it would do no good for Amelia to see where he had grown up, to see what he had come from. He was a man from humble origins, the product of parents with minimal education. Amelia was a woman who had only ever moved in the highest levels of society. People like his parents never came into her orbit.

They were the invisible people who cleaned her house, cooked her meals, shoed her horses, and performed all those other tasks that members of Society took for granted. Now she was to meet some of those invisible people and come to the realisation that they would be her future in-laws.

Everything she had said suggested that she would not judge him for his origins, but that did not stop that nagging sensation from rising within him. The one that was never too far away. The one that told him that he would never be good enough, that he would always be judged, and would always be seen as inferior. Hadn't Lydia's father made that clear, laughing in his face when he had asked for his daughter's hand in marriage? Hadn't Lydia confirmed it, telling him not to be so foolish when he suggested they elope? Now there was the danger that Amelia would do the same. She would be confronted by his origins and the realisation of just how different they were.

They entered the house, where the butler was waiting for them. 'Cook has asked when you would like luncheon to be served.'

Leo almost embraced the man. 'Now, thank you, Hobson.' He turned to Amelia. 'We can't possibly visit my family until after lunch.'

She frowned and Leo was sure she was about to present some counter argument.

'And I'm sure Aunt Beryl is in need of something to eat, even if you aren't. Plus,' he raced on before she could deny this, 'an afternoon visit I am sure would be more acceptable to my parents.'

That did the trick and she nodded her agreement. All he had to do now was think of a reason why an afternoon visit would be unacceptable.

He tried. He failed. And after lunch found himself seated beside Amelia heading towards the local village and a visit he was sure would be uncomfortable for all concerned. He'd decided to take the small, one-horse gig and drive himself, rather than the carriage with the liveried servants, knowing his parents would be further disconcerted if he arrived in a grand manner, and would worry what the neighbours might think.

He gave a small flick of the reins and tried to still his thoughts. He always prided himself on his ability to quickly adapt and to turn things to his advantage. Wasn't this upcoming marriage proof of that? And yet, the gripping in his stomach and the tightness in his shoulders suggested that in this instance that ability was letting him down.

He needed to think this out rationally. He was about to introduce his intended to his parents. For many men such a meeting would be reason enough for a certain level of agitation. But Leo was not most men. It had been a long time since he had experienced nervousness. He'd overcome too much in his life to be fearful of anything or anyone ever again. And yet, this was a unique situation. He had never introduced a young lady to his parents before.

At least Amelia did not seem to share his trepidation about meeting her future in-laws, if her happy chattering was any indication.

'Do you know, this is the first time I've visited Cornwall?' she said with a delighted smile while looking around at the passing scenery. 'It really is rather beautiful.'

He cast a glance at the hedges, wildflowers and trees lining the narrow country lane as if seeing them through her eyes, and had to admit it was a pleasant sight. 'My parents love this area and my mother could never understand why I wanted to live in London.'

'I must say, I agree with her. Why would anyone want to move from such a glorious setting, and doesn't the air smell divine?' She inhaled deeply.

'London is where the money is. If I hadn't lived in London it's unlikely I would ever have been able to buy the Fitzherbert estate. This area is picturesque, but you can't live off pretty scenery. No one respects you because you come from a quaint village.'

He could hear the terseness in his voice and he did not want to be like that. This weekend was all about convincing her that their marriage was a good idea and that would not happen if he allowed his own agitation to get in the way of achieving that goal.

'It's a shame that you can't now just enjoy the fruits of your labours and spend more time in this glorious countryside.'

He looked around and for a moment wondered whether she was right. It would be good to stop fighting. He flicked the reins, shocked at such an uncharacteristically weak thought. He could never stop fighting. Fortunes could be lost much more easily than they could be won. He was rich now, but he could never rest. Men

like him would always be a target. There were too many
men who wanted to take him down and see him destroyed. He would never let that happen and the only
way to ensure it never did was to continue to work and
acquire greater wealth.

He brought the gig to a halt in front of his parents'
humble cottage. The smithy was attached to the house,
and even though Leo provided his parents with enough
money so they could retire in comfort his father insisted
on continuing to work, and today was no different. A
fire burned brightly in the furnace at the back of the
smithy. The sound of metal hammering on metal rang
out in the otherwise quiet neighbourhood as his father
pounded at the red-hot end of a rod of iron. He was
dressed exactly as he always had been during Leo's
childhood, his sleeves rolled up above his elbows, with
a thick leather apron to protect him from sparks and a
cloth cap on his head.

Leo's happiest memories during his school years,
perhaps his only happy memories, were of helping his
father in the smithy during the holidays, and the sound
and sight of his father at work went some way towards
assuaging his agitation.

His father looked up, and for a moment stared at the
guests walking up his pathway without recognition.
Then he placed the iron rod into a nearby metal bucket
of water, causing hissing steam to fill the smithy, removed his apron, rolled down his sleeves and walked
towards them.

'Son,' he said, the word sounding almost like an honorific rather than a greeting. Then his eyes flicked to Amelia and he doffed his flat cap.

'Father, this is Lady Amelia. The young lady I told you about, my bride-to-be. Lady Amelia, this is my father, Mr Tom Devenish.'

His father clenched his cap tightly in his hands. 'My lady,' he said, lowering his gaze. Leo's heart ached for him. Subservience to those they considered their betters was second nature to his parents, as it once would have been to him, and still would be if his life had not taken a different course. But his parents were good people, better than many he met among the upper echelons of society, and should not have to defer to anyone.

'Please, call me Amelia.'

He flicked a quick glance at Leo, who nodded to inform him that yes, he could call her by her given name alone.

'I reckon you'll be wanting to see your mam,' he said, looking towards the house as if he couldn't get away from his son fast enough. Before they could answer he turned and walked back to the smithy, rolling up his sleeves as he went, seemingly desperate to return to work.

The door opened and his mother rushed out. 'Leo,' she called, hurrying down the path. 'You should'a told us you were going to visit.' She looked at Amelia. 'And bringing your young lady as well without giving me time to prepare…' Her gaze quickly took in Amelia's fine clothes. Her smile died. She lowered her eyes and curtseyed.

'This is Amelia,' Leo said. 'Amelia, may I present my mother, Mrs Margaret Devenish?'

His mother gave Amelia another quick look, lowered her eyes again and made another curtsey.

Amelia stepped forward and took both his mother's hands in hers. 'I am so pleased to meet you. And it's all my fault that we're being so rude and visiting without letting you know. I wanted to meet you, so I insisted that Leo bring me immediately.'

'No need to apologise, my lady,' his mother said, without looking up.

'Are you going to invite us in, Mam?' Leo said, certain that otherwise they would remain in the pathway for the entire visit, his mother frozen by indecision.

'Of course.' His mother stood aside so they could enter and followed behind like the deferential servant she had been trained to be.

Amelia and Leo took their seats at the scrubbed pine table while his mother hovered near the coal stove.

'I was just saying to Leo what a beautiful area this is and how he was so lucky to have been born here,' Amelia said.

'Oh, yes, my lady, it's a right beautiful area.'

'Please, call me Amelia.'

His mother sent a glance towards Leo, as if unsure whether she could take such a liberty. She had spent the early part of her life as a servant, where she was not even allowed to speak to members of the household unless spoken to, never mind call them by their name, and certainly not their given name. Such an adjustment was not going to come easily to her.

'Will you be wanting a cup of tea?' she said, looking from Leo and Amelia to the kettle as if it were unlikely that such eminent people would do something so ordinary.

'That would be lovely,' Amelia said, standing up. 'Allow me to help.'

A look of horror crossed his mother's face. 'No, no, my lady, you sit down. I'll do it.'

'Please, call me Amelia,' she repeated. 'And I would love to help. Where do you keep the cups and saucers?' She spotted some crockery on a shelf above the stove and lifted them down.

'Oh, no, my la... Amelia. Those are for family. I'll get the good cups.' She moved towards the door. 'And perhaps you'd like to go through to the parlour while I make it.'

'But we are family,' Amelia replied. 'And this kitchen is so warm and cosy. We're happy here, aren't we, Leo?'

His mother stared at her as if unsure what to make of this strange woman who was placing cups and saucers on the table, either oblivious to the discomfort in the room or refusing to let it affect her. She looked to Leo for guidance and all he could do was smile in reassurance.

She turned her back on them, busying herself with making the tea, while Amelia described the scenery they had passed on their trip to the cottage.

'The wildflowers are still putting on such a lovely display. That's something you never see in London. And the air...' She inhaled deeply as if still able to smell the freshness of the countryside. 'I do not think I have ever smelt air so clean. It is as if our smoggy London lungs are finally learning how they're supposed to breathe.'

His mother merely turned and smiled politely, then went back to her tea making.

'I suspect this is the prettiest corner in the whole of England. You're so blessed to live here, and Leo was certainly lucky to spend his early years in such beautiful surroundings. I was saying to him on the drive over I can't understand why he does not spend more time here rather than in London.'

As she continued to chatter on, he could see the tension in his mother's shoulders slowly releasing.

'That's exactly what I think,' she said as she placed the brown pottery teapot on the table. 'Leo will have to take you for a walk along the coast. He used to spend ever such a lot of time there when he was a lad. Usually pretending he was a pirate or a smuggler.'

'What was he like when he was a boy? I want to hear all about it.'

A smile lit up his mother's face, something that had not happened in his presence for some time. 'He was a right scamp, always into something, but he was as bright as a button.'

'I can well imagine.' Amelia looked at Leo and also smiled. 'He's not much different now.'

'Would you like scones and jam?' his mother said before Leo could add anything to the conversation. 'I made them earlier for Tom's lunch, but there's some left over, and there's some lovely strawberry jam.'

'Oh, yes, please,' Amelia said, as if scones and jam was the most delicious dish she had ever been offered.

His mother crossed the room and picked up a plate covered with a blue and white checked cloth and proudly placed it on the table, along with a pot of jam and some cream. 'The strawberries come from Leo's glasshouse. The servants always bring us some. It's such a treat.'

Leo made sure his parents wanted for nothing and had fresh produce sent over regularly.

She smiled at Amelia. 'Please, help yourself.'

They both took a bite of their scones, and Amelia's eyes grew wide in appreciation, much to his mother's pleasure.

She devoured her scone and reached for another. 'So tell me more about Leo when he was a child,' she asked as she smothered her scone with cream and jam.

'Oh, he played such inventive games—pirates, smugglers and knights. He used to stage famous battles he'd heard about at school and organise all the other children into the different armies.'

Leo couldn't help but laugh. He hadn't thought of that for years, and all the fun he'd had with the other village children. Even though he was younger than many of his fellow soldiers he always took the role of the general leading his troops to victory.

His mother also smiled at her memories. 'The teacher at the local school said he had never had such a clever student. He learnt to read and write so quickly and was very good with his sums.'

Leo could hear the pride in her voice. She was proud of what her ten-year-old son could do but was ashamed that his wealth and power now rivalled that of some of the most established families in England.

As if she had read his mind her smile faded. She looked down at the table, moving an invisible crumb with her finger. 'It was the teacher who encouraged us to let Lord Fitzherbert send him off to that fancy school. We didn't really want to at first, but the teacher convinced us that it would be the best thing for Leo.'

Leo had never heard that before and had always assumed his parents had been grateful to Lord Fitzherbert for sending him away to school.

'That was kind of Lord Fitzherbert,' Amelia said, looking from mother to son. 'Was he a philanthropist?'

Both mother and son laughed mirthlessly at this comment.

'We'd never known him to do anything else charitable,' his mother said. 'That's why it was such a surprise that he gave Leo this opportunity.'

'So why did he single you out? Was it because you were so clever at school?' Amelia asked him.

'I doubt that he knew anything about me,' he replied, the scone suddenly tasting like ash in his mouth.

Amelia frowned and turned back to his mother for an explanation.

'That's something I've often wondered as well,' she said. 'His Lordship never did anything for no one ever again, to my recollection, and he never paid me nor Tom no heed, even though he was paying for our son's education. I don't know if he even knew that Leo was mine.'

They both looked to Leo for an explanation. He drew in a deep breath and exhaled slowly. He had never told his mother the story and had certainly never shared it with any of the women in his life, but it seemed he had no choice but to tell them now.

'I was an experiment.'

'An experiment?' both women said, looking from him to each other then back at him.

He nodded as if it was of no real importance, determined to keep his voice matter-of-fact, so neither would know the true extent of the pain that cruel act had caused him.

'It happened the day you took me to the big house when you were called to work because Lord Fitzherbert had important visitors attending a house party.'

'Oh, I remember that day. I couldn't find anyone to look after you, so I brought you with me and gave you strict instructions to stay out of the way of the other servants.' She turned to Amelia. 'I could have got into ever such a lot of trouble, but he did as he was told and no one noticed him.'

'That's because I went exploring.'

His mother gasped, as if the event had only just happened and she was in danger of being punished for some transgression.

'You did say he was a bit of a scamp,' Amelia said with a little laugh, and patted his mother's hand in solace.

They both turned back to him, and he braced himself as he remembered how his life had changed irrevocably from that moment.

'So what happened? How did you become an experiment?' Amelia asked.

'My explorations took me to the library. When I first

walked into that book-lined room I was amazed. I'd never seen so many books before, all in one place. As if discovering a pirate's treasure trove, I removed book after book from the shelves in total amazement. Then I found a botanical text with beautiful drawings of plants, and was gazing at it in wonderment when Lord Fitzherbert and several of his guests walked in.'

His mother's hand covered her mouth and her eyes grew wide.

'What did they say? What did they do?' both women asked.

He fought to ignore the churning in his stomach, determined not to reveal the anxiety these memories aroused. 'They were highly amused, as if they'd found an animal at the zoo attempting to read a book,' he said with a forced laugh, as if recounting an amusing anecdote.

'That's appalling,' Amelia whispered.

He wasn't fooling either woman with his laughter or attempt to lighten the mood. And perhaps to do so was being condescending. Amelia had asked to hear the story and was not some flibbertigibbet who needed to be sheltered from the realities of life. That was yet another of her qualities he admired. And his mother was looking at him with both concern and curiosity, as if finally getting the answers to questions she had long pondered.

'One guest argued that Lord Fitzherbert's attitude was wrong and objected to the other's laughter. Not because he considered it insulting to me, but because he believed there was no reason why a member of the lower orders shouldn't be interested in botany if given the opportunity and education.'

'Quite right,' Amelia murmured.

'The discussion continued, and they hardly seemed aware of me as anything other than an object to be observed and studied. All I wanted to do was to escape, back to Mam, but the men were blocking the exit. I was forced to remain as their argument got more heated.'

'How could they be so insensitive and not realise they were upsetting a young boy?' Amelia said, and his mother nodded slowly, as if to make further criticism of the people she considered her betters would be an offence.

'I suspect whether the lower orders actually have feelings could have been another subject for debate between them,' Leo said.

Amelia shook her head slowly, and she exhaled her disapproval.

'The argument raged for some time, until Lord Fitzherbert made a wager. He said he would prove that no matter how much education you gave the lower orders they would never amount to anything. He pointed at me and said that he would pay for "that boy" to have the best education money could buy. He was convinced that no matter what advantages I was given I would still end up with status no higher than a servant. The two men shook on it and my fate was sealed.'

'Oh, son. We never knew any of this.' His mother reached across the table and took his hand. 'We always wondered why the Earl was being so generous, but the teacher told us not to look a gift horse in the mouth and to just accept it as unexpected good fortune. He told us we had to think of your future, that not many boys were given such an opportunity and we'd be selfish to turn it down.' She looked from Leo to Amelia, her face full of appeal that they would understand. 'And it was for the best.' She smiled, the edges of her lips quivering. 'It was. Just look at him now.'

'It must have been hard for you, to lose your son,' Amelia said quietly.

His mother nodded. 'It was. We missed him sorely when he was away. But his letters were always full of all sorts of exciting tales, playing cricket and studying Latin and whatnot.'

Leo swallowed down the bile rising up his throat, remembering those letters and the lies he wrote. He had never revealed to his parents the true torment of his school years. They had been so proud to send their son off to school, and so excited to hear about all he had learnt when he returned for the holidays, he could not burden them with the knowledge that he had suffered for years at the hands of bullies.

'But I suspected he wasn't as happy as he claimed. Were you, son?'

Leo's chest clenched, as if someone was squeezing his heart. 'It was the making of me,' he said dismissively as the two women stared back at him with matching looks of compassion he did not want. This meeting was becoming uncomfortable, but not in the way he had imagined.

'But it did break my heart to part with him. We only saw him during the holidays, and he changed more and more each time he returned.' His mother bit her lip as if she had said too much. 'For the better, of course,' she added quickly. 'He had ever such nice manners and such a lovely way of talking.'

He had changed?

His memories were of parents who had become increasingly distant but the sadness in his mother's eyes told another story. She tried to smile, but the quivering in her lip made a lie of any happiness. Such a sight would break his heart if his heart hadn't been strongly reinforced so that it was no longer capable of bending, never mind breaking.

'It was a terrible thing to do, parting a mother and son,' Amelia said quietly. 'All the lovely manners in the world cannot make up for that.'

A small tear appeared in his mother's eye. She quickly lifted the pot to refresh their cups, an unnecessary action as they had hardly touched their tea.

'I kept trying to tell myself it was all for the best. Each time he returned for the holidays I wanted to stop him going back to that school but I knew that was just me being selfish. After all, boys like him never got such an opportunity.'

She smiled tremulously. 'I did worry ever so much when he was away and fretted about the way it was changing him, but knew I had to keep my objections to myself. I don't mean the manners and the way of talking, but because he went from such a happy, carefree boy to one who was angry all the time. I still don't know if it was a good idea him getting all that education. Sometimes, I must admit, I think, yes, he's become rich because of it, but at what cost?'

She bit her lip as if she had revealed too much.

Amelia took hold of her hand. The two women's heads had moved closer together and they were talking about him as if he were no longer present.

'I think they were mean to him, those other boys, I'm sure of it,' his mother said quietly. 'If he had just gone to the local school, he would have still got an education. Maybe he wouldn't have learnt all those things like Greek and Latin, but he also wouldn't have changed so much. I feel like I lost my boy when they sent him off to that posh school.'

'I'm still here, Mam,' he said, wondering if he should inform these two women that they were talking about a man who was capable of buying an estate out from under an earl, whom politicians feared and members of the highest ranks of society deferred to. He was not a man who needed anyone's pity.

His mother reached over and squeezed his hand, and for a brief moment tears welled up in Leo's eyes before he quickly blinked them away, shocked by how this sentimental exchange had affected even him.

'I'll leave you two to talk,' he said, standing up and heading for the door before either woman could see the bizarre effect this conversation was having on him. 'I'll see if Pa wants help in the smithy.'

With that he closed the door behind him, paused, took in a slow, deep breath and headed over towards his father. 'I'll give you a hand, Pa,' he said, taking off his jacket, rolling up his sleeves and grabbing a spare leather apron hanging from a hook.

He attempted to focus on pounding the metal, hoping the hard physical work would drive out all that his mother had just said.

Several horseshoes had to be abandoned, due to his hitting the metal with plenty of strength but little finesse. But as he settled into the rhythm of the work his agitated state calmed, and he carefully crafted each horseshoe, rather than hitting it with ferocity as if it were his enemy.

He could see why his father continued with such work, even though his son's wealth meant he no longer had to work for a living. There was satisfaction to be gained from creating something with one's own hands.

'I think your young lady might be ready to leave,' his father said, looking towards the cottage.

Leo turned and saw Amelia and his mother standing at the doorway.

'Best you clean yourself up, son, before you go back to your fancy house.' He indicated the water-filled trough at the edge of the smithy. It was a long time since Leo had washed in such a manner. Stripping off his shirt, he took the cloth and wiped off the sweat from his face and chest, quickly dried himself and pulled on his shirt and jacket. When he turned to Amelia she was still staring at him, her hand clasping the string of pearls around her neck.

'Goodbye, Pa,' he said.

'Bye, son, and thanks for your help.'

Leo wondered how much help he could actually provide to a skilled craftsman, but he was grateful for his father's thanks.

'It's been lovely to see you again, son,' his mother

said when he joined them. 'And to meet your young lady. You will come again, won't you?'

'Of course we will,' Amelia answered for both of them. 'And I'm sure Leo would love to see more of you at his home here in Cornwall and in London.'

They both turned to look at him. 'You and Father know you are welcome at any time.'

Amelia gave his mother a kiss on the cheek and they walked back down the path. Before they reached the gate his mother took hold of his arm and drew him back. 'You've got a good one there, son. I reckon she's going to make you a good wife.'

Leo looked in her direction. Amelia had left the path, walked over to the smithy and was chatting to his father. Like everything else since her arrival at his estate, this visit had not been what he had expected, but he did have to agree with his mother that he had indeed got a good one there.

Chapter Fifteen

Pull yourself together, Amelia admonished herself as they drove back through the countryside.

But that command did nothing to drive out the image of Leo, shirtless, ripples of water coursing down the sculpted muscles of his chest. Her fingers had itched to run themselves along those hard muscles, her lips had tingled at the thought of kissing them, her tongue had wanted to lick and explore, to follow the line of the water as it moved down his chest and his stomach. She gulped, remembering the line of dark hairs on his stomach that disappeared into the trousers slung low on his hips.

Amelia had felt those muscles up against her when they had kissed, but seeing them in all their naked glory had left her awestruck by such virile, powerful masculinity. She had often imagined what they were like, but the sight of him without his shirt on had only proved to her that she had an inadequate imagination. She could never have visualised such masculine perfection if she had not seen it for herself, and now she knew it was an image that was going to continue to torment her.

Behave yourself, Amelia admonished herself again, squirming on her seat to try and relieve the tension gripping her in places well-brought-up young ladies should not be thinking about.

'Thank you,' he said, breaking into her fevered thoughts.

'Thank me? For what?'

For my decidedly impure thoughts? For continuing to imagine you with your shirt off, your muscles rippling, your skin glowing with perspiration?

'For today. For that visit. For being so gracious with my parents.'

'Oh, I did nothing. Really. It was a pleasant visit and I liked your parents.' Amelia squirmed once again, but this time it was guilt that was making her uncomfortable. She should not have insisted on this visit. His mother was now convinced that Leo would soon be married. *'I'm so pleased he has met you,'* she had said when Leo left the room. *'He deserves to be loved by a good woman, one who will make him happy, like he used to be when he was a lad.'*

'I'm sorry,' she said, the words slipping out.

'Sorry?'

'I'm sorry for everything that has happened to you. Lord Fitzherbert was heartless to use you in the way he did. It wasn't just cruel to you, but to your parents as well,' she said quietly. 'It was simply appalling that he deprived a mother of her only child just so he could win a stupid bet.'

His flick of the reins was the only indication he had heard her.

'Except he lost,' he said quietly.

'Everyone lost.'

They sank into silence, moving through the countryside but seeing nothing of the tranquil scenery.

He found it hard to talk about. He had lost so much. If he had remained in his home and not been sent off to boarding school he would have spent his days working side by side with his father, exchanging jokes and conversation, before returning to the cottage, where his mother would serve them a hearty meal.

He would have grown up with a warm, loving family. Perhaps he would have met and fallen in love with a local lass and raised his own family among people he had known his whole life, people who cared about him.

He now had wealth, power and prestige, but Amelia had always sensed a deep sadness behind his confident exterior. Now she knew the reason why.

Sadness washed over her. He had achieved so much in material terms but in exchange he had lost so much more.

He had been badly treated and had a right to be angry with the men who had used him for their own entertainment, but it was a tragedy that he continued to rage against the world. He thought he was punishing Lord Fitzherbert and his friends, and punishing those who had mistreated him at school, but the only person he was now punishing was himself.

'No, I won,' he finally said as they drove through the gold and black wrought-iron gates at the entrance to his estate. 'I proved conclusively to Lord Fitzherbert and his friends that I was capable of being educated and making something of myself.' He paused briefly. 'And it was a wager I'm pleased to say he came to regret.'

She could hear the anger and bitterness in his voice and once again wanted to reach out to him, to somehow try and make this better, to heal his wounds.

'Yes, he lost the bet and you proved him wrong, but I believe you also lost too much.'

'Nonsense. I had my revenge. I proved Lord Fitzherbert wrong. And now I own all this.' He looked along the drive, towards the stately home dominating the landscape.

Amelia did not look up, her gaze moving instead to his hands, which were gripping the reins so tightly the leather had become wrapped around his white-knuckled fingers. She reached out and lightly touched his hand. He said nothing, but slowly his grip loosened.

'To further prove him wrong I have established schools throughout the district and hired skilled teachers so more young people can have the advantage of a good education, without having to be ripped away from their parents.'

It was the first time she had heard him admit that losing his parents had been hard on him.

'Was your mother right? Were you treated badly at school?' she asked quietly.

He stiffened beside her and she wondered whether she should have probed a wound that was obviously so raw.

'Yes, it was hell,' he said almost inaudibly.

Once again, she reached out and touched his hand. This time he transferred the reins to one hand and held hers gently. Warmth coursed through her as his thumb gently stroked her skin.

'After a childhood playing with my friends, I discovered that not all children take their pleasure from enjoying each other's company. Some children get pleasure from tormenting others, ones they have singled out as weaker than themselves. Some children know how to be brutal and relish finding new and inventive ways to demean and humiliate others.'

He spoke so quietly she had to lean towards him to hear.

'I have since taken my own pleasure in making every one of those callous boys suffer, one way or another.'

'Did that heal your pain?'

The gig came to a halt in front of the house. He turned to face her, his dark eyebrows drawn together as if what she had said was so outlandish he was struggling to find a reply.

'It certainly caused *them* a lot of pain,' he finally said with a laugh that contained no humour. He jumped down and offered her his hand.

Amelia's heart broke for the boy who had suffered so much, for the mother who had lost her only child, and for the man who could not let go of his torment.

She took his hand and climbed down. He was so much more complex than the man she had thought him when they had first met. Then she had dismissed him as nothing more than a hard-hearted businessman, a man who knew women found him attractive and exploited that attraction. She had despised him for the ease with which he moved through the world, like some sort of conquering hero, acquiring new businesses and women wherever he went.

It was that misconception that had resulted in her taking pleasure in exposing him in *The Ladies' Enquirer*. It was that misconception that had led to his being coerced into this engagement. It had led to his being forced to marry a woman he did not love, a woman he would have barely noticed if she had not unintentionally forced her way into his life.

Shame shot through her. He did not deserve this. After all he had suffered, he deserved to be happy, and not to be thrust into an unwanted, loveless marriage.

She should tell him the truth, here and now, and put an end to this deception. She was not only lying to Leo but had now also lied to his parents. When his mother had told her how pleased she was that Leo had found a woman who could love and care for him, it had caused Amelia to shrivel inside with guilt. She really was a terrible woman, and it was time she made this right, to stop all these lies.

Aunt Beryl appeared at the top of the stairs, smiling her greeting, and walked down to meet them. The words that would free him froze on Amelia's lips. Telling him the truth would release him from an unwanted marriage, but it would have terrible consequences. Her father would disinherit her. That she knew she could bear, somehow, but she could never see Aunt Beryl thrown out of the home she had lived in for the past twenty-one years with nowhere else to go.

If she set Leo free, her innocent, lovely aunt would be the one to pay the price.

It was all wrong, so wrong, but until she found a way to ensure Aunt Beryl's financial security she would have to continue lying to this man, a man who did not deserve her lies.

Before Aunt Beryl could politely ask about their visit, Leo bowed to them both, obviously anxious to get away. 'I will see you both at dinner,' he said, then rapidly moved up the stairs two at a time and disappeared through the large doors.

'Oh, dear. Did the visit to his parents go badly?'

'No, not exactly,' Amelia said, still staring up the stone stairs. Once again he had run away, just as he had done at his mother's house, as if the pain had become more than he could bear.

'Why? What happened? What's wrong?'

She turned back to her aunt and smiled. 'Nothing's wrong. Leo's parents are a delight. His mother is warm and loving, as one would expect a mother to be.'

Aunt Beryl raised one eyebrow as if suspecting Amelia was not telling her the entire truth.

'Oh, all right,' she said. 'His mother told me things about Leo's childhood that have made me see him in quite a different light.'

Aunt Beryl tilted her head. 'Is that a good thing or a bad thing?'

'It explains a lot,' Amelia responded, looking back up the stairs. 'So that is a good thing, I believe.'

'Then it was a successful visit,' her aunt declared, taking Amelia's arm and walking up the stairs.

Amelia was not as convinced as her aunt. She was now seeing Leo in a clearer light, could understand more about the nature of the man, but that didn't mean the solutions to her own problems were any more apparent. Nor did she know what she was going to do with this new insight into Leo Devenish's character.

'Did it heal your pain?'

That was what she had said to him. It was a question Leo had never contemplated. He had not known how to answer it when she asked and was still confused by what it meant. But then, so much of today had left him confused.

As James helped him into his dinner jacket he tried to make sense of all that had happened during the day.

Nothing about his visit to his parents had been as he'd expected. He most certainly had not expected his mother to reveal how she had not wanted him to go away to school, nor had he expected her to claim that he had become an angry man.

He was not angry. Was he? Amelia had said nothing to contradict his mother. Instead she had looked at him with compassion. Was that how Amelia saw him? As an angry man who lashed out at others? And was she right? Was he holding on to his pain and anger? Was he continuing to exact revenge on the world, at the expense of his own happiness?

Amelia had certainly given him pause for thought, unlike any of the women in his life.

He had told no one of the torment he had experienced at school, not even Lydia, especially not Lydia. One thing school had taught him was to never, ever appear weak. The moment you did so others would pounce.

He had even suspected he would have been diminished in Lydia's eyes if he had told her about the bullying he had received at the hands of the aristocratic young men who were part of her social set.

But with Amelia it was different. He had not felt weak when he had revealed his past suffering to her. It did not make sense, but it was as if exposing his weaknesses had made him stronger.

'Did it heal your pain?'

Taking revenge on the men who had tormented him as boys, becoming so powerful he was all but untouchable, having wealth that enabled him to buy this estate and much more, no, none of that had healed him, if it was healing that he required. But right now, the tightness in his chest that never left him had loosened its relentless hold. The gripping of his jaw had relaxed. There was a lightness to his being that he had never experienced before.

Was that what she meant by healing?

He shook his head as if to force out that thought. He needed his relentless drive, and if it was anger that fuelled it, then he needed his anger. That was what made him a success. He was still the target of other men. They could still take away everything he had. He could never let his guard down and he never would.

And yet, all he wanted to do right now was to spend a pleasant evening in Amelia's company. He had accepted that he would marry her, and this weekend was all about convincing her that she too should accept it— even, hopefully, look forward to it.

But that was not why he wanted to be with her. He

just wanted her company. To enjoy being in her presence. For the first time in as long as he could remember, he had no ulterior motive, he was seeking no personal gain. He just wanted to be with a woman he was coming to…

His thoughts ended abruptly. Coming to what? Not love. Never love. He had loved once before and would never do that again. If he was worried that his time with Amelia was weakening him, crushing his anger and relentless drive, then love would weaken him to the extent that it could destroy him. It had taken him a long time to recover from Lydia's crushing blow. No, it was not love. She was a woman he admired. One who would make an ideal wife for a man such as him. Nothing more.

Thoughts of her parted lips entered his mind. It was not admiration he had felt when she suggested a walk in the woodland. That had been lust, pure, or perhaps not so pure, lust. How could he admire a woman and lust after her like a randy schoolboy at the same time?

That was another question he did not have an answer for. It seemed there was much about the way he felt about Lady Amelia that was beyond his understanding.

'I believe the maroon gown with the black lace would be perfect for tonight,' Aunt Beryl informed Minnie. 'And style her hair in that fancy French fashion you do so well.'

As Minnie helped Amelia into her gown and brushed out her long hair, Aunt Beryl fussed around her, seemingly as nervous as she was, although what her aunt had to be so anxious about, Amelia had no idea.

And her aunt's behaviour was doing nothing to soothe Amelia's agitated nerves. The excitement that had been simmering under the surface since she had arrived at Leo's estate was starting to boil up inside her again, and she was finding it hard to sit still as Minnie combed, curled and ornately styled her hair.

Amelia was not certain the gown was the best choice. It was the most daring in her collection, with its low-cut neckline, and off-the-shoulder short sleeves. Amelia pulled up the lace around the neckline, trying to cover up her decolletage, worried that it might look as if she was trying to seduce Leo Devenish.

'You don't think this is a bit revealing?' she asked Minnie and Aunt Beryl.

Aunt Beryl swatted her hand away. 'No, it's perfect. Mr Devenish won't be able to resist you in such a gown.'

Amelia doubted that very much. A slight blush tinged her cheeks as she remembered her attempt to encourage Leo to kiss her when she had first arrived. He had certainly been able to resist her then, and she hoped this gown would not be interpreted as yet another clumsy attempt to get him to kiss her.

'When he sees you looking like that Mr Devenish will probably fall in love with you all over again and make another heartfelt proposal,' her aunt said, placing her hands on her heart.

The bubbling in Amelia's stomach instantly changed to an uncomfortable gripping sensation, and Amelia wanted to rip off this foolish gown. It didn't matter how she dressed. Leo would not be making a second proposal as he had never made a first one. He was marrying her for one reason and one reason only, because he had no choice. Dressing up for him, imagining him kissing her again, it was all so silly and pointless. No matter how she looked, no matter what he thought of her, he would marry her because he believed he had to. What she should be concentrating on was finding a way out of this dilemma, not wearing fancy gowns, not styling her hair in the latest fashion.

She needed to keep her flights of fancy under control. She was not in love with him. He was not in love with her. He had kissed her twice, but it was obvious those kisses meant much more to her than they did to him. And damn it all, they did mean a lot to her, so much so that their memory affected her judgement and caused her to act foolishly. Tonight she would have to maintain her dignity and not reveal how desperately she wanted him to kiss her again. He could never know that his kisses had ignited something within her that only he could quench.

'Stop worrying,' Aunt Beryl said. 'You look beautiful.' She turned to Minnie for confirmation.

'Indeed you do, my lady. I don't believe I've ever seen you looking more lovely. Your cheeks are blooming, your eyes sparkling.'

'That's what a woman in love looks like,' Aunt Beryl said, and both women sighed.

Love? Was that what she was feeling for Leo? She hoped not. It was bad enough being fiercely attracted to him. It would be a disaster if she was in love with him as well. No, love was something she would never allow herself to feel for him.

'Thank you, Minnie. I won't be needing you again, so you can retire for the night,' she said, dismissing her lady's maid.

Aunt Beryl and Amelia walked down the sweeping staircase to the drawing room, Amelia's nerves becoming more agitated with every step.

She entered the drawing room. Leo stood up. His eyes locked on to hers, then slowly moved down her body. Any regrets Amelia might have had at the way she had dressed evaporated as she saw the appreciation in his gaze. Amelia knew the gown accentuated her womanly shape, nipping in her waist, lifting her breasts, and showing off the curve of her hips. It was a peculiar feeling, one she had never experienced before, but it was as if she had dressed for him, was presenting herself to him for his pleasure.

'Amelia,' he said quietly, almost to himself, the word seemingly holding greater meaning than merely being her name. He signalled to a chair and Amelia walked across the room, conscious with every step that his eyes were fixed on her.

'Oh, dear,' Aunt Beryl said, still standing in the doorway. 'I seem to have come down with a headache.'

Amelia and Leo turned to face her.

'Should I call for the doctor?' Leo asked.

'Oh, no, I believe all I need is an early night. If you would be so kind as to arrange for a tray to be sent up to my room?'

This was most unusual. Amelia had never known Aunt Beryl to have a headache before, and she had been perfectly all right when they were dressing for dinner.

'I'll come up with you,' Amelia said, crossing the room towards her aunt.

'No,' Aunt Beryl stated with more strength than one would expect from someone suffering from a headache. 'No,' she repeated, placing the back of her hand on her forehead. 'I just need to rest, alone, then I'll be perfectly all right. Go and enjoy yourself with your young man.'

Amelia cringed. Leo was not her 'young man', but now was not the time to point this out to her aunt.

The door shut behind Aunt Beryl. Slowly Amelia turned round to face him.

He looked down at her and smiled. 'You look beautiful tonight,' he said.

Amelia knew she was not a beautiful woman, no one had ever before told her so, but under his appreciative gaze she could almost believe that she was.

'Thank you,' she murmured.

He looked towards the door. 'I do hope your aunt will be all right. Perhaps I *should* call for the doctor.'

'I don't think that will be necessary. I believe my aunt has decided to forgo her chaperoning duties for this evening and that is the cause of her sudden headache.'

He raised his eyebrows and smiled. 'I'm growing more and more fond of your aunt every day.'

Amelia gave a small laugh.

'Shall we?' He took her hand and led her down the hallway to the dining room. Despite the fact she was wearing gloves, Amelia's hand reacted to his touch, a tingling sensation rippling up her arm and shooting into her heart.

They entered the elegant dining room, and he escorted her to her chair. Amelia doubted she would be able to eat a thing, she was so agitated. As he pushed in her chair, she inhaled his familiar masculine scent of musk and bergamot, which did nothing to assuage her increasing agitation.

They sat in silence as the footman served the soup and poured the wine.

'That will be all, thank you, Arthur,' Leo said. 'We'll call you when we're ready for the next course.'

The footman bowed and departed, leaving them alone. Amelia lifted the spoon to her lips and was horrified to see that her hand was shaking. She had no need to be nervous. She had been alone with Leo before, and yet every nerve in her body seemed alive and all she was aware of was the man sitting beside her at the table.

'This is a lovely room,' she said, desperately trying to make the requisite polite conversation.

'All the more lovely because it has been graced by your presence.'

She looked at him and saw him cringe. Was he feeling as awkward as she was? Surely not. Leo Devenish was not a man to feel awkward. Even when Lady Madeline had tossed the contents of a brandy balloon in his face he had not looked uncomfortable.

'I'm sorry, that was rather gauche, wasn't it?'

She laughed. 'A little bit.'

'But I meant it. You do look lovely tonight, Amelia.' He reached over and swept back one of the curls Minnie had artfully draped across her naked shoulders. His finger lightly stroked the exposed skin, causing Amelia to sigh again as she tilted her head towards his hand.

'You truly are the most beautiful woman I have ever seen,' he said, his voice as quiet as a gentle caress.

Amelia's rational mind suspected he had said the same thing to countless women. After all, he'd had many truly beautiful women in his life, women much more attractive and sophisticated than Amelia. This was probably part of his tried-and-true seduction routine, but she didn't care. She loved hearing him say it, and if he did have seduction on his mind, that too was something she would not object to.

His fingers lingered on her skin, causing the rhythm of her heart to accelerate. Was it about to happen? Oh, how she hoped it was. She might never have another chance to experience what it was like to be taken by a man, and it was an experience she wanted. And she wanted it with this man, Leo Devenish.

'I'm afraid I don't appear to have any appetite tonight,' she said, looking down at her full soup bowl, hoping he would say, *To hell with dinner* and draw her into his arms.

He didn't. Instead, his hand left her shoulder. He picked up the silver bell and gave it a small ring to summon the footmen. They entered, carrying several terrines. Leo and Amelia sat in silence as one footman removed the soup bowls and another served the next course.

The footmen departed and Amelia moved the food around on her plate. Perhaps she should stop being so subtle and come straight out and tell him what she wanted, and it wasn't salmon in hollandaise sauce. It wasn't any food at all.

'Is the salmon not to your liking?' he asked.

Amelia picked up a morsel of fish and placed it in her mouth. 'It's delicious.' It was. It just wasn't what she wanted. 'But I'm afraid, as I said, I'm not terribly hungry tonight.'

'Are you unwell?'

I'm as unwell as Aunt Beryl.

'No, I just don't have much of an appetite.'

'Then would you prefer to adjourn to the drawing room?'

Yes.

'Oh, but I don't want to keep you from your dinner.'

He stood up and held out his hand towards her. 'I doubt very much that I will suffer if I miss one meal.'

She took his hand and tried not to smile with too much glee as he escorted her out of the dining room and back to the drawing room.

He led her towards a chair, but she kept on walking and sat on the divan, indicating for him to sit beside her in a bold move that surprised even her.

As he did so, her heart was pounding so loudly she was sure he must be able to hear it. This was it. She was hopefully about to be seduced by a man whose experience was legendary.

Was it deliberate that his strong thighs were almost touching hers? She hoped so. Although their legs were not actually making contact, she was sure she could feel the warmth of his body against hers. The temptation to move a little bit closer was all but overwhelming. She gave in to that temptation and closed the gap between them.

A small sigh escaped her lips as the strong muscles of his thigh lightly touched her leg.

She turned to face him. 'I wouldn't object if we kissed again,' she said, then lightly bit her bottom lip as her daring words sent heat rushing to her cheeks. 'After all, we are engaged.' The heat intensified, not just because of her boldness this time but also because of her lie. They might be engaged but she was determined that engagement would never lead to a marriage.

He smiled, slowly and seductively, drawing Amelia's eyes to those lovely, full lips, lips that she had felt before on hers, lips she was desperate to feel again.

'You really are a delight,' he said.

Did one kiss a delightful woman? She hoped so.

His finger lightly stroked along her bottom lip, causing her to gasp and part her lips in expectation. 'Delightful, beautiful and oh, so innocent.'

This was torture, pure, exquisite torture. He had to kiss her now. To not do so would be beyond cruelty. She tilted back her head. Her lips parted in invitation. She closed her eyes. 'I don't have to be innocent,' she whispered. 'You can put an end to that.'

His tormenting thumb withdrew and disappointment flooded her.

She opened her eyes. This was terrible. Was he going to not kiss her because she was an innocent? That was hardly her fault.

'We are engaged,' she reminded him. 'There's nothing wrong with an engaged couple kissing.'

She held her breath as his gaze moved to her lips.

'No one could object to our kissing now,' she repeated. 'Especially not me.'

It worked. His lips were immediately on hers, hard and insistent. Any sense of guilt flew out of her mind as his arms wrapped around her, holding her tightly. All she could do now was feel. Feel his lips on hers, his body hard against hers, his arms encircling her.

And she kissed him back with a passion that took her by surprise, as if the floodgates that had held back her emotions had been thrown open and she was giving full vent to all she felt for him. Her fingers wove into his thick black hair, holding him to her, and her lips drank in his masculine taste. Her body pressed hard up against his, needing his touch to relieve the pounding desire building inside her.

His tongue lightly stroked her bottom lip and she sighed softly, parting her lips further and inviting him in. He accepted her invitation, his tongue probing and tasting, filling her up.

She wanted him so much, wanted more than just his kisses. She wanted to feel his hands on every inch of her sensitive skin, wanted to explore his body with her hands, her lips, her tongue.

The strength of her desire for him making her reckless, she withdrew from his kisses and whispered in his ear, 'Touch me, caress me.'

In one smooth gesture he wrapped an arm around her waist, another under her legs and she found herself lying back on the divan, with Leo looking down at her, desire sparking in his eyes.

He paused for a moment. She held her breath and

waited. Was he expecting her to now object to what she had all but begged for? How could she possibly object to what she wanted so badly, what she had to have? Unable to speak, to express in words what she wanted, she reached up to him, her hands encircling his head.

Responding to her unspoken consent, his hungry lips were once again on hers. He wanted her as much as she wanted him. This passionate, powerful man, this man who had taken so many desirable women as his lovers, wanted her. He had said she was beautiful, and as he kissed her with such unbridled desire she did feel beautiful.

But she wanted more, much more. If he wasn't going to give her his caresses, she would have to take them. Acting on instinct, she rubbed her breasts against his hard chest, her nipples tightening under the friction, causing her aching desire to build in intensity, pounding through her and making her insensible with need.

His lips still on hers, his hand moved down her neck, gently caressing the sensitive skin. His touch traced along her naked shoulders, then across the mounds of her breasts.

Not thinking, just acting, she took hold of his hand and moved it lower, sliding it inside her gown.

'Amelia, are you sure?' he asked, his breath soft against her neck.

'Yes,' she said on a gasp.

His hand cupped her breast, and her gasps turned to soft moans.

When his fingers moved to the tight bud and squeezed it gently, she shamelessly cried out in pleasure.

Could any feeling be more exquisite? Amelia doubted it. His finger and thumb still tormenting her nipple, he kissed her neck, nuzzling the sensitive skin. His kisses moved down to her shoulders, following the path of his caresses, and across her swelling breasts.

His other hand slipped inside her dress. Cupping both breasts, he lifted them out of the confines of her gown, exposing them to his gaze.

The kissing stopped. The caresses stopped. She opened her eyes, and through a fog of yearning looked up at him. He was staring down at her, his brown eyes smoky, his breath coming in rapid, strangled breaths. She knew he liked what he saw and Amelia doubted it was possible to feel more sensual.

'My beautiful, beautiful, Amelia, I want you so much,' he whispered, his voice husky.

'Then have me,' she murmured.

He lightly kissed each nipple, causing Amelia to repeatedly gasp out a breathy 'yes'. He cupped both breasts, pressing them close together, his tormenting mouth moving from one to the other, sucking and nuzzling. When he ran his teeth lightly over the tight, hard bud Amelia was sure she was about to explode with the burning tension building inside her.

Then she did. As if a charge had been detonated deep inside, shockwaves rippled out, starting at the site of his tongue and resonating through every part of her body.

'Oh!' she cried out loudly. 'Oh, oh…' She collapsed back onto the divan. 'That was…that was…' That was indescribable.

She smiled at him. His hands were still holding her

breasts and he was smiling up at her, that lovely, seductive smile. It was all so shameless, but oh, so glorious.

'Thank you,' she said, not sure if that was the correct response, but she was certainly grateful for what she had just experienced and would like to experience it again, often.

'My pleasure,' he said with a laugh. He lightly kissed each nipple again, as if saying goodbye, and lifted up the lacy top of her gown. But she did not want this to be over, not yet.

Her heart, which had been slowing from its frantic pounding, once again began to accelerate. She pushed his hands away from her dress.

He looked down at her, his eyebrows raised in question, his lovely lips turned up in a smile.

'I want more,' she whispered, wrapping her arms around him, sweeping them along the hard muscles of his back, cupping his firm buttocks and pulling him towards her.

She was unsure what she wanted from him, but knew she had to feel his body against hers, wanted him pressed against her most intimate part, which was calling out for his touch. She arched herself up off the divan. Still holding his buttocks, she rubbed herself against his hips and parted her legs so she could draw him closer to her, needing him to relieve her throbbing need.

He lifted himself off her and took her in his arms. 'We can't,' he whispered in her ear. 'Not until we are married.'

'But…but…'

But we will never marry and I want you so much. I need you so much, she wanted to say, but couldn't.

'Oh, Amelia, you are so tempting.'

'Then be tempted.' Amelia did not feel above begging for him to relieve the consuming need that had once again taken her over.

He kissed her once more.

'I can't,' he whispered, while at the same time taking hold of the fabric of her gown and bundling it up around her waist.

'You can,' she said on a sigh, then gasped as his hand slid up the inside of her thigh, caressing the naked skin above her silk stocking. It was glorious, but not what she wanted. The throbbing between her legs told her what she needed. Taking hold of his hand, she moved it to the site of the throbbing and rubbed against his hand, knowing this was what she had to have.

'Oh, Amelia,' he said on a gasp as his hand entered her drawers and cupped her sex.

'Yes!' she cried out.

His fingers stroked and parted her feminine folds. She lay back, knowing this was what she needed, knowing he could give her what she had to have. When his finger moved inside her, Amelia's body shuddered in consent and under a will of their own her legs parted wider. This was what the pounding in her body had been crying out for. A release that only he could provide. Her back arched, urging him on. Slowly, gently, he pushed deeper and deeper inside her, his palm stroking her, the rhythm slow at first, then faster and faster, matching her own insistent rocking.

Her moans coming louder and louder in time with his stroking, a wave surged up within her, growing higher and higher with each caress.

She had thought the touch of his lips on her nipples had been the greatest pleasure it was possible to experience, but as his hand rubbed between her legs, as his fingers pushed deeper inside her, she found herself being lifted up to an even greater peak of pleasure.

'Oh, yes, yes, Leo, yes!' she cried out as she was thrust up to a towering crest and exquisite ecstasy crashed over her, leaving her gasping for air.

Her heart still pounding to a vigorous tempo, her body exhausted, she smiled in complete satisfaction. 'That was wonderful,' she gasped out. 'I'm pleased we didn't wait until our wedding night.'

He gave a small laugh. 'Oh, Amelia, you are priceless.'

She lifted herself up onto one elbow. 'What? Why is that funny?'

'There's a lot more to making love than what we just did.'

'There is?'

He laughed again and lightly kissed her lips.

'Then let's do it,' she said, lying back down and parting her legs, desperate to experience any other magic he had in store for her.

He pulled down her skirt, and lifted up the front of her gown, her breasts disappearing under the lacy fabric. 'As much as it pains me, and believe me, it pains me in ways you'll never understand, I will not take your virginity until our wedding night.'

Hadn't he already taken her virginity? It certainly felt as if something momentous had just happened. Having no mother, Amelia had never been told what to expect from the marriage bed. Aunt Beryl had never married, so could explain nothing to her. All she had said was Amelia would have to take her guidance from her husband. At her finishing school she had been told that submitting to your husband in the marriage bed was a woman's duty, but no one had told her it could be earth-shatteringly enjoyable.

And he said there was more to come. If he was indeed insisting they wait until they marry, Amelia was almost tempted to put aside all of her reasons for not marrying just so she could taste every ecstasy this glorious man could give her. But that would be far too selfish. She was not going to marry him; she would not do that to him. But somehow she had to convince him there was no need to wait until their wedding night to show her every glorious way in which they could make love.

Chapter Sixteen

Leo should not have done that and thank God he had stopped when he did. It had been hard to do so, in more ways than one, but he had never deflowered a virgin and he wasn't about to start now. He could wait until their wedding night, where their marriage could be consummated in their marriage bed, in the age-old tradition. She deserved to lose her virginity in the proper place at the proper time and in the proper way, not in some furtive manner on the drawing-room furniture.

He took her hands and gently lifted her to her feet. She would never know what strength of will it was taking for him not to rip her clothing off, and to lose himself deep within her folds. He tried to console himself that the waiting would be worth it, but right now that felt like no consolation at all.

She was so beautiful, the most beautiful woman he had ever known, and he did not just mean her appearance. There was something captivating about her that caused him to lose himself whenever he was with her.

And he had never seen a woman look more radiant as

she had been when she reacted to his touch. Lying back, her lips parted as she gasped, her eyes hooded, that pink blush flushing across her cheeks, neck and breasts, she had been nothing short of dazzling and it was a sight he would never forget.

Although, right now, it was perhaps something he should try not to think about if he was to remain determined to wait the long months until they were man and wife.

'I believe it would be best if I bid you goodnight,' he said, taking her hand and lightly kissing her palm. 'We should not have done what we did, but I have no regrets.'

She shook her head, then nodded, her eyes wide. 'No, no, I have no regrets either, except maybe we could—' She pointed back to the divan.

'I will see you in the morning,' he interrupted, turned and strode out of the room. It was rude to leave her in such a manner, but if he remained in her presence any longer he was sure he would not be able to keep to his vow and resist the urge to strip her of her virginity.

Returning to his room, he dismissed his valet. Under the circumstances it would be more discreet if he undressed himself. But he knew he would not sleep. Instead, he paced up and down, going over and over everything that had happened that day. Her arrival, the visit to his parents, and then their passionate encounter on the divan.

He had never met a woman like her. She was unique, as was the intensity of his feelings towards her. The power of that emotion reduced how he felt about Lydia to something resembling an adolescent crush. Could he be falling in love with Lady Amelia? Was that the strange sensation that was possessing him? Was that why he wanted to stroke and caress her every time he saw her? Was that why, when he looked at her, she seemed bathed in a golden glow? Was that love? No, it couldn't be, it was just lust, a lust more powerful than any he had felt before, but still just lust.

A knock on the door broke through his tormented wondering. What on earth could James want? He did not know. In agitation he pulled opened the door to a sight that literally took his breath away. Amelia, her blonde hair released from its clips and flowing down her back and over her shoulders, and dressed only in a nightgown and robe.

Without speaking, she took his hand and led him to his bed. He had to stop this. Now. It was wrong. But he said nothing as she climbed onto his bed and removed her robe. As if struck dumb he stood looking down at her, knowing he should say something to stop this, but unable to do or say anything.

When he didn't answer, didn't move, she loosened the tie at the neck of her nightgown and pushed it off her shoulders. He groaned. That was the only sound he was capable of, a mindless, animal groan of desire. The gown moved lower, exposing her beautiful, full breasts, the tight nipples pointing up at him in invitation.

He was lost. Before he was even aware that he had moved he was on the bed. His arms were around her, his lips had claimed her, his body was on top of hers.

His hands moved to the waistband of his breeches, tugging at the buttons. Fabric ripped, buttons popped as she joined his frantic effort to free him from the restricting garment.

Pushing up her nightgown, he moved her legs apart. 'Are you sure, Amelia?' he asked, praying that she would say no and he would stop this madness.

'Yes, I'm sure,' she whispered in his ear.

He positioned himself at her opening, entering her but a fraction. As her tight sheath closed around him, drawing him in, he released another animal groan of pleasure. Temptation was calling out to him, demanding that he thrust himself deep inside her to relieve the pressure that was stronger and harder than he had ever experienced before.

But he wouldn't do that. She was a virgin. He had to be gentle. Slowly, he eased himself into her, watching her expression for any sign of pain. She smiled up at him and her legs wrapped themselves around his waist.

'I don't want to hurt you,' he said as he moved further inside.

'You won't. You can't.'

Her hands slid down his back and cupped his buttocks, pushing him forward. Slowly, inch by inch, he was drawn inside her wet sex until he was fully encased. Her eyes were closed. In pleasure? So she could bear the pain? He had to know.

'Amelia?' he asked.

She didn't answer, but her hands gripped his buttocks tighter, her back arched, and she moved herself along his shaft. It was all the answer he needed. Still maintaining a level of control he did not think himself capable of, he slowly withdrew and entered her again.

Leo shuddered with pleasure with each stroke, loving the feeling of her tightly around him, loving the feeling of making her his. He looked down at her, at her beautiful face, her lips parted as she panted in pleasure, her eyes closed, her hair spread out across the pillow.

The glorious sight was almost more than he could bear and once again he was forced to exercise control. Pausing, he kissed her lips, her neck, her breasts, loving the taste of her silky skin. The grip of her fingers on his buttocks tightened, her legs wrapping themselves higher around his back as she angled herself on the bed to take him deeper inside her.

'You are so lovely,' he murmured. His words inadequate to describe the extent of his feelings for her, he entered her faster and deeper, her groans growing louder with each thrust, her arching back matching his rhythm.

'Yes, yes!' she cried out as her shuddering sex gripped him tightly, her fingernails dug into the skin of his buttocks and she collapsed back onto the bed, still panting for breath.

His heart pounding so hard as if trying to escape from his chest, he withdrew from her and released his own pleasure into the bedlinen. What he had just done was wrong, but he would not make things worse by impregnating his bride-to-be before their wedding day.

Gathering her in his arms, he kissed her forehead, her cheeks and her still gasping lips. 'I'm sorry,' he murmured, nuzzling into her neck.

'Sorry? What on earth have you to be sorry about? That was...' She shook her head. 'It was...'

'It was fast.'

'Mmm, yes, it was. Lovely.'

He laughed and kissed her again. 'Your first time should not have been like that. I should have taken things slowly, gently. I didn't even take my clothes off properly.'

'Oh, well,' she said, sitting up and undoing the buttons of his rumpled shirt. 'You can always make up for it on my second time.'

Laughing, he took her in his arms, knowing that a second time would not be nearly enough.

It was wrong. Amelia knew what she had done was wrong, scandalous and deceptive.

He said they had to wait till their wedding night, but she knew there would never be a wedding night. So she tricked him. It was such a terrible thing to do, but after what she had experienced in the drawing room she had lost all sense of what was right and wrong. All she knew was she wanted him, wanted him to make love to her completely, to show her all that could happen between a man and a woman.

And she knew, despite what he said, he had been fighting against his desire to take her. She had seen that look on his face when he left her in the drawing room. It was desire as intense as her own. Desire for her. That had given her the courage to do what she would once have thought unimaginable, to come to a man's room and offer herself to him.

Yes, it had been wrong, but by God it felt right. And it continued to feel right, throughout the night. As promised, he made love to her again, slowly, kissing every inch of her body, including parts that had initially shocked her, until she had lain back in the bed, her legs around his shoulders and surrendered herself to a pleasure that had left her reeling.

The teachers at her finishing school had told her to submit to her husband. And that was what she did, again and again. Although, as the night went on, submission was not the word one would use to describe her behaviour. Leo showed her so many ways to give and receive pleasure that by the time light started to show around the edges of the curtains she doubted there was much more she could learn.

She positioned herself above him, looking at the glorious sleeping man. Every inch of him was magnificent, those strong muscles that she was now free to gaze at to her heart's content, that handsome face, those sensual lips that she could kiss whenever she felt like it. And she felt like it now. She leaned down and lightly skimmed his lips with her own, causing his eyes to open.

'My love,' he whispered. 'You are so beautiful.' It was wonderful to hear, but still there was always that nagging thought that he had said that to many women before her.

'I bet you say that to all the women you've had in your bed,' she said, her voice teasing, her mind meaning every word.

He raised himself up onto one arm, his face serious. 'No, there's been no one like you.'

'What, you've never been forced to marry before?' she continued, still trying hard to keep her voice light. 'There's been no one you've wanted to marry?'

Including me?

'There was someone once,' he said, lying back and staring up at the ceiling.

Amelia's heart lurched. 'Who was she?' she asked, her tone neutral, both wanting and not wanting to hear the answer.

'Lydia Bedford.' It was the first time Leo had said that name out loud since she had curtly and callously rejected him. He waited for the shockwaves that the thought of Lydia always sent rushing through him. None came.

'You asked her to marry you?' Amelia asked quietly.

'Yes.' He lifted himself back up on one arm, and looked down at her. With her hair tousled from last night's lovemaking, her red lips swollen from their kisses, her lithe body naked and tempting, he wondered how he could ever have found any other woman attractive.

'What happened?'

He shrugged and lay back down. 'She turned me down.' He gave a small laugh. Then stopped, shocked by his reaction. How could he be amused by something that had once hurt so much? 'I was young and I thought I was in love.'

Until he met Amelia, Lydia had been everything he had wanted in a wife, beautiful, cultured, and the epitome of gracious womanhood. He had been lost from the moment he had laid eyes on her. An innocent, at that time, he had not known she was playing with the affections of the self-made man of dubious origins for her own amusement.

'Didn't Lydia Bedford marry Lord Featherstone?'

'Yes, she married him after she turned me down.'

'Lord Featherstone?' She scowled, causing Leo to laugh. 'Why would she marry him?'

'The answer to that is in his name. Lord Featherstone. "Ladies marry titled gentlemen," she informed me.' At the time it had cut Leo so deeply he had thought he would never recover. So many times he had replayed her words, reliving the way they had been slowly enunciated, as if she were speaking to the slow, clumsy blacksmith's son he had suddenly felt like. '"We have had fun, and I have thoroughly enjoyed all our time together, but Father is right—we cannot possibly marry."' Remembering those words usually filled him with pain, anger, shame, but now he felt nothing. Nothing at all. That was strange. It was as if he was recounting something that had happened a long time ago to a different man.

'That's appalling. You must have loved her very much.'

He shrugged. 'I thought I did, but as I said, I was young and did not know what love was.' He ran his hand lightly down the centre of her chest, between those glorious, tempting breasts. 'But let's not waste time talking of the past.' There were much better ways to spend their time than talking of the past.

'It's morning already,' she said, pointing to the window, where the light at the edges of the curtains was changing from the soft grey of pre-dawn to pale yellow as the sun rose. 'I must go,' she said, still lying on the bed. 'If my maid finds my bed chamber empty she will be scandalised.'

His hand slowly moved from her breastbone to

lightly circle her nipple, causing her to gasp. 'And you wouldn't want to scandalise the servants.' He leaned down and lightly kissed her stomach.

She moved sensually under his touch. 'And Aunt Beryl might be shocked.'

'You wouldn't want to shock Aunt Beryl,' he added, his kisses moving down her body.

Her legs parted, causing him to smile.

'Oh, all right, one more time, then I really must go,' she said.

He laughed, taking her in his arms and kissing her waiting lips. 'Amelia, my love, you really are precious.'

Once again, he had called her his love. Those words came so easily from his lips, but did he mean it? Was she his love? As her legs wrapped around him, that familiar surge of desire rose up inside him, making thought impossible. But now was not the time to think. Now was the time to surrender to the pleasure of making love to this beautiful, enchanting woman.

Chapter Seventeen

Was Aunt Beryl looking at her strangely? Had her lady's maid raised a curious eyebrow when she brought in the hot water for her morning wash? Were the servants paying her more attention than usual?

As Amelia sat at the breakfast table, drinking her morning cup of tea, she was sure everyone must know what she had been up to last night. After all, she had changed so much they must be able to tell that something was different about her.

She looked across the table at Leo. He sent her a secret smile, causing a little shiver to ripple through her. It seemed all he had to do now was look at her for her body to react.

One of the most sensible decisions she had ever made was to ignore his command that they wait until their wedding night. If she had done so, they would be waiting for ever and she would not have experienced last night's ecstasy.

So she had lied to him by omission and tricked him for her own ends. Again.

Another quiver rippled through her. This time it felt decidedly like guilt. Leo still did not know there would be no wedding. She had delayed her father by saying she did not wish to wed until the end of the Season, claiming the need to have the perfect wedding dress designed and made for her. If she had not extricated herself from her perilous financial position by then, she would have to come up with another reason to delay.

After last night, part of her was tempted to forget all about her plan to free Leo from this unwanted arrangement. Lying in his bed, his arms around her, she had imagined being his wife, spending endless hours making love to him, waking every morning in his arms. But deep down she knew that to do so would be unfair. He was marrying her to save her reputation, a reputation she gave not a fig about. He did not love her and would not have made love to her last night if it wasn't for this forced arrangement.

She looked down at her breakfast. No, despite what she had just experienced, she would not be so selfish as to tie him to a marriage he did not want. She still had to make the magazine profitable so she could pay Aunt Beryl back all the money she had loaned her and have enough money so that if her father made true on his threat, her lovely, innocent aunt would not suffer for her behaviour. Once that was done she would set Leo free.

She looked over at Aunt Beryl, who was eating her breakfast and happily talking to Leo. He caught her eye and smiled again, that heart-melting smile that held her captive. She rubbed her fingers together, just itching to touch him again, and longed for the time when they would be alone.

She could now see why women like Lady Madeline were willing to make complete fools of themselves over him. Lady Madeline had experienced the same delights she had and had been furious when he had taken that pleasure away.

A small knot formed in the middle of her chest. Leo had made her writhe in pleasure last night. He had shown her sensual delights that she had not known existed. Just as he had done with so many women before her and would no doubt do with many women after her.

And like Lady Madeline she had fallen hopelessly under his spell. But unlike Lady Madeline Amelia was determined she would move on from Leo with complete decorum, even if it made her die inside to see him with another.

But that would not be happening this weekend. She smiled to herself, and that naughty, impish side of herself that she had hitherto not known existed rose once more to the surface. She still had one more day and one more night to enjoy herself in his arms. And by God, she was going to do so.

He had set out to woo his future bride, not seduce her, although he had not actually seduced her. Technically, she had seduced him. Surely, that exonerated him from any guilt he should be feeling. He had never before taken a young lady's virginity, and had never lain with a debutante, and deep down he knew he should not have done so last night.

Despite knowing it was wrong, any guilt he was ex-periencing was not as large as the immense satisfac-tion he felt this morning. He should not have taken her virginity, but at least he would be marrying her. That, surely, should keep that residual, gnawing guilt at bay.

He had promised to marry her when her father caught him kissing her, now he had deflowered her, a sin that no father would ever forgive, and he was lucky that all he had to do to make amends was end his life as a bach-elor and become shackled by the chains of matrimony.

He had accepted it when her father insisted they wed, had even seen advantages to such a marriage that was not of his making, and now could see another unex-pected advantage to having Amelia in his life.

He would have this beautiful, sensual woman in his bed night after night. He had never experienced any-thing like what happened last night. He'd had more women in his bed than he could possibly remember, some far more experienced than his innocent bride-to-be had been, but none had made him feel the way she did. When she touched him, she sent emotions cours-ing through his body that were more than just physi-cal pleasure.

It was as if their lovemaking had joined them, and not just on a physical level. He was a practical man, a rational man, not given to foolish emotions, but it was as if they had become one during their lovemaking, as if both their bodies and their souls had united.

He had lost himself entirely to her.

Even now, looking at her beautiful face across the breakfast table, all he wanted to do was hold and caress her again. Such a thing had never happened before. As ashamed as he was to admit it, with all the other women in his life, once he had made love to them, all he had wanted was for them to leave, as quickly and with as little fuss as possible, so he could get back to work. But with Amelia it was different. He never wanted her to leave his side.

It seemed instead of wooing his future bride, she had wooed him, and changed him from a man who was making the best of things to one who was happily entering the state of matrimony.

One would almost think that he had fallen in love. He almost recoiled at that thought, then pushed it away and continued to drink his coffee. Of course he wasn't in love. He'd declared that he would never suffer that vulnerable state again, never put himself in a position where anyone could hurt him.

He was too rich and powerful for any male to ever hurt him, and after Lydia his heart had become armoured so that no woman could hurt him either.

No, what he was feeling for Amelia was lust, a lust stronger than one he had ever experienced before, but still it was just lust. And he could see no reason why lust alone could not be the basis for a happy marriage. It wasn't exactly in the wedding vows. He was yet to hear a vicar suggest that a man lust after his wife until death do they part, but right now, his lust for Amelia was something he was sure would last a lifetime.

Aunt Beryl made her excuses the moment breakfast was over, as if sensing that Leo and Amelia wanted to be alone.

'Would you like to take that walk in the woodland now?' he asked as soon as the door shut behind her.

Amelia giggled. 'I thought you said it would be inappropriate for us to be alone in the woods, where no one can see us.'

'I did, but right now I have a burning need to be inappropriate.'

She giggled again. 'That's interesting. I suspect your need is burning in exactly the same place as mine.'

'Then I think we have no choice but to quench that fire.'

'Yes. Although it seems no matter how often we quench it, it doesn't take long for that fire to start smouldering again.'

He stood up and took her hand. 'You really are a little minx, aren't you?' He pulled her into his arms and kissed her, long, slowly and deeply. 'My beautiful, precious little minx.'

He might not have wanted her before they were forced into this engagement, but there was no denying that he wanted her now, unceasingly.

'We could go back up to my bed chamber,' he whispered in her ear.

'You promised me the woods and I want the woods.'

She really was incorrigible. Another loveable quality that he couldn't get enough of.

'Then the woods it will be.'

As he led her by the hand down the path and towards the trees a delicious sense of recklessness swept over Amelia. This was so naughty. She was sure even married couples were not supposed to be so wanton, but being with Leo made her wanton, and knowing that it would not be for ever made her determined to take every opportunity to explore that new-found wantonness, wherever it took her.

And that was exactly what she did. They passed their day in much the same way as they had passed last evening, forgoing luncheon so they could continue to feast on each other. By dinnertime they knew they would have to return to the house so they could dine with Aunt Beryl.

Although when they arrived back at the house, they were informed that Aunt Beryl had another of her uncharacteristic headaches and had asked to have her meal served in her bed chamber.

'I, too, seem to have a headache,' Amelia said. Leo's brow furrowed in concern until she sent him a conspiratorial wink. 'I would like to have my meal served in my bed chamber also.'

'Yes, I seemed to have caught a bit too much of the sun as well. It must have been all that time I spent outside today,' Leo said, proving to Amelia that he was no actor. 'Would you be kind enough to serve my meal in my bed chamber as well? I won't require much, and can you please leave it on a tray outside my room?'

'Mine, too, please,' Amelia said, more quickly than was needed. 'Tray, outside room, yes, perfect.'

'Very good, sir, my lady,' the footman said with a bow.

Amelia and Leo held their laughter until the man

had departed, took each other's hand and rushed up the stairs to Leo's bed chamber.

The trays remained outside their rooms until the small hours of the morning, when, finally overcome with hunger for more than each other, they retrieved them and held a picnic among the tousled sheets.

When the morning came, Amelia sneaked back to her room and deposited the empty tray at her door.

Today she would be returning to London, back to reality, but Amelia was sure this weekend she had amassed a trove of glorious memories to last her a lifetime.

Chapter Eighteen

The elevated mood that had Amelia floating on a cloud drifted away as the railway carriage took her back to London, and a sense of melancholy descended. The time with Leo had been magical, but that was all it had been, magic, an illusion she had conjured up through her own deceptions.

She was now returning to reality. What she had experienced had changed her in ways she could not put into words, but she could not let it change her resolve to put all of her wrongs to right. But, oh, how she wished she could forget about righting a wrong.

She could barely acknowledge it even to herself, but what she really wanted was to pretend their engagement was real, that during their time together at his estate they had merely expressed their love and consummated their future as man and wife. Then she would not have to extricate herself from this engagement. She could go through with the marriage and spend the rest of her life with a man who made her feel things, experience things that she had hitherto not known existed.

But deep down she knew that would never do. Even if *The Ladies' Enquirer* never turned a profit. Even if she was never able to pay Aunt Beryl back. Even if she did have to marry Leo so her aunt would be safe, she could not continue to lie to him. He deserved the truth. Lying to him had been unacceptable behaviour before the weekend but was even worse now. After what they had shared, she could not hold on to her secrets. She had to tell him everything she had done and hope he could find it in his heart to forgive her, and even better, to understand the reasons for her behaviour.

'Cheer up, my dear,' Aunt Beryl said, patting her knee. 'You'll see him again soon. And it won't be long now till your wedding day. We really must start making arrangements to have your special gown made.'

'There's plenty of time for that. The marriage will not take place until the end of the Season.'

Aunt Beryl frowned, so Amelia forced herself to smile. 'But of course, I'm very excited about the wedding gown. Let's visit the dressmaker as soon as we arrive back in London.' That caused her aunt to smile, which was some consolation for Amelia's continued lies and deceptions.

Once they arrived home, before she had even taken off her hat and coat, Amelia made further excuses to delay the visit to the dressmaker, telling her aunt it was essential she visit her office immediately. Lies and more lies. Charles was not expecting her until the next day, but she took a hansom cab to *The Ladies' Enquirer's* office, where she was greeted by an uncharacteristically joyful Charles.

'Lady Amelia, did you have a pleasant weekend?' he asked, almost singing the words.

'Yes,' she replied. Her voice rose in a question as she regarded his elevated mood. 'I take it your weekend was rather pleasant as well?'

'What? Oh, yes, I suppose it was, but today was even better. On Friday we received a summons to a meeting with your bank manager.'

Amelia's heart sank, remembering the last time she had spoken to that condescending man, although Charles's smiling face suggested this time it could not be all bad news.

'I thought it best not to delay, so I made an appointment with him immediately.' He paused, still smiling at her, like a comic delaying the punchline for greatest effect.

She signalled he should continue.

'I saw him first thing this morning and he was most impressed by the way we have turned around the magazine, which has made a substantial profit for the first time.' He paused once again, as if teasing out his news.

'Go on.'

'He said that the increases in sales and advertising revenue gave the bank reason to be optimistic.'

Again he paused, again Amelia asked him to continue.

'He's granted us the loan!' he cried out. 'He said the changes to the magazine proves that we know the industry and what our readers want, so that gives them confidence to give us a small loan.' Charles did an unexpected jig on the spot. 'It's not much, but it's enough to expand our distribution, take on staff, do all the extra things we wanted to do, which will lead to bigger profits and maybe an even more generous loan.'

Amelia's heart seemingly took flight, and she placed her hands on her chest as if to stop it escaping.

And more importantly I can pay Aunt Beryl back the money I owe her.

'Oh, that is wonderful news!'

Charles continued to list all the ways they could improve *The Ladies' Enquirer* to attract even more subscribers and advertisers.

Amelia nodded along with every suggestion, knowing the bank manager had answered all of her prayers and solved all of her problems.

Now you can set Leo Devenish free.

Her euphoria evaporated as quickly as it had appeared. There was now absolutely no reason for her to continue with this fake engagement. Aunt Beryl was safe. Her father had no power over her. Leo could now be told the entire truth. Then he could decide for himself whether he wanted to go through with a marriage that had been forced upon him, to a woman he had hardly even noticed before her father had given him no choice but to marry her.

The bank manager's granting the loan was the best and the worst thing that could happen to Amelia. If this had happened a few short months ago there would be no dilemma, no conflicting emotions. All she would be feeling was happiness that she had saved her magazine and could pay back her aunt. And happiness should be what she was feeling now. The magazine's future was secure. Her aunt was saved. Her father could no longer threaten her with throwing Aunt Beryl out on the street if she did not marry Leo. She could tell Leo the truth and free him from a forced marriage. Wasn't it everything she wanted?

And didn't it prove what a terrible, selfish woman she was that she was not bursting with pleasure that everything had worked out for the best? To her immense shame, part of her wished the bank manager had never granted the loan, that she would find no other way out of her predicament and would be forced to marry Leo.

Part of her wished she did not have to do what she knew she must, tell Leo the truth and set him free.

Amelia's appointment with the bank manager had been stressful, but she would happily exchange a meeting with a panel of condescending bank managers than one with Leo Devenish where she had to finally reveal the truth. With her stomach twisting and turning she arrived at his office five minutes early in a desperate attempt to calm herself before this vital meeting.

She could have taken the coward's way out and written him a letter but she knew she had to face him and face up to everything she had done. She could have arranged to meet him, invited him over to her house, visited him at his Mayfair townhouse, but she knew there was a danger that she would become distracted and conveniently forget all she had to say to him.

So she had arranged to meet at his office, where all they could do was talk.

'I have an appointment to see Mr Devenish,' she informed the secretary, who sent her a curious look before pulling his face back into a professional, passive expression. 'Please take a seat, my lady,' he said, pointing to the leather couch against the wall.

She kept her hand on her churning stomach, sat down and tried to still her whirling thoughts and to once again go over the words she had already repeatedly rehearsed.

The adjoining door opened, and Leo entered the waiting room. 'Amelia. I thought I heard your voice. How lovely to see you. Come through. I've only got five minutes, as I've an appointment with the owner of *The Ladies' Enquirer*.'

Like a lamb to the slaughter, she meekly followed him into his office. The moment he shut the door behind them he took her in his arms. 'As I said, I've only got five minutes, but there's a lot I can do in five minutes.' The reason for her visit slipped her mind as his lips claimed hers and she was enveloped in his masculine strength. And she kissed him back. After all, what was the harm in forgetting all other concerns and just enjoying this moment, especially as it might very well be the last time she would find herself in Leo Devenish's arms?

But she had tricked him long enough. Yes, she wanted his kisses, wanted them with all of her heart, but she had to tell him the truth. She forced herself to break from his arms and take a step backwards.

'Leo, I need to talk to you.'

He smiled. 'That's a shame. I can think of a much better way to use this precious time than talking.' He stopped smiling and placed his hand under her chin, tilting her face upwards. 'What's wrong, Amelia? Why are you looking so worried?'

She swallowed, closed her eyes briefly and forced herself to breathe slowly and deeply. 'We've got more than five minutes. Your appointment is with me. I am the owner of *The Ladies' Enquirer*.'

He smiled, then his eyebrows drew together as if he was sure this was a jest but was struggling to see how it was funny.

She took another step backwards, unable to think clearly when his body was close to hers. 'It's true. I'm the owner of *The Ladies' Enquirer*.' She looked down and drew in another series of steadying breaths. 'And I wrote the *Tittle-Tattle* column.'

The residue of a smile died completely. 'What are you telling me, Amelia?'

On weak legs she moved to the nearest chair, sure that if she didn't sit down soon she would collapse under the weight of all that she was going to tell him. 'I'm so sorry.'

'I don't understand.' He sat across from her, his face as hard as marble. 'I believe you need to explain yourself.'

She paused, fighting hard to remember her well-rehearsed words, which had suddenly deserted her.

'A year or so ago I borrowed money from Aunt Beryl to start the type of magazine I wanted to read, one that had intelligent articles for women with an enquiring mind. At that time there was no magazine like it on the market and I was sure I could make it a success.'

She waited for him to make some comment. He said

nothing, merely stared at her, his dark brown eyes unwavering as he waited for her to continue.

'The magazine immediately acquired a small number of regular subscribers, but barely enough to cover publication costs. I'd hoped the number would grow, but it didn't. The way things were going I'd never have sufficient funds to pay back my aunt.' She swallowed. 'So I tried to get a loan from a bank but the manager all but laughed at the idea of lending money to a woman.'

Once again she waited for him to make a comment, hoping to see compassion in his eyes, but all she saw was the cold stare of a stone-hearted businessman.

'It was your suggestion that turned the fortunes of the magazine around.' She wasn't intending to flatter him, just tell him the truth, but deep down she hoped that this revelation would soften that hard expression. It didn't.

'I don't know if you remember, but at a dinner party, you said *The Ladies' Enquirer* needed a gossip column to attract a wider audience. So I wrote the *Tittle-Tattle* column.'

'Of course I remember. So it was you who wrote about the incident between me and Lady Madeline?' This statement was delivered in a flat tone, as if without judgement, but that didn't stop Amelia from wincing at her betrayal.

'Yes,' was all she could bring herself to say, unable to formulate a justification for her actions.

'What about the next column? The one that told the world that I had kissed you, that the Lion was now after fresh meat and had devoured the innocent Lamb. Did you write that as well?'

'I did,' she said, her voice little more than a whisper.

His stare remained unwavering, the only change in his expression being the slight flaring of the nose, and tightening of the jaw.

'What on earth made you do that?' he finally asked in a controlled tone. 'What were you thinking? Why would you ruin your own reputation?'

'I told you I care nothing for my reputation,' she rushed on, leaning towards him, beseeching him to understand. 'And I knew it would throw your suspicions away from me.' She sighed at the memory. 'Not that you suspected me anyway. You assumed it had to be a man behind the magazine.'

He stared at her, and Amelia hoped he was starting to understand her. 'You are right. I know that men can be callous, but I made the mistake of thinking that women are better than that, that a woman would not deliberately destroy another woman's reputation, especially one who was innocent.' His jaw once again tightened.

'Lady Madeline?' Innocent was not a word she would usually associate with his former lover.

'You...' he said, his voice rising. 'You were the one I thought was innocent. When I read that column, I wanted to destroy *The Ladies' Enquirer*. I wanted to cause all sorts of harm to the owner, bring the man who wrote that column to his knees for what he had done to you. Now you're telling me...' He stopped, inhaling and exhaling slowly.

Amelia lowered her head, shame gripping her. 'I know. I'm sorry.'

'And what of our engagement? Was that something you planned as well? Was that why you kissed me? Was that why you wrote about it? To force me into marriage?'

'No, no, of course not.' She stood up, then sat back down again, not sure how to make him understand. 'I never expected that to happen. If Father hadn't come home when he did, if he hadn't barged in on us, if we hadn't been kissing… No, none of this was planned.'

'And yet you agreed to it. That suggests to me that you were compliant with your father's wishes.'

'No, I wasn't. He made me.'

He waited for her to explain.

'Father said if I didn't marry you, he would take it out on Aunt Beryl. He said he'd throw her out on the street. She is completely dependent on him financially, or at least she was. Now that *The Ladies' Enquirer* is making a profit, I'll be able to pay back the money she loaned me and provide her with an income if Father withdraws his financial support. It won't be in the style she is used to, but she'll be comfortable enough.'

She looked up at him in appeal, hoping he would understand that she had never meant to force him into this unwanted marriage. He continued to stare at her, his face revealing nothing.

'I had to agree with the engagement,' she repeated and watched his face for signs of understanding. It remained unflinching. 'But now, you see, we don't have to go through with it. We don't have to marry.'

'You agreed to this marriage to save Aunt Beryl?'

'Yes, yes. I never meant to force you into it.' Finally, he was starting to understand.

'And now that you have your own money you wish to call it off.'

'I wish to give you back your freedom.'

'And what of everything we shared this weekend?'

Heat exploded onto Amelia's cheeks. 'That was… well, it was lovely,' was all she could say, as ineffectual as that was.

'I deflowered a virgin.'

Amelia bit the inside of her bottom lip. His voice was so emotionless as if what had happened between them could be reduced to a short, factual statement.

'I will still have to marry you,' he continued, his voice still flat. 'As a result of my actions your chances of securing another husband have been severely downgraded.'

Amelia squirmed in her seat. He was talking about something so beautiful, something that had turned her world on its axis, as if he were discussing the value of a commodity that was no longer rated as highly as it once had been.

'No one knows what happened between us,' she whispered, pain and humiliation gripping her. 'It can remain our secret, and I most certainly do not expect you to marry me because you…deflowered me.'

'I have no choice.'

Amelia had not known what to expect when she entered his office, but she knew what she had hoped for. She had hoped he would say he did not care that she had tricked him, lied to him and forced him into this engagement, because he still wanted her. Instead, she was faced with a man who was still determined to marry, but only because he believed it the honourable thing to do.

She did not want that, and she did not want him if the only reason he wanted to marry her was because of some misguided sense of propriety and a need to pay the price for taking her virginity.

'But I do not want to marry you.' A series of lies had got them into this disastrous situation, and it seemed only a lie would get them out if it. She did not want Leo Devenish to marry her because he had to, and it was obvious that was the only reason he would. She had been right all along. Men like him did not fall in love with women like her. Men like him did not fall in love at all. They had affairs with women like Lady Madeline, women who were beautiful, sophisticated and experienced.

The only reason he had ever shown her any interest was because she had been forced on him. She might not be as desirable as Lady Madeline, but at least *she* could hold on to her dignity in the face of his coldness towards her.

His eyes drilled into hers and she was forced to lower them. 'I do not wish to marry you. I wish to call off the engagement.'

He stood up. 'Then we have nothing more to say to each other. Now, if you'll excuse me, I have other appointments this morning. My secretary will see you out.'

He walked behind his expansive oak desk, placing a barrier between them, and leafed through a pile of papers.

Amelia stood up and took a step towards him. 'Leo?'

He looked up. 'I'll leave the arrangements to you. I believe that in such cases it is customary for the young woman to announce the termination of the engagement. No one in Society is likely to think any less of you. I'm sure they will assume that you finally came to your senses and managed to extricate yourself from an engagement to a man who was beneath you.'

'No, I—'

'This appointment is over, Lady Amelia. As I said, my secretary will see you out.' He sat down, dipped his pen in the inkwell and commenced writing, leaving Amelia with no choice but to walk away.

Chapter Nineteen

Leo threw his pen down on the desk the moment the door closed quietly behind her, black ink spattering across a contract that no longer seemed important.

He clasped his head in his hands. He had thought her different. He had actually thought that there was something unique about Lady Amelia Lambourne. What they had shared at the weekend had been so special to him, and he had given himself entirely, something he would have once thought impossible. And it had all been lies. She had fooled him completely.

When they had visited his parents and she had been so at ease in his mother's kitchen he had believed she was someone who saw the real person beneath the exterior, not the class from which they came, and treated them according to who they were, not the family they came from.

When he had bared his soul to her, told her about his torments at school, he had done so because he thought she would understand. Now he regretted letting his guard down in such a foolish manner. She was not different, not special, not unique. She was exactly the same as every other member of her class. How could he possibly have thought that she might actually want to marry the son of a blacksmith? Just like Lydia, she had her own reasons for playing with him. Lydia had seen him as someone she could flirt with, someone to amuse herself with, before she found a titled man to marry. Amelia saw him as a way to save her floundering magazine.

Just like Lydia, Lady Amelia had used the boy from the lower orders for her own ends.

And yet it had not been just a bit of harmless fun for Amelia. Unlike Lydia, she had done more than flirt with him. A woman from her class was supposed to remain a virgin until she wed. Their virginity was not given lightly.

Only after providing the heir and at least one spare was an aristocratic woman allowed to have affairs. If anyone knew what they had shared when alone at his Cornwall estate, no man from her class would consider her suitable as a bride, especially gormless twits like the Vacuous Viscounts. Had she been using him then as well?

He had promised not to reveal what had happened between them, but she had said nothing, had not thanked him for his assurances of secrecy. Was he now going to feature in a third scandal as the rogue who deflowered the innocent debutante?

Leo had no idea. All he knew was he had been used. Once again, he had been played, and allowed himself to be a pawn in the game of an aristocratic woman.

It served him right. He had forgotten all the lessons he had learnt in the school playground, all those painful truths the aristocracy had literally beaten into him. He had forgotten the disdain on Lydia's father's face when he had asked for her hand, had forgotten her look of confusion then amusement when he had suggested they run away and elope.

He was an outsider and always would be. It didn't matter how rich, how powerful he became, they would always look down on him. And it had taken Lady Amelia to remind him of that fact.

He picked up a blotter and attempted to undo the damage he had caused. The ink smeared further across the page. He grabbed it, crushed it into a tight ball and threw it across the room.

'Parsons,' he called out, summoning his secretary. 'Contact the bank and tell them I require another copy of the Somerville contract.'

Parson looked at the ball of paper lying in the middle of the floor but said nothing, merely picked it up, bowed and departed.

Leo had wasted enough time. He needed to focus on his work. That was what protected him from women like Lady Amelia, from her class, and everyone who ever had the audacity to try and treat him badly because he was merely a blacksmith's son.

At least that was what he would do, if the damn words on the documents in front of him would stop swirling before his eyes.

He pushed away the papers unread. This would not do. He would not let that woman affect him. She meant nothing to him, just as he meant nothing to her. Just like Lydia, he had been a mere dalliance, even if she had taken that dalliance much further than Lydia ever had.

The irony was not lost on Leo. He'd had so many women in his bed, women who meant as little to him as he did to them. He had never had to maintain his guard to avoid being hurt by them because those women could never hurt him.

But with Amelia, he had surrendered himself, had allowed himself to feel for the first time since Lydia. And by God he was feeling now. As if a constricting metal band had suddenly wrapped itself around his chest, and a thick fog had descended on his mind, his body was seemingly in the clutches of a debilitating illness. He shook his head, to try and drive away the confusion. This would not do. No one affected him like this. No one could hurt him. Not even Lady Amelia. He was stronger than this. He would survive this. He had to.

Amelia had done it. She had told him the truth. She should now be feeling a certain amount of satisfaction that finally she had put things to rights. But if this was elation she could happily live without it. Every part of her body was weighed down by the cold way in which he had received her news. But she could not surrender to self-pity. She had brought this on herself, so bear it she must, and with as much stoicism as she could muster.

She had told the truth to Leo, and now she must tell the truth to her father. He needed to know that her engagement was over and she would not be marrying anyone just to save him from embarrassment in front of his friends at his club.

She entered her father's book-lined study, to find him leaning back in his chair, a cigar in hand, a newspaper open on the table. The room was rarely, if ever, used for studying. Her father never read. Instead the study was a room where he could smoke and savour a glass or two of brandy.

'Father, I need to talk to you.'

'What is it, Amelia?' He looked down at the newspaper spread out in front of him as if too busy perusing the latest news to talk to his daughter. 'If it's anything to do with the wedding, talk to Beryl. I want nothing to do with this abomination of a marriage.'

'That's what I wish to talk to you about, Father. There will be no marriage.'

He folded up the unread newspaper and sighed. 'We have already discussed this, Amelia. You will be marrying him. I don't like it any more than you do, but I will not be made to look a fool in front of my friends.'

'I have told Mr Devenish that we are not going to marry.'

'Well, you can go and tell him that you are. And if that scoundrel thinks he's weaselling out of this I'm more than happy to remind him that he has no choice but to do the honourable thing and restore your reputation. No man will take liberties with my daughter and not pay the price, even a blacksmith's son—especially not a blacksmith's son.'

'No, you won't, Father. We are not going to marry and you cannot make us.'

His eyes narrowed. 'And you're prepared to see Beryl suffer, are you?'

'No, of course not.'

'Good.' He took a long draw on his cigar and flicked his hand towards the door to indicate that she should leave.

'If you cut off Aunt Beryl financially then I intend to support her myself.'

He looked up at her, his eyes wide, then he broke into laughter.

She placed her hands firmly on her hips. 'I am the owner of a successful magazine, *The Ladies' Enquirer*, which is starting to make a healthy return. If you won't support Aunt Beryl, then she can live off the proceeds of the magazine.'

His laughter stopped, to be replaced by a scornful frown. 'Have you completely lost your mind? You? The owner of a magazine? What on earth are you talking about? You're just a chit of a girl. Girls do not own magazines.'

'This girl does. And she owns a magazine that is daily growing in subscription numbers and is rapidly attracting substantial advertising revenue.'

He stared at her, as if trying to digest what she was saying. 'That nonsense aside, you will still be marrying Devenish.' He grinned victoriously. 'I will tell him that if he doesn't marry you, I will sue him for breach of promise. See how he likes that.'

'And if you do so our family will become an even greater topic of conversation. Your friends at your club will have even more to laugh about. Do you really want them discussing how your daughter was compromised by the son of a blacksmith, and then you had to take the man to court because he wouldn't marry her?'

Colour flushed her father's face, from his neck up to his hairline, turning it a deep shade of red.

'I thought not.' With that she turned and walked out of his study.

Next, she had to tell Aunt Beryl that the wedding was off. That too was not going to be an easy conversation, as her aunt had grown very fond of Leo.

In an attempt to soften her news, she firstly told her aunt of the magazine's success and that her money would be returned to her, with a healthy interest payment. Then she informed her aunt that the wedding would not be taking place. The reaction was as expected. Her aunt was shocked and saddened. Then she tried to convince Amelia that it mattered not how the engagement had come about and, as Leo was perfect for her, she should go through with the marriage.

Amelia had to agree that Leo was indeed perfect for her, so perfect it hurt, but that meant nothing. She was not perfect for him, and she would not force a man into an unwanted marriage, any man, even one she wanted as badly as she wanted Leo Devenish.

When she realised Amelia's mind was made up, her aunt took her in her arms, which was much harder to endure than her father's wrath. Amelia had to fight not to let the tears she had been holding back since she left Leo's office from gushing out in an uncontrollable flood.

'I'm so sorry, Amelia,' her aunt said, gently rocking her as she had often done when Amelia was a child. 'I could see that you were falling in love with him, and I was sure he was in love with you.'

Amelia swallowed down those unshed tears. 'I'm not sure what I feel for Leo Devenish,' she said. 'But I know that he doesn't love me.' If her aunt had seen his cold expression, then she too would have no doubts as to Leo's lack of feeling for her.

Disentangling herself from her aunt's warm, comforting embrace, Amelia knew she still had more people to tell, and they needed to be told as soon as possible. Rumours always escaped, as if by magic, and she wanted her friends to hear her news before it made it onto the gossip circuit.

She sent notes out to Emily, Georgina and Irene, and called them all to her home. Their excited faces and chatter when they arrived and handed hats and coats to the waiting servants, suggested they assumed they were being summoned to hear good news.

As soon as they seated themselves in the drawing room all three asked her about her visit to Leo's estate, which she answered with as few words as possible, saying it was very pleasant, that his estate was opulent and he had been a gracious host to herself and Aunt Beryl.

This elicited raised eyebrows and exchanges of confused looks, but she would reveal nothing until they were all seated and tea had been served.

Adopting Leo's matter-of-fact manner, she told them all that had happened in his office, determined to keep her emotions in check. Once she had finished her three friends stared back at her, with matching looks of concern.

'Are you sure that is what you want?' Emily asked.

'Yes,' Amelia said to her unconvinced audience.

'We all know that you didn't want to make Mr Devenish marry you, but haven't your feelings towards him changed since then?' Georgina asked, her voice tentative. 'You seemed to be having such fun together when you were courting. You always looked so happy. Like a couple in love.'

'All pretence,' Amelia said dismissively.

'Really?' Irene asked.

'Oh, all right. Yes, it's true that I have feelings for Leo... Mr Devenish. But that's all that has changed. The situation has not. We were forced into this engagement and now we no longer have to marry.'

'And what did Mr Devenish have to say about your calling off the engagement?' Emily asked.

'He took the news...' Amelia paused as the memory of his cold, hard eyes entered her mind. 'I believe he is pleased all has been resolved in an acceptable manner.'

The three friends looked at each other and appeared to be having an unspoken conversation.

'And what about you, Amelia? Do you think all has been resolved in an acceptable manner?' Irene asked.

'Yes.' That was true. She did not want to marry a man who was only marrying her because he believed he had to. So this had to be an acceptable outcome.

Three sets of eyebrows rose as her friends waited for her to elaborate.

'Oh, all right. Yes, perhaps what I secretly wanted was for him to fall at my feet and say that he wanted to marry me anyway, but that didn't happen. So there's nothing more to be said on the matter.'

Her friends stood up and moved towards her. She held up her hands to stop them. 'Please, don't console me, don't be nice and don't say kind things. If you do, I'm sure I'll burst into tears.'

'Is there anything wrong with bursting into tears? It might be exactly what you need right now,' Irene said.

'No, I want to put this all behind me.' Amelia sat up straighter and lifted her chin. 'Please, sit down.'

Her friends remained standing.

'This is all for the best,' she said, slightly louder than necessary. 'Don't you remember how we discussed all the ways I could get out of this marriage? Don't you remember how difficult it was? Don't you remember consoling me for being trapped by my father and by Society's silly conventions?'

None of her friends replied, but thankfully they all took their seats.

'We all just want what's best for you, Amelia, what makes you happy,' Emily said.

'Well, this is what's best. This is what makes me happy.'

Three concerned faces gazed back at her.

'Oh, all right. So I'm not happy now, but I will be soon. I'm sure of it. I'll be able to take some satisfaction in freeing a man who doesn't love me from an unwanted marriage.' Amelia forced herself to smile. 'I have finally told Leo the truth. That alone should be enough to make me happy.'

Amelia had hoped that would be the end of it, but instead her friends once again left their seats and, defying her wishes, embraced her, causing those tears that she had been fighting so hard to keep in check to flow down her cheeks.

Chapter Twenty

Leo Devenish knew himself to be resilient. If he hadn't been he would never have survived his school days, he would never have become the successful businessman he now was, he'd never have made it in a society where all the odds were stacked against him.

That resilience would take him through this latest upset. He knew it would. It had to. He could not continue to feel this way for an eternity. He could not possibly spend the rest of his life thinking about Lady Amelia, remembering her lovely smile and delightful melodic laugh. He could not go on imagining he saw her on the street, only to be both disappointed and relieved when another woman turned around and he discovered it wasn't her.

And he could not continue to imagine how she looked when they made love, could not constantly be tormented by the memory of her beautiful body as she arched and writhed beneath him in pleasure. He most certainly had to take control of himself and drive that image from his mind.

Soon, he was certain, he would be free. Finding another woman to warm his bed was one way to make himself forget all about her. But to his amazement he had completely lost interest in the fairer sex. He did not want another woman in his bed. He wanted Amelia. No woman had made him feel the way she did, and he suspected no one ever would again. When he'd made love to Amelia it had been so much more than a physical pleasure, although the physical pleasure had reached heights he had not realised possible. But she had opened something up in him, something that had closed down a long time ago, a tantalising feeling he could barely remember. One best described as happiness.

With Amelia he had laughed, he had enjoyed himself, he had experienced a lightness of spirit that he had lost long ago. And now that joyfulness had gone as quickly as it had arrived and he was left feeling as if part of himself had been ripped away.

This is what you get for allowing a woman to strip away the armour you have carefully built around yourself.

And the tragedy was, he needed that armour now, more than ever before, but it had gone, leaving him raw and vulnerable. His armour had repelled the school bullies and protected him from the rival businessmen he went up against every day. It made him impervious to the aristocrats who looked down their imperious noses at him. Yet pretty little Amelia had not only pierced his armour but also left him exposed to her wounding arrows.

He looked down at the work piling up on his desk

and tried to focus, then turned his chair and stared out of the window, down at the people bustling along the busy London street.

Throwing himself into his business ventures was another method he had hoped would cauterise his wounds, but that too held no appeal. What did it matter if he became richer and more powerful? It would not fill the gnawing hole in his chest that was with him when he woke in the morning and was still there when he retired for the night.

If attempting to salve the pain in the pointless pursuit of another woman was not going to work, and acquiring more power, prestige and wealth held no appeal, Leo was at a loss as to what to do.

He strode out of his office, telling his secretary he would be spending some time at his Cornwall estate. Like an injured animal retreating to lick his wounds, he boarded the next train out of London, telling his valet that his services would not be required.

However, on arrival, instead of heading straight to his estate, he walked through the village to his parents' cottage. His mother greeted him with open arms, her reservations towards her successful son no longer evident.

Bracing himself, he told her that he and Amelia would not be marrying, news which she accepted with disappointment, compassion and a consoling cup of tea.

Not long ago, he would not have even bothered to tell his parents such a thing, but he appreciated his mother's comforting words and her attempt to heal him with affection. When his father came in to join them, he greeted the news by asking Leo if he'd be interested in helping out in the smithy, something Leo was surprisingly eager to do.

As the two men worked side by side, sweating under the heat of the furnace and the physicality of the work, Leo was able to briefly forget about Amelia. But when they stopped for some much-needed food and drink, she came back into his mind.

It had been many years since he had spent this amount of time with his parents, and he had never turned to them in time of need, believing himself to no longer need the help of anyone. He had Amelia to thank for reconnecting him with his family and showing him that even when you were a success, even when you had immense power and wealth, you still needed the people who cared about you.

Sitting beside one another, Leo and his taciturn father stared out at the surrounding countryside and ate their meal in silence.

'Loved the lass, did you, son?' his father finally said, the question asked as casually as one would make a comment on the weather.

But there was nothing casual about the consideration Leo gave to such an enormous question. Did he love Amelia? Would that account for the warmth that flooded through him every time they were together? Was that why she continued to grow more and more beautiful in his eyes every time he looked at her? Was that why losing her had left such an empty pit deep inside him?

'Yes, I believe I did,' he responded.

'Then you should fight for her.'

Leo drank his mug of tea as he considered this state-ment. His father did not understand. Men like him had no weapons with which to fight for a woman like Lady Amelia. Men like him were doomed to defeat, no mat-ter what.

'It's not that easy,' he finally responded.

'Nothing worth having ever comes easily. And she seemed to me to be a lass worth having.'

Leo knew his father was right. The lass certainly was worth having, but what was the point of fighting when you were destined to lose? Instead, he needed to find a way to protect himself, to build up his defences once again, to return to being the man he was before Amelia Lambourne swept into his life.

Once the meal was over, he and his father returned to work and continued hammering out horseshoes in companionable silence for the rest of the day.

Their work finished, the two men washed up and his mother served them another hearty meal. The pain in his chest never once released its tight grip, but with his mother fussing around him Leo experienced a sense of belonging which had been missing from his life for such a long time.

That evening he agreed to spend the night at his parents' cottage, having no wish to return to his large, lonely estate. Lying on his bed in a room that was lit-tle bigger than the four-poster bed he would have slept in at his home, he knew that as much as he was angry with Amelia, as much as he wished this never-ending pain would go away, he did not regret her coming into his life. She had changed him, improved him. The mere fact that he was here, tonight, in his parents' home, was proof of that. He was wrong when he dismissed her as being just like all the other women of her class. She really was unique in so many ways.

She had hurt him, she had used him, but he could not turn his love for her into hate, as much as he wished he could. Nor could he blame himself for falling in love with such a woman. How could he not fall in love with her?

No other woman of his acquaintance would have the ambition and drive to set up and run her own magazine. And she had done so for the best of all reasons, to provide women with a voice for their social and political concerns. She had entered a competitive, cut-throat industry but had managed to maintain her humanity as she did so. Unlike himself, she was not driven purely by profit. How could he not admire such a woman?

Even the lies she had told him were to save her magazine and her Aunt Beryl.

It was hardly her fault that he had fallen in love with her, and yet causing him to fall in love with her was something for which he would never forgive her.

Leo could delay it no longer. After a few days he said goodbye to his parents, promising to return soon and often, and he took the train back to London.

Along with his secretary, a pile of work greeted him at his office. On top of the contracts that demanded Leo's immediate signature was an envelope addressed to him in an unfamiliar feminine hand. Ignoring the pressing needs of work, he took his letter opener and slit open the envelope.

It was from Amelia's aunt Beryl, of all people, informing him that she had recently come into some money and would appreciate his financial advice on how best to invest it.

There was a certain irony in Aunt Beryl's request. She had money because Amelia had managed to make *The Ladies' Enquirer* profitable. She had done so by adding a gossip column, which had inadvertently been his suggestion. That column had featured him and had led both to their engagement and the end of the engagement. Now the aunt wanted his help to make that money grow.

He penned a note to Amelia's aunt, informing her that he would be delighted to assist her and she was welcome to visit him at his office any time that was convenient, then handed the note to his secretary to arrange delivery.

Leo was fond of Aunt Beryl and despite what had happened between him and Amelia he was more than happy to help. Amelia had said that her aunt was financially dependent on her father for support, so it would give him added satisfaction if he could take away some of the power the snobbish Earl of Kingsland wielded over the women in his family.

A few hours later another note arrived from Aunt Beryl, suggesting that instead of a meeting at his office they should take afternoon tea together at the Savoy the next day. It was not the usual place in which Leo conducted business, but if it would make the aunt feel more comfortable then Leo could see no harm in such an arrangement. He penned another note of acceptance and once again buried himself in the mounting pile of business correspondence.

The next day he entered the Savoy and found himself in a decidedly feminine environment. Groups of women sat around tables, each woman wearing an absurdly large hat bedecked with feathers, ribbons and artificial flowers, making it impossible to see where Aunt Beryl had hidden herself.

The head waiter led him to a table in the corner, where the aunt had already ordered tea for two, along with a three-tiered server bearing scones, cakes and sandwiches. This most certainly was not how he usually conducted business meetings.

He bowed to Aunt Beryl and took his seat.

'I'm so pleased you were able to make it, Mr Devenish,' she said, dismissing the waiter and pouring him a cup of tea.

'My pleasure, Miss Simpson,' he said, waving away her offer of a rather dainty cake with pink icing.

'Please, call me Aunt Beryl, or even Beryl, if you want to be really risqué.'

'Aunt Beryl it is, then.' He'd been risqué enough with the women of this family. 'So, I'm assuming that the money you have come into is not an enormous sum and that you would prefer to invest it in a conservative scheme where the returns might not be as large but you will not be putting it at such a high risk.'

Aunt Beryl nodded, but he could see he did not have her entire attention and she seemed more interested in looking around the room than focusing on discussing maximising the return on her money.

'There are several good schemes available at the moment that I think you should consider—'

'Oh, it looks as if we have company,' she interrupted.

Leo turned round to see who she was indicating and saw Amelia approaching. His heart lurched within his chest as the head waiter led her across the room towards them. She looked as beautiful as ever, dressed in a soft blue gown that matched the colour of her eyes, and her blonde hair tied back in a tight bun at the nape of her creamy neck.

Remembering himself, he stood up. She saw him above the sea of ladies in large hats and halted in her tracks. She looked towards the door, back at Leo and her aunt, then her pretty face became defiant and she strode across the room towards their table.

He could only hope that she did not think that this was any of his idea, and that he had staged some sort of ambush.

'What is the meaning of this?' Amelia said, glaring from him to her aunt.

'Sit down, dear, and have a cup of tea.' Her aunt poured the second cup and moved it towards the empty chair.

'You never said that he would be joining us.'

'He's not joining *us*, dear. I'm leaving,' Aunt Beryl said, rising to her feet.

'Then so am I,' Amelia said, still standing.

'No, you are not. You are going to sit down, take afternoon tea, and make polite conversation with Mr

Devenish. If you don't, all it will prove is that I did not do my job properly and I have raised a rude young lady who should know better.'

Amelia huffed out a sigh and with much flouncing of skirts sat down.

'Right, I'll leave you two to talk.' And without further comment Aunt Beryl left the room.

They sat in silence for a moment or two, staring everywhere except at each other, as if afraid to make eye contact.

'This was not my idea,' Leo finally said. 'And it quite obviously wasn't yours either.'

'It most certainly was not.'

'So, Aunt Beryl wants us to make polite conversation.'

They continued to look around the room as if making polite conversation was something with which neither was familiar.

'I went to visit my parents last week,' he said, for want of anything else to talk about.

'Oh, how are they? I hope you gave them my regards.'

'No, not exactly, but they are both well. And they both expressed their disappointment at what happened between us.'

She blushed and lowered her eyes. 'Yes, I'm sorry about that. I liked your parents immensely and did not mean to trick them as well.'

'No, I suppose not. That was something reserved for me alone.'

'No, I—'

'I'm sorry, Amelia. I doubt that constitutes polite

conversation. So, tell me, how is *The Ladies' Enquirer*? I hear that it continues to grow in popularity?'

'Yes. And I suppose it would be polite of me to say thank you. If it hadn't been for your good idea about the gossip column it would not be such a success.'

They both sank back into silence, and Leo tried not to think about that gossip column and all the troubles it had caused. And he certainly did not want to think about how the column had brought this beautiful, enchanting woman into his life and into his bed.

'I'm sorry—' they said at once, then exchanged pinched smiles.

'I'm sorry for deceiving you,' she said quietly.

He shrugged. 'You're a businesswoman. Sometimes we have to resort to deception to survive and prosper. You were worried I might take over your business and you did what was necessary to stop that. Believe me, I have done much worse on my climb to the top.'

'Yes, but I did not want to deceive *you*. I hated the deception.'

'Which particular deception are you talking about? The one where you printed stories about me in the paper? Or the one where you agreed to our engagement despite knowing you would never marry me? Or was it…?' He paused, not able to ask if she had deceived him when she was in his bed. Was her reaction all faked? Was the way she cried out his name in ecstasy all staged? He doubted it. No woman was that good an actress.

She blushed and lightly bit her bottom lip. 'I regret all my deceptions.' Then she gave a doleful smile. 'While I regret deceiving you, I don't regret having known you. And I don't just mean because you inadvertently helped my magazine to become a success.' She moved slightly in her chair, looked down at the table then back up at him. 'Let's just say how to succeed in business wasn't the only thing you taught me.'

He raised his eyebrows and her blush deepened, but he was pleased to see she also smiled.

'I was happy to oblige,' he said, also smiling.

She laughed lightly, then her face became more serious. 'But I *am* sorry I tricked you. I should have told you that I planned to get out of the marriage as soon as I could pay Aunt Beryl back. But I was worried that Father would find out and Aunt Beryl would suffer.' She reached out across the table towards him, then, as if remembering herself, withdrew her gloved hand. 'Otherwise, I would have told you immediately that you did not have to go through with it.'

'And if the magazine never made a profit, would you have married me?'

She shrugged one slim shoulder. 'I would never have done that to you. I would have found a way to put a stop to this forced marriage.'

'Would marriage to me have been such a trial for you?'

'No, of course not, but a forced marriage is not what I want, and not what you deserve. Neither of us wishes to marry, but if we did, we should be free to marry if and when we want to, not because we are forced to by stupid social conventions and to stop people gossiping about us.'

He nodded and once again they sank into silence, their untouched tea growing cold. As he stared at the crisp white tablecloth the conversation with his father came back to him.

'Loved the lass, did you, son?'

He had admitted to himself and his father that he did indeed love Amelia. And this might be the last conversation he had with the woman he loved.

'Then you should fight for her.'

He had fought for so much in his life, and none of those things, not power, not wealth, seemed important now. But Amelia was. Nothing was more important than his love for her. He knew how to fight to achieve his goals in business, but this was a battle for which he was hopelessly ill prepared. But he had to at least try.

He drew in a deep breath to gather his resources and order his spinning thoughts.

'I need to make a confession,' he finally forced himself to say.

She tilted her head in question, her eyes narrowing as if she was wary as to what he might say.

'I judged you harshly for your behaviour and regret doing so.'

Coward. Tell her how you feel.

'I more than anyone should have known how hard it was for you. You were trying to establish a magazine with the entire world against you, including your father and, I'm sorry to say, me. You were struggling to keep a magazine going and I made things so much worse by threatening to take it over.'

'Well, you didn't know.'

'I do now. What you have done is so impressive, and I would like to help you make it an even greater success. I would love to be of assistance in any way I can.'

You're still being a coward. You've used that word. Love. So now tell her you love her.

'You taught me that we all need each other's help at some time. So please, let me repay that by helping you.'

'Oh. Does that mean you have forgiven me?'

'There is nothing to forgive. Everything you did was for the best of reasons. You wanted to protect your aunt, so you had to marry me. You thought I wanted my freedom and had been compromised into marrying you, and you wanted neither of us to be forced into marriage. All it shows is that you have a considerate nature. You were ambitious to make your magazine a success and you feared that I might ruin your dream. And you are right. It is an intelligent read for intelligent women, just like you, and it should be owned by a woman, just like you.'

She gave him a sweet smile that melted his heart. 'Thank you.'

'But I, too, must apologise for my behaviour,' he added.

She shook her head slowly, her gloved hands turned up in question.

He looked around the room at the chattering women. He doubted any of them would hear a word he said over the noise of their conversation, and the clinking of cups on saucers, but he leaned forward anyway and lowered his voice. 'I should not have seduced you.'

And if I was a better man I really would be sorry,

but having you in my bed has been too wonderful to cause real regret.

Her gloved hand covered her mouth and she gave a small laugh, as colour once again tinged her cheeks. 'If I remember correctly it was I who seduced you. Don't you remember that I came to your room and gave you no choice?'

He moved uncomfortably on his chair. How could he possibly forget the memory of her entering his bed chamber, dressed only in her nightgown and robe? That image appeared before him repeatedly and was doing so now, in all its intoxicating glory.

'But I should have…or at least I shouldn't have… If I'd known I wouldn't have…that the engagement was…' He sighed at his bumbling attempts to explain. 'It was wrong.'

Her hand covered his. 'It was not wrong. Not for me.' She lightly bit the edge of her lip once again and withdrew her hand. 'I suppose the only thing that was wrong was that I led you to believe that we were to be married, so… I sort of tricked you into having your wicked way with me.' She sent him a tentative smile, causing him to laugh.

'Believe me, on that occasion I was happy to be tricked, and have had no regrets since.'

'No, me neither.'

He smiled at her, then his smile died. 'No, that's not true. I do have regrets.'

Her head tilted in question.

'I regret that it was not real.'

'Oh, yes, I am sorry about that. I—'

He took hold of her hand and gently squeezed it. 'You have nothing to apologise for, Amelia. Nothing at all. Meeting you is the most wonderful thing that has ever happened to me.'

She stared at him, wide-eyed. 'It was?'

'Yes. You have affected me in ways I would not have thought possible.'

'I have?' Her eyes grew even wider.

'And I'm so sorry I judged you harshly.'

She shook her head. 'It was no more than I deserved.'

'No, you deserve to be respected and admired.' *And loved.* 'I have another confession to make to you.'

'You do?'

'I told you about Lydia Bedford.'

'Yes,' she whispered, lowering her eyes then looking back up at him. 'You were in love with her once.'

'I *thought* I was in love with her, but now I wonder if I ever knew what love was.'

Until now. Tell her.

'I also thought I knew what pain was like when she rejected me. She all but laughed in my face at the audacity of a man from such lowly origins thinking she would deign to marry him. That was why I reacted the way I did when you called off our marriage. I assumed you too did not want to be associated with a blacksmith's son.'

'No, Leo, I didn't… I never… I'm sorry.'

'Again, you have nothing to be sorry for. I know that you are nothing like Lydia.'

Because I love you. You are the woman I truly love, have only ever loved.

'And I am not the man I was when I attempted to court Lydia.'

Tell her, man, for God's sake, tell her.

'I'm not the man I was when you first met me.'

Coward, stop avoiding it.

'I mentioned that I visited my parents last week?' She nodded.

'It was then that I realised how much you had changed me. You brought my parents and me back together, and for that I will be eternally grateful to you.'

'All I did was insist that we visit them.'

'No, you did so much more. You showed me how much I had lost, and what I could regain. My mother said that I had been a playful child before I went away to school. She was right. That school ripped all the joy out of my life, and my life since then has been equally joyless. Yes, it's been successful and from the outside it would look as if I was enjoying myself, but I've been dead inside for so long I didn't even realise it. Until I met you. With you I felt alive, I felt joy and happiness.'

She stared at him, as if unsure what he was saying.

'As I said, I thought I was in love with Lydia, but that was because I didn't know what love was, until I met you.'

Her mouth formed a round circle and her eyes grew even bigger. 'Oh.'

'Amelia, I am in love with you.' He had finally said them, the words that he had been so afraid of saying out loud, but now they sounded like such an inadequate expression of the enormity of what he felt. 'I can hardly express what I feel for you. It is as if you have possessed me, my heart and my soul. You have brought so much happiness into my life, made me see the world through different eyes, made me different. All I can say is you are a beautiful woman with a beautiful soul.'

She continued to stare back at him as if dazed, her pretty lips parted, her blue eyes wide, her eyebrows raised.

'It would do me the greatest honour in the world if you would allow me to court you properly, to try and prove to you that I am worthy of you, and hopefully you will grow to love me as well.'

'No, there's no need to do that.'

As if a fist had struck him in the chest, he physically recoiled and his hand covered his wounded heart.

She leaned forward and placed her hands on his arms. 'Oh, that was clumsy of me. What I mean is, you don't have to do anything. You don't have to prove yourself to me. I am in love with you, hopelessly and completely.'

It was his turn to stare back at her with a dazed expression. 'Oh, Amelia,' he said when the words finally sank in. He still didn't know how to tell her what he was feeling but he knew what he wanted to do. Throw aside the small round table that separated them, take her in his arms, here and now, in the middle of the restaurant, and kiss her.

'And there's no need to court me,' she continued.

'But—'

She held up her hands to stop his words. 'We've already done the courtship. Let's go straight to the marriage. I for one can't wait any longer for our honeymoon.'

He stared at her for a moment, then laughed loudly

enough to turn heads at the neighbouring tables. 'Amelia, you are priceless. But if we are to marry, there is one thing I must do.'

He stood up, moved around the small table, knelt down in front of her and took her hand in his, causing the babble of voices to still. 'Lady Amelia, will you do me the greatest honour and consent to becoming my wife? I love you with all my heart and soul, and promise that if you marry me I will devote my life to your happiness.'

The room had grown silent as the watching ladies waited for her answer.

'Of course I will,' Amelia said, leaning down and kissing him.

A small gasp went out from the lunching ladies.

They'd already caused a scene, so Leo decided he might as well give the ladies something to really talk about. Standing up, he pulled Amelia to her feet, took her in his arms and kissed her again, causing a louder gasp to be emitted from their audience. Then the chattering resumed at an increased volume, proving once again how much everyone loved to gossip.

'That was lovely,' Amelia said when he finally released her from his embrace. 'But I can think of a much better way for us to celebrate our engagement, one that would be rather too scandalous for the tearoom at the Savoy. So perhaps we should retire to your townhouse.'

Without comment he took her hand and led her out of the hotel, anxious to get her into his carriage and back into his bed. As they passed through the foyer, neither noticed Aunt Beryl, taking tea and smiling contentedly as she raised a toast to them with her teacup.

Epilogue

The wedding of an earl's only daughter traditionally brought out all of Society. That was not the case for Amelia and Leo. They chose to have a quiet wedding, and against convention held it at his estate. Both Amelia and Leo wanted to ensure his parents felt comfortable attending the nuptials and suspected that would not happen if they hosted a lavish Society wedding.

Instead, they opened up Leo's estate to all of his tenants and the entire village. Her father was scandalised, which added to Amelia's enjoyment of the day. At one stage he had refused to give her away unless she conformed, held a conventional wedding at her family estate and invited members of all the leading families of their acquaintance. Amelia responded to this threat by telling him that one of the tenant farmers would be more than happy to give her away. Finally the Earl reluctantly relented, as Amelia had known he would. After all, if it got back to the men at his club that his daughter had been given away by a tenant farmer, he would be a laughing stock, and he would not abide that.

So with as much dignity as he could muster he walked his daughter up the aisle of the village church in front of tenant farmers, servants, butchers, bakers and other people with whom he wouldn't usually deign to mix.

The wedding breakfast was held outside and there was a country fete atmosphere throughout the day. In the evening, a local band of musicians assembled and dancing was held, with all the villagers, tenants and servants taking part. Even her father started to loosen up at that stage, and Amelia saw him swing one woman after another around the dance floor. This was either due to the infectious music, the enthusiasm of the locals, or the free-flowing tankards of ale. Whatever it was, Amelia was pleased to see him enjoying himself. He even danced with Aunt Beryl, which surprised both Amelia and her aunt.

Her three best friends, Emily, Georgina and Irene, had no reservations about getting into the spirit of the occasion. After fulfilling their role as bridesmaids, they took to the dance floor with abandon, enjoying the reels and jigs with more enthusiasm than Amelia had ever seen them show for quadrilles and waltzes at formal balls.

'What would Miss Halliwell say if she could see us now?' Irene called out to Amelia as they flew past each other during a rather vigorous reel.

'Young ladies, you must float like a cloud on the dance floor,' all four responded in Miss Halliwell's prim voice, followed by much laughter as they vigorously joined in the required foot-stamping and hand-clapping. Their behaviour resembled a thunderstorm more than a gently floating cloud, and their smiling faces showed how much they enjoyed such mayhem.

Charles, Amelia's assistant, also had no problems enjoying the evening to the full, and was seen on the dance floor with several local lasses and had more than one dance with Amelia's lady's maid. He had been worried when Amelia had informed him that she was to marry, wondering what it meant for the future of *The Ladies' Enquirer*. Then was relieved when she had informed him that her marriage would change nothing and she would continue to be the owner and editor, with him at her side.

Leo, however, had decided that marriage would be a good time to make some changes, and had vowed to do what Amelia had suggested, and spend time enjoying the fruits of his labours, saying the pursuit of greater power suddenly seemed like a pointless activity.

And if his behaviour during the wedding was any indication, he would have no problem enjoying himself. When they weren't dancing Leo and Amelia circulated and spoke to each guest in turn. Many of them had known Leo since before he attended school. Despite the fact that he had owned the estate for many years, most greeted him as if they had not seen him since he was a young boy. While some were uncomfortable with Amelia on first meeting her, they soon thawed and chatted happily with her, sharing gossip about the village. As she watched her husband talking and laughing with his neighbours, Amelia knew that the walls that had divided him from his family and the people he had spent his early childhood with had now completely crumbled.

'It looks like you were missed,' Amelia said, after one boyhood friend had finished recounting a tale of Leo organising them into mounting a siege on the local bakery, which had resulted in the baker's finally relenting and giving them all currant buns just to make them go away. A tale that had caused much laughter and slapping of backs.

'They miss the boy I was, not the man I became.' He smiled down at her. 'Now they are greeting a new man, and they all have you to thank for that.'

'I think you give me more credit than I deserve.'

'I do not think that possible.' His smile faded for the first time since they had exchanged their vows and his face became serious. 'You have restored me, my love. You have taught me how to love, laugh and take pleasure in life. I don't know how I can ever thank you for that, but I promise I will spend the rest of my life trying.'

'That sounds like a wonderful idea,' she said with a laugh. 'And I think you should start by once again dancing with your wife.'

He led her out onto the floor and they joined the revellers, laughing and spinning around until they were dizzy.

When the villagers finally left in the early hours of the morning, and their house guests had retired for the night, Leo took Amelia in his arms and kissed her with a passion that left her reeling more decidedly than the vigorous country dances ever could.

'I cannot believe it is possible to be this happy,' he said, as they swayed to silent music. 'And I owe it all to you, my beautiful bride.'

Amelia hardly heard his words, as her focus was taken by the arms that were holding her close, protecting her from the world, filling her with his strength and those tempting lips that were so close to her own.

'Have I told you how much I love you?'

She laughed lightly. 'Not in the last ten minutes or so.'

He cupped her chin, lifted her face and gazed down into her eyes. 'That is rather remiss of me. But I don't believe the words exist that can express how much I love you.'

'If you can't tell me with words, I believe there are other ways in which you can show me,' she said with a smile.

And with that he scooped her up in his arms and carried her into their home.

* * * * *

If you enjoyed this story, make sure to look out for the next book in Eva Shepherd's Rebellious Young Ladies miniseries

And whilst you're waiting, why not check out her Those Roguish Rosemonts miniseries?

A Dance to Save the Debutante
Tempting the Sensible Lady Violet
Falling for the Forbidden Duke

WOOING HIS CONVENIENT WIFE (Regency)
The Patterdale Siblings • by Annie Burrows

Jasper's out of options when feisty stranger Penelope offers him a lifeline—marriage. It's a practical match...until an inconvenient desire to share the marriage bed changes everything!

AWAKENING HIS SHY DUCHESS (Regency)
The Irresistible Dukes • by Christine Merrill

Evan is stunned when Madeline takes a tumble fleeing a ball...and accidentally falls into him! Now the situation forces them somewhere the duke didn't want to be—the altar!

THE GOVERNESS AND THE BROODING DUKE (Regency)
by Millie Adams

Employed to tame the Duke of Westmere's disobedient children, Mary should avoid entanglement with their widower father. If only she didn't crave the forbidden intimacy of their moments alone...

HER GRACE'S DARING PROPOSAL (Regency)
by Joanna Johnson

Widowed duchess Isabelle's wealth has made her the target of fortune hunters. A convenient marriage to mercenary Joseph will protect her but could also put her heart in danger...

THE EARL'S EGYPTIAN HEIRESS (Victorian)
by Heba Helmy

Ranya's mission is clear: restore her family's honor by retrieving the deed to their business from the Earl of Warrington. Until she finds herself enthralled by the new earl, Owen...

A KNIGHT FOR THE RUNAWAY NUN (Medieval)
Convent Brides • by Carol Townend

Having left the convent before taking her Holy Orders, Lady Bernadette is horrified when her father wants her wed! The only solution—marrying childhood friend Sir Hugo.

Get 3 FREE REWARDS!

We'll send you 2 FREE Books <u>plus</u> a FREE Mystery Gift.

FREE Value Over **$20**

Both the **Harlequin® Historical** and **Harlequin® Romance** series feature compelling novels filled with emotion and simmering romance.

Get 3 FREE REWARDS!

We'll send you 2 FREE Books <u>plus</u> a FREE Mystery Gift.

Both the **Harlequin® Desire** and **Harlequin Presents®** series feature compelling novels filled with passion, sensuality and intriguing scandals.

HARLEQUIN
PLUS

Try the best multimedia subscription service for romance readers like you!

Read, Watch and Play.

Experience the easiest way to get the romance content you crave.

Start your **FREE TRIAL** at
<u>www.harlequinplus.com/freetrial</u>.